DYING TO TELL

Val Collins

The main character in this book is Aoife. This is a very common Irish name and is pronounced "eee-fah". A bit like Eva with an 'f'.

Most of the other names in this book are English but I have included Irish names for some minor characters.

Grainne (Grawn-Yah) – in most of my books
Ciaran (Kier-awn) – Irish for Kieran
Sadhb (Syve)
Dearbhla (Dervla)
Aoibhinn (Ay-veen)
Fionn - (Fyunn)

These are all common Irish names. If you would like to hear them pronounced, check out my Instagram post here:

https://www.instagram.com/p/CndXtaLh6fl/

Dying To Tell is the fifth book in the Aoife Walsh Thriller Series. All five books are standalone thrillers and can be read in any order. The other books in the series are Girl Targeted, Only Lies Remain, The Silent Speak and Where Loyalties Lie. You can check out all my books on my website here:

https://valcollinsbooks.com/books/

PROLOGUE

MATT SHUT HIS eyes and took several deep breaths. After a few minutes he felt his pulse begin to slow. *Good. Breathe in, hold. Breathe out. Okay, now do it again. And again. That's better. Now think. How are you going to get out of this?* Images popped into his mind and he jerked his head to one side to dislodge them. *The people who caused this aren't important right now*, he reminded himself. *What matters is figuring out a way to...* His eyes flew open. *What the—? Is that...? Oh dear God, no!* He squeezed his eyes shut like a kid who believed things he couldn't see would disappear. His heart beat so fast he felt the room spin. For a second he wondered if he was having a heart attack. The idea was so ridiculous he almost laughed. *What difference would it make now? What difference would anything make?*

ONE

THE MAN SETTLED down on the sunbed and looked around. It was as he'd feared; not one unattached female. Such a pity he hadn't been able to get here earlier in the season. A family who had been occupying several sunbeds moved away and there she was, on the last sunbed in the row, staring out at the ocean. She was a little older than his eldest daughter, twenty-four or twenty-five, maybe, with alabaster skin and carrot-red hair. Not beautiful, definitely well below his usual standard, but she was pretty enough and he'd never been with a redhead before. She'd do. He was about to make his move when he noticed the towel, iPad and shades on the sunbed beside her. Was her friend male or female? It would be a mistake to rush in. What if her friend turned out to be a goddess? He could wait. He finished his drink, eyes roaming the beach in case a prettier girl walked by.

About fifteen minutes later, movement caught his attention and he looked her way again. The girl was now shoving the items from the second sunbed into her bag. So she was alone after all? He sat up, ready to catch her eye and give her the smile that had never yet failed him. But she hurried past without even a glance in his direction. He was amazed to find he was quite annoyed.

Why did he care if that chit of a girl didn't notice him? It took him two whole minutes to decide to follow her, a decision he regretted almost immediately when she strode up the road like a commuter who could see her train in the distance. Should he go back to the beach? A girl who walked that fast was way too uptight for his taste. No, he was up now, he might as well get a nice cold drink from the hotel bar.

The girl was talking to the receptionist when he entered the lobby. He'd definitely been right about her. Look at that frown! Her face would be destroyed in another few years if she kept that up. He took a seat as far away from the door as possible and had just ordered a drink when the girl rushed out of the hotel again. All that running around. What kind of a holiday was that? Somebody really needed to teach that girl how to relax.

Twenty minutes later, she sprinted past him to the receptionist desk. There was a hysterical note to her voice, and her hands were flying in all directions. Curiosity got the better of the man and he moved to a seat nearer the reception desk.

'Matt was lying on the sunbed beside me,' he heard her say. 'I fell asleep and when I woke up, he was gone.'

The receptionist muttered something the man didn't catch. The girl's voice rose.

'You told me already that he didn't return to the hotel today. I want you to call the police right away.'

The receptionist picked up the phone and muttered into it. The man's Italian was limited, but he was pretty sure he caught 'hysterical' mentioned more than once. Three minutes later he saw the short, stout hotel manager straighten his tie and pat his greying moustache as he hurried to the receptionist desk. The manager muttered something in a conciliatory tone, put his hand on the girl's arm and tried to lead her away from the desk. The girl shook him off.

'I am not going anywhere. I have walked the entire beach twice. I've checked our room. Nobody has seen Matt in hours. I want you to get the police over here this minute.'

'Madam, you must not be upset. Your husband is enjoying the Italian sun. He will return momentarily.'

'Something has happened to him. I know it. He'd never disappear without telling me.'

'But you were asleep, yes? He didn't want to disturb you, so he went sightseeing, perhaps? If he has not returned by tonight, then we will contact the police.'

'My husband would never disappear without a word. Something terrible has happened. You have to call the police right away. This is an emergency.'

'Madam, the sea here is calm. You say your husband is a strong swimmer. He could not drown. If he had been in an accident, the police would have contacted the hotels. Please, go upstairs and rest. I'll have a waiter bring you a nice cold drink. When you wake your husband will be—'

'So you're not going to phone the police? Fine. I'll call the Irish embassy and they can handle it.' The girl ran out of the lobby, the hotel manager in hot pursuit.

The man shook his head. The receptionist had been right. The girl was hysterical. If his own wife called the police every time he went chasing a young girl, they'd never get anything else done. *Didn't the girl say the Irish embassy? It's always raining over there. Everyone knows they can't cope with the sun. The girl probably has sunstroke. Tomorrow she'll be embarrassed by the fuss she caused.* A pair of long shapely legs caught the man's attention, wiping all thought of unstable Irish girls from his mind.

༄

The following morning, the man stood at the receptionist desk. His foot tapped against the floor as he waited for the receptionist to finish her phone call. As the minutes passed, his grip on his suitcase grew so tight his knuckles ached. He needed to get out of here now. Wasn't it the receptionist's job to check him out? Why couldn't she do her job while she chatted away on what was probably a personal call? Two seconds later, he'd had enough.

'Excuse me.'

The receptionist smiled and held up one finger to indicate she'd be with him in a moment. The man's face reddened. This was intolerable. He was about to speak again when the receptionist's eyes widened and she hurriedly finished her phone call. The man glanced behind to see two men in police uniform. His heart pounded against his chest as he moved to one side, picked up a hotel brochure and pretended to read it. He couldn't follow all of the conversation between the police and the receptionist, but he understood it had something to do with an Irish man who was missing. That damned Irish redhead. Couldn't she have waited a few hours until he'd managed to get out of the country? He couldn't risk the police questioning him. The man took a seat in the reception area and waited until the hotel manager led the police to a private office. Then he rushed to the reception desk. Elbowing an elderly couple to one side, the man insisted he had to leave immediately or he would miss his plane. He settled his bill with the cash he had taken from the ATM earlier that morning and almost ran out of the building. He jumped into a waiting taxi. As it pulled into the traffic, he sank into the seat and let out a long sigh. Earlier that morning, he'd worried he'd never make it out of the hotel in one piece, but the future was looking brighter already. Nobody would ever be able to link him to the fake name and address in the hotel records. He would be safe now.

Almost a month later, the man was scrolling through his newsfeed as he waited for his youngest to finish her ballet class. It was the red hair that caught his attention. The Irish girl was in an airport, head down, dragging two large suitcases behind her. The headline read, *Newlywed returns home alone.*

TWO

AOIFE DIDN'T HEAR the click-click of the high heels hurrying towards her. Even the chair scraping across the floor didn't immediately catch her attention.

'Sorry I'm late. Work is hectic as usual. I must have been out of my mind when I decided to become a lawyer.'

'Huh?' Aoife looked up from her phone. 'Oh, hi, Orla. Hang on a sec.'

Orla stopped a passing waiter and ordered a coffee. She checked her text messages, then turned to her friend, but Aoife's eyes were still glued to her phone.

'What's going on?'

Aoife slipped her phone into her bag. 'Sorry, I just had great news. Remember I mentioned that an editor I've done some work for has contacts at the *Irish Times*?'

'Oh my God! You're writing for the *Times*? Aoife!'

Aoife laughed. 'It's only one feature.'

'But, Aoife, it's the *Times*.'

Aoife's eyes shone. 'I know.'

'Is it the missing people feature you told me about?'

'Yeah. I pitched them an entire series, but I knew that was

a long shot. They liked the idea, but they want a different journalist reporting on each case.' She grinned at Orla. 'The brilliant thing is they said I could do the first story and I get to choose the subject. Isn't that amazing?'

'I can't believe it! Have you decided who you're going to write about?'

'Nicole Gallagher. Do you remember her? She was all over the papers last year.'

'Her husband disappeared, didn't he?'

Aoife nodded. 'On their honeymoon. Can you imagine?'

'Has she agreed to speak to you?'

'She just messaged me now. We're meeting tomorrow.'

'That's really brilliant, Aoife. I'm so happy for you. If you keep going on like this, you'll be able to give up all those horrible temping jobs soon.'

'I hope so. I'd really love to be working from home full-time before I get pregnant again.'

'Are you planning on having kids immediately?'

'We thought it would be best to wait a year or two. I want Amy totally used to her new family before we disrupt her life any further.'

'Is she okay about the wedding?'

'To her it's just a party and a chance to wear a fancy dress. She doesn't remember a time when Conor wasn't in her life. Her latest thing is parading up and down the hall, flinging potpourri everywhere.' Aoife laughed. 'She says she's practising to be a flower girl.'

'Talking of which'—Orla thanked the waitress, who put a cup of black coffee on the table—'did you check out the links I sent you?'

'Links?'

'Aoife! For God's sake! The wedding's in four months. You have to choose a dress. What are you waiting for?'

'Oh, there's no rush. It's not like we're doing the big white wedding thing. It will only be family and a few friends, and we're having the reception in the garden.'

'Have you at least ordered the marquee?'

'I think Conor did that.'

'You think! Aoife! Do you want to get married or not?'

Aoife laughed. 'Of course I want to get married. I just don't have any interest in what I wear or where we eat or any of that stuff. I did the whole big white wedding thing before, remember? And look how that worked out.'

'That was because you chose the wrong man. This time it will be completely different.'

'Yeah, well, I didn't know I'd chosen the wrong man at the time and I still hated every minute of the entire day.'

'You were a teenager, Aoife, and your parents were barely cold in their graves. A big family wedding was the last thing you needed. Besides, I wasn't there, was I? This time you are going to have a ball. I take my bridesmaid's duties very seriously and you are going to have the best day of your entire life, whether you want it or not. I won't hear any arguments.'

'Orla, I have people to inter—'

'No "Orlas". I am making an appointment for you and we are going to pick out your dress.'

'But—'

Orla held up a hand. 'No buts. I'll give you a choice of three different days, but you are going to one of them if I have to drag you there by the hair.'

THREE

Aoife was well used to interviewing people and it rarely cost her a second thought, but this time it felt different. Her mouth was dry and her hands clammy as she parked opposite Block 2 in the apartment complex. This time there was so much at stake. If she did a good job, she'd be able to pitch to every editor in the country. It could really kick-start her career.

Nicole's apartment was in Sandymount. It was an expensive area, within walking distance of both the ocean and the city centre. Judging from the size of the apartments and the age of the majority of cars parked near her, Aoife assumed most of the apartments were rented. In a largely futile attempt to make the four concrete boxes look inviting, tiny green triangles separated the four apartment blocks and the exteriors were freshly painted.

Aoife took deep breaths as she climbed the stairs to the second floor. She wiped her hands on her leggings before knocking on the door. It was opened by a woman a few years younger than herself wearing skinny jeans and a grey hoodie. She wore no make-up and her red hair was tied into a loose plait which was pulled over one shoulder, Katniss Everdeen style. Aoife could count on the fingers of one hand the number of natural redheads she had seen in her life, but the freckles that covered every inch of Nicole's face left no doubt that her hair colour was natural. There were dark circles under her eyes, and although her lips formed a smile as she greeted Aoife, her eyes were dull and lifeless.

Nicole led Aoife into a large room which comprised the entire living area. The kitchen ran along one wall, opposite which was a tiny breakfast bar with two stools. Directly opposite the kitchen was a peach-coloured three-seater sofa which faced a wall-mounted flat-screen TV. Almost touching the back of the sofa was an oval glass table with four chairs. French doors led to a decent-sized balcony with a round table and two chairs.

'I know,' Nicole said when she saw Aoife looking outside. 'Whose bright idea was it to waste so much space on a balcony? It might make sense if we had a sea view, but you'd need a skyscraper to catch a glimpse of the sea from here.' She took two mugs from the cupboard. 'Coffee?'

'You're the first journalist I've spoken to in a long time,' Nicole said, putting two mugs of coffee on the table. She took a seat opposite Aoife.

'Thanks for agreeing to talk to me.'

'To be honest, I'm not sure this is a good idea. I'm sick to death of people saying Matt ran out on me and I just can't accept it. He didn't, you know.'

'What do you think happened?'

'I don't think, I have absolutely no doubt what happened.' Her eyes filled with tears, but she blinked them away. 'Matt is dead.'

There was a knock on the door and Nicole went to answer it. 'My neighbour,' she said when she returned a few moments later. 'Checking up on me. I barely knew anyone in this building before Matt died—now I've no idea what I'd do without them. They've all been so good.'

'You're very lucky.'

'You have no idea. In the beginning, when I didn't want to get out of bed, they brought food. After a few weeks, they insisted on dragging me outside for some fresh air. I would never have believed strangers could be so kind.'

'They sound amazing.'

'They really are. And they won't even let me thank them. They insist I did them a favour. The other apartment blocks in this complex are mostly full of strangers, but they say it's thanks to me that in this block we've all become close friends.' She gave a sad smile. 'At least one positive thing came from Matt's death.'

'Why are you so sure Matt's dead? He's still listed as missing, isn't he?'

'There's no other possible explanation.' Nicole picked up her mug. 'Oh, I know what people say. Believe me, I've heard it all—he had another wife, another family, he was in debt, in trouble with the law. It's all nonsense. I knew Matt. He wouldn't have left me without a word. Not under any circumstances.'

'Tell me about him. How did you and Matt meet?'

Nicole's eyes took on a faraway look, but her memories didn't appear to give her much pleasure. 'In Nepal. Both of us booked the same hiking tour to the Everest base camp. Matt and I were the only two Irish people, so we spent a lot of time together. I mentioned returning to Ireland and looking for a full-time job. We were both in IT, so when Matt returned a few months later, he texted me and asked if I had any good contacts.

I said he could stay with me for a while until he found a place of his own. He never left.'

'Who did he work for?'

'Mostly he worked freelance. He talked me into doing the same. It gave us the best of both worlds—a home base and regular extended holidays.'

'You both worked from this apartment?'

'I like working at this table, or in good weather I move out to the balcony. Matt worked in the bedroom.'

'How long were you together before you got married?'

'Three months.' She caught the surprise on Aoife's face. 'You think I hadn't known him very long and that I have no idea what Matt is capable of. You're wrong.'

'People can surprise you.'

Nicole shook her head. 'Not Matt. I knew him as well as it's possible to know another human being. And Matt knew me. My mother…' She twisted the wedding ring on her left finger. 'Aoife, I don't want you writing about Matt's family or mine. That's confidential.'

'I keep my promises, Nicole. You'll get to read every word of my story before it's printed, and I'll remove anything confidential that's not essential to the story.'

'Right. Well, this is completely irrelevant, so it stays between us. Okay?'

Aoife nodded.

'My mother has substance abuse issues. I rarely saw her growing up, but every year or so she'd turn up at my grandmother's house, make a big fuss of me, and just when I was beginning to think that this time everything would be alright, she'd disappear. She never once said goodbye. It took me years to accept she'd never change. If Matt wanted to leave me, he'd have told me. At the very least, he'd have sent me an email, or even a text. He'd never disappear without a word. He knew what that would do to me.'

'The last time you saw Matt was on the beach, right?'

'Yes. He was on the sunbed beside me before I fell asleep. When I woke up, there was no sign of him.'

'And he left all his things behind?'

Nicole nodded. 'His passport was in the hotel safe. His bank account has never been touched. He's never used his credit cards. His phone has been switched off since the day he disappeared. He's never contacted his parents.'

'What does his family think happened?'

'You'd have to ask them. I only met his mother once. I've never met his father.'

'Why is that?'

'When Matt told them we were getting married, they tried to talk him out of it. There was a big fight and Matt said if that's the way they felt, he wasn't inviting them to the wedding. I tried to talk him round, but he said they weren't a close family and he only told them we were getting married out of a sense of obligation.'

'Did Matt say why they weren't close?'

'The only thing that matters to them is what others think of them. Everything was framed in terms of the neighbours. It wasn't "you'll be late for school", it was "the neighbours will see you're running late again". They cared how their son reflected on them, but they didn't give a damn about Matt.'

'He told you that?'

'Not exactly. Matt was very reluctant to discuss his childhood. All he would say was it was no big deal, that his parents had never been abusive and he'd wanted for nothing. But I knew his relationship with them bothered him more than he let on.

Once I met his mother, I understood why. A block of ice would have more warmth.'

'You met his mother after Matt died?'

Nicole nodded. 'When I came back from Italy, I called to their house. The police had already told them Matt was missing, but they'd made no attempt to contact me. It didn't seem right ignoring them. I was dumb enough to assume that at the very least they'd have questions about Matt's disappearance.'

'They didn't want to discuss it?'

'His mother wouldn't even let me inside the door. She said it was my fault her son ran away. She accused me of lying about being pregnant and—'

'You were pregnant?'

'No, I was never pregnant and Matt knew that. His mother thinks I lied to him. She believes there was no other possible reason Matt would want to marry somebody he'd only known for such a short time. She said I put him under too much pressure, that he was too young to be a husband and father and that if I hadn't forced him into a commitment, none of this would have happened.'

'Can I speak to Matt's parents?'

'You could try, I suppose, but they won't want to be interviewed. I'll text you their contact details. They live in Glenageary.'

'Great. Now this is a human-interest story, so my readers will want to feel they really know Matt. Did he have an Instagram account?'

'He had one when he travelled, but he hasn't posted since then.'

'Could you forward the photos on his phone?'

'I can't. There was a break-in here a few weeks after I returned from Italy. There wasn't much to take, but they got both our laptops.'

'Weren't his photos saved to the cloud?'

'No, he'd used up his free storage when he was travelling and he didn't think it was worthwhile buying more. We generally used my phone for photos. It's got a much better camera. I can send you those pics if you like?'

'That would be great, thanks. But those pics are a record of your life together. I'm looking for something that gives me a feeling of Matt as an individual. Could you send me his bank and credit card statements for the six months before he disappeared?'

'How would they help?'

'You can tell a lot about a person from their financial records.'

'Okay. It can't do any harm, I suppose.'

'I'd also like to speak to Matt's friends. Could you give me a list?'

'I'll send you the wedding guest list. Everyone we knew was there, and it was the last time any of them saw him.'

'And I'd like to speak to your neighbours.'

'Matt had a few clients in the complex, but he didn't know them well. Mostly he gave them remote assistance. He knew the people on our floor to say hello to but that was about it. As I said, I only became close to the neighbours after Matt died.'

'I'd still like to speak to them, if that's okay with you.'

'Sure. I'll let them know I'm fine with it.'

Nicole printed out the bank statements and handed them to Aoife.

'Thanks. You mentioned on the phone that you hired an Italian firm of private investigators. Did they come up with anything?'

'They only have one lead that seems promising. When they

spoke to all the hotel staff, one of the receptionists mentioned a man she thought had been acting strangely. According to her, the man's eyes followed me every time I entered the reception area that day.'

'Men often watch young, pretty women.'

'The odd thing about this guy was he checked in the day Matt disappeared and checked out the following morning. He'd reserved the room for a week.'

'That's unusual. He could have had an emergency of some kind.'

'That's what I thought, but the detectives felt it was worth following up on. They bribed the receptionist to give them a copy of the man's passport, but when she checked the file it was missing.'

'Could she have misfiled it?'

'Maybe. But when the investigators checked out his address, it was fake. They think he gave a fake name too.'

'How is that possible? Didn't the receptionist look at the passport when she registered him?'

'She doesn't remember the man checking in. It had been a very busy day with lots of people coming and going, but she's adamant she took a copy of everybody's passport and confirmed their photo and name matched the passport details.'

'How do the detectives explain that?'

'They're not sure, but one thing is certain, that man went to a lot of trouble to hide his identity. Why would he do that, Aoife?'

'I don't know.'

'I think it's because he's either Matt's murderer or he knows something about his death.'

FOUR

THE MINUTE SHE reached her car, Aoife phoned the Gallaghers' landline and left a message. She doubted she would even get a response, but that evening she received a text with directions to the Gallagher home and a request that she arrive at 10.15 the following morning. The text was unsigned. Who arranged meetings for 10.15? Why not ten o'clock or ten thirty?

Matt's parents lived on a quiet street lined with mature trees. The houses were all large red-bricked buildings separated by generous gardens. The residents obviously didn't believe in house numbers. The houses were distinguished by their names—'The Pines', 'Prospect House', etc. One was even called 'Sea View' although there was no sea in sight. The Gallaghers' home was 'Aurora'. The gates opened onto a large, paved area. Two octagonal steps led to a glass door with a black frame. The bell was answered by a small, elderly lady who introduced herself as 'Mrs Gallagher'. Aoife guessed she was in her late seventies. That would make her in her fifties when Matt was born. Matt's grandmother, maybe? Mrs Gallagher was a little too thin to be considered elegant, but her style was classic and expensive. She wore a well-cut navy skirt, white blouse, navy cardigan and navy patent kitten-heeled shoes. Her light brown hair was cut into short layers. She looked Aoife up and down and from the frown and her pursed lips, Aoife guessed she didn't approve of jeans or leather jackets.

'Follow me, please.' Her tone was frosty and her posture stiff. Disapproval practically seeped from her pores.

They walked through a short corridor into a large, high-ceilinged octagonal hallway. It was bright, airy and cheerful, a stark contrast to Mrs Gallagher. The large room Aoife was led into seemed a better fit. The dark, heavy furniture was appropriately oppressive. It was as if every attempt had been made to diminish the room's natural beauty. Even the stunning bay windows were half hidden by multicoloured floral curtains. Mrs Gallagher motioned for Aoife to take a seat on the dark brown sofa. She perched on the edge of a chair opposite, her head erect and her back ramrod straight.

Aoife was unsure how to begin. What was this woman's relationship to Matt?

'Will we be joined by Matt's father?'

Mrs Gallagher pursed her lips. 'My husband spends most mornings on the golf course.' She caught the surprise on Aoife's face and her frown deepened. 'We believed we were unable to have children. Matthew was something of a surprise.'

'Thank you for agreeing to speak to me, Mrs Gallagher.' Aoife waited, but Mrs Gallagher didn't respond. Nor did she ask to be called by her first name. 'I've spoken to Nicole,' Aoife continued. 'She—'

'The only reason I agreed to speak to you is to explain that Matthew is not a suitable subject for your article. My son is not missing. He realised his marriage was a mistake and he couldn't face telling the girl, so he ran away. He'll return when he is ready.'

'Have you heard from Matt, Mrs Gallagher?'

'I have not. Nor do I expect to. Matthew was very angry when his father and I advised him against marrying that girl. We were right, obviously, but that will add to Matthew's anger.'

'Why are you so sure your son is alive?'

'I do not subscribe to the theory that bodies can disappear into thin air. If Matthew was dead, his body would have been found by now.'

'His wife disagrees.'

'Of course she does. She wants Matthew declared legally dead.'

'Why would she want that?'

'Because she thinks she can get her thieving hands on my son's money.'

'Matt had money?'

'He's the only grandchild on either side of the family. Both sets of grandparents left money in trust for him. He'll have access to it on his thirtieth birthday. I said to the police, keep an eye on that money. On Matthew's thirtieth birthday, he'll get in touch with our solicitors. I'd stake my life on it.'

'Is there much money involved?'

'About five million.'

In an attempt to stifle a whistle, Aoife had a fit of coughing. Matt's mother watched impassively. When Aoife made two unsuccessful attempts to speak, both interrupted by a fit of coughing, Mrs Gallagher gave an exasperated sigh and left the room. A few minutes later she returned with a glass of tap water.

'Thank you,' Aoife said when she had recovered her breath. 'That's a lot of money.'

'It certainly is, and it's the reason that girl wants everyone to believe Matthew is dead. She thinks she'll inherit everything.'

'And will she?'

The older woman shrugged. 'It depends on the terms of the trust. I don't imagine his grandparents envisaged Matthew disappearing without a trace.'

'I get the impression you don't like Nicole.'

'You are correct.'

'May I ask why?'

Mrs Gallagher's mouth twisted into a sneer. 'She is not the kind of person I would wish to associate with.'

'Why is that?'

'Do you know her mother is a drug addict?'

'Nicole mentioned there were issues.'

Mrs Gallagher snorted. 'Issues! The woman's been in prison for shoplifting. That's the kind of family my son married into—criminals!' Her face flushed a dark red. 'My husband and I devoted our whole lives to building a reputation as honest, decent, upstanding citizens and that's what our own son does to us—marries a criminal and then'—her voice rose—'in case there was a single person in the country who didn't know about it, he runs away and has the whole sordid tale spread all over the media. It's all I can do to hold my head up in public.'

'How do you think Matt is supporting himself at the moment? He hasn't tried to access his bank account or use his credit card.'

Mrs Gallagher shrugged. 'He works in IT. There are always people willing to pay cash for that type of work. Matthew can look after himself.'

'It must be a difficult life, though. Wouldn't it be a lot easier to tell Nicole he wanted a divorce?'

'Obviously, but Matthew wouldn't see it that way.'

'I don't understand.'

'Are you familiar with the saying "The apple doesn't fall far from the tree"?'

Aoife nodded.

'My husband is a talented businessman and has many stellar qualities. Unfortunately, our son inherited his main failing.'

'And that is?'

'The men in my family are weak. Neither of them could stand up to anyone if their lives depended on it. At the first sight of confrontation, they turn and run. Matthew would rather walk away from his life than tell that girl unpleasant truths.'

'Such as?'

'That their marriage was a mistake, of course.'

'But they'd been married less than a week.'

'Huh! Believe me, you can know a marriage is a mistake within hours.'

'I see. Would your husband be willing to speak to me?'

Mrs Gallagher stood. 'I believe I have adequately explained why speaking to any member of my family would be a waste of time.' She opened the door to the hall and waited for Aoife to join her. 'I'll show you out.'

FIVE

'NICOLE THINKS THE man in the hotel was the murderer.'

Conor switched on the kettle. 'It's possible, I suppose. But why would any murderer check into the same hotel as his victim? Where is the hotel, by the way?'

'Bari in Italy. I looked it up. It's a city by the sea, so you can have a city and beach holiday in one. It looks amazing. Isn't it an awful pity I don't have a richer client? I could get free trips to Italy to interview the hotel staff.'

'Is the hotel nice?'

'The Colonnina? It's nice but not luxurious. They have a very mixed clientele—holidaymakers and businessmen. It's very near the airport.'

"So they must have businessmen who get up early and holidaymakers who are still wandering around in the early hours. I don't think you'd stay in a hotel like that if you intended to murder one of the guests. Too much coming and going. It seems unnecessarily risky.'

'I don't know, Conor. Maybe the murderer didn't intend to kill Matt. They could have had an argument that got out of control.'

'True. I'm not convinced, though.'

'No, I'm not either.'

Amy bounded into the room, Supergirl balanced on her head. 'Coffee time!'

'Change into your pyjamas first, Amy.'

When she was gone, Aoife put her arms around Conor and they kissed passionately. They reluctantly drew apart when they heard Amy's footsteps on the stairs. Conor took out three mugs and filled two with coffee and one with tepid water. Aoife and a pyjama-clad Amy followed him into the sitting room. Amy plonked down on the sofa between them. Conor handed her the mug of water and she took a big gulp.

'What do you say?' Aoife asked.

'Thanks, Moaney.' Amy wiped her mouth with the back of her hand. She grabbed the red tiles and pulled the Connect 4 stand closer. 'You have to be yellow this time, Moaney.'

Conor picked up the yellow tiles. 'Okay, but tonight I'm going to win.'

'No, you can't win.' Amy giggled. 'I'm the world champion.'

Aoife switched on her laptop and did an internet search for Matt's father. The photo she found was ten years out of date, but Aoife figured she would still recognise him. When Conor saw she was working, he kept Amy busy, insisting she had to give him one more chance to win. Aoife smiled at Amy's shouts of triumph and Conor's pretend groans. A few more Google searches and she had confirmed that the nearest golf club to the Gallaghers' home was in Killiney and that Matt's father was a member. When she checked her emails, she found Nicole had already emailed her the wedding guest list—two hundred names.

By this time Conor had played ten games of Connect 4.

Aoife took pity on him and switched on the TV. All thoughts of Connect 4 forgotten, Amy stretched out on the floor and within a few seconds was completely engrossed in a Disney movie. When she fell asleep, Conor carried her upstairs.

'How's the article going?' he asked when he returned.

'Early days yet. It's a good thing I'm between temping contracts. I have about two hundred and fifty people to speak to. It's going to take forever.'

'What did you think of Matt's mother?'

Aoife filled him in on their conversation.

'Do you think she's right?' Conor asked.

'That Matt is alive? No. Whatever his mother says, I can't see him giving up his life rather than ask for a divorce. It's odd they haven't found his body yet, though.'

'If it was an accident, they probably would have.'

'Which means Nicole is right and Matt was murdered.'

Conor nodded. 'And statistically speaking, the murderer is probably his wife.'

'They were married less than a week, Conor, and Nicole is the one insisting Matt is dead. If she murdered him, she'd want everyone to believe he walked out on her so the police wouldn't investigate.'

'Not if she's after Matt's money. A court has to declare him dead before she'll be able to touch it.'

'But that would take years, Conor. Wouldn't it?'

'No. They changed the law a few years ago. Now the entire process can be completed within twelve months if there's reasonable evidence to suggest the missing person is dead.'

'Nicole isn't a murderer. It's obvious she loved Matt, and she even hired an Italian firm of private investigators when the

Italian police weren't doing enough to find him. That's got to have cost a fortune.'

'You have to spend money to make money.'

Aoife aimed a pretend blow at him. Conor ducked and grinned.

'Seriously though, Aoife, half the murderers in the world claim they loved their victims. A spouse is the most likely suspect even when there isn't any money involved.'

'I doubt Nicole knew about Matt's inheritance. Their apartment is tiny. And it's rented.'

'That's interesting. Matt didn't want his wife to know he was going to come into a lot of money. I wonder why?'

SIX

THERE WAS TORRENTIAL rain the following morning. It started just after Aoife walked Amy to her classroom. In the three minutes it took to walk back to the car, she was drenched to the skin. What the hell was happening to Irish weather? Was this global warming? Ireland never used to have rain like this. She'd have to forget her plans to talk to Matt's father today. Nobody would play golf in this weather.

Aoife tossed her soaking wet clothes into the washing machine and, having changed into sweats, spent the morning phoning everyone on Nicole and Matt's wedding list. By noon, she had crossed ninety-two people off her list. All were friends of Matt's from his school and college years. He'd sent them the odd WhatsApp message with photos from his travels, but the wedding was the first time they'd spoken to him in years, and even then, they barely got past congratulations. The first time they'd seen Nicole was when she walked down the aisle. Aoife made appointments to speak to Matt's best man, a school friend he occasionally played squash with, and every relative on the guest list. Then she drove to Nicole's.

⁂

'Five million! I don't believe it. Matt would have told me if he had that kind of money.'

'He doesn't have it yet. He'll inherit it when he turns thirty.'

'But that's just three years away. His mother is lying. She has to be.'

'Matt never mentioned anything about future plans? Buying a house, maybe?'

'We discussed where we'd like to live. Matt wanted a house by the sea. We both spent all our money travelling, so I didn't think it was a serious conversation. I said we should start saving for a dep…' Her voice trailed off and she looked down at her wedding ring.

'Yes?'

'Now that I think about it, Matt was very reluctant to discuss buying a house. He said our twenties are for travelling and our thirties for settling down. Maybe that was because he was thinking of his inheritance. But why wouldn't he say so?'

'I don't know. Did Matt leave a will?'

'No. We had access to each other's bank accounts and we don't own any property. The only thing he left was his car. As he's still officially alive, I figured I could do what I wanted with it. One of the neighbours offered me cash, so I sold it.'

'To somebody in this building?'

'No. He lives in one of the other blocks. Katie upstairs took care of it. I didn't want to know.'

'Of course. Nicole, did you get a chance to ask your neighbours if they would speak to me?'

'They're all fine with it. Do you want to start now?'

'Would anybody be free at such short notice?'

'Most of the apartments are empty during the day. Vicky works shifts, so she's here at odd hours, but I know she's working today. Katie's your best bet. She works from home and she's usually happy to take a break. I'll introduce you and I'll see if I can line anybody else up for today.'

Katie wore skinny jeans and a crop top that exposed her entire midriff. There wasn't one inch of fat to be seen and her body had the toned look of someone who spent hours each week in the gym. Her long, shiny dark hair was tied back in a ponytail and she wore pink-and-white runners. Her apartment was an exact copy of Nicole's. Even the furniture was identical. Katie and Nicole exchanged smiles when they noticed Aoife's surprise.

'Everyone gets a shock if they see more than one of these apartments,' Katie said. 'The entire complex was purchased by some American company. I guess it was cheaper to buy the furniture in bulk. I suppose we could add our own touch, but it hardly seems worth it. Most of us don't plan to stay here very long.'

Katie cleared a laptop and files from the kitchen table. 'Nicole, are you staying? I can get you something to drink.'

'Thanks, Katie, I'll leave you two alone. Anyway, I wouldn't drink anything you keep in this place. How you can get through the day without coffee is beyond me.'

Katie grinned. 'Sometimes I don't. Whenever I'm in town I pop into Bewley's, but don't tell Greg. He's convinced the stuff will kill me. Aoife, I can offer you orange juice or'—she picked up a large plastic container filled with a thick green concoction—'would you prefer an energy drink?'

'A glass of water is fine, thanks.'

When they were alone, Aoife said, 'Nicole mentioned how great all her neighbours have been.'

'Somebody had to help the poor girl. Did you see those photos of her landing at the airport? She didn't have a single person with her for support. We couldn't let her go through this alone.'

'Nicole didn't have any friends who could help?'

'Not people she's close to. She went travelling straight out of college and she lost touch with most of her friends over the years.'

'Hadn't she been back six months before Matt disappeared?'

'Yes, and she made a few friends at work, but then she and Matt became an item. You know what it's like, they were still at the spending-every-moment-with-each-other stage.'

'Nicole was lucky to have you.'

'We're lucky to have her too.'

'How well did you know Matt?'

'We said hi when we ran into each other in the lift or the car park. That's about it.'

'Did anyone else in the building know him better?'

There was a slight pause before Katie replied, 'No.'

'You don't seem very sure.'

'I'm sure.'

'Okay, well, I'm going to go door to door over the next few days, so I might find out more information then.'

'Door to door?' Katie put down her drink and muttered, 'Damn.'

'Is something wrong?'

'All Nicole has now is her memories of Matt and he becomes more saintlike every day. If you were to find out anything that destroyed her memory, it would kill her.'

'What could I find out?'

'Nothing. Forget it. It's time I went back to work.' She pushed back her chair and went to rise.

'Katie, if I don't know what I'm supposed to be keeping secret, I could accidentally let it slip to Nicole.'

Katie slumped back into the chair. 'I suppose you have a point. I didn't know Matt and I have no idea if this is true or not, but there are rumours that Matt was having an affair.'

SEVEN

KATIE WAS UNABLE to give any more information about Matt's affair.

'I didn't want to know about it and I refused to discuss it any time the subject was raised.'

'Who did you hear discussing it?'

'Several people.'

'You can't think of any of their names?'

'Well, the first person who mentioned it to me was Vicky. Her apartment is at the end of this corridor. I heard it several times since, but I can't remember exactly who mentioned it.'

Aoife was able to interview another three of Nicole's neighbours. None of them had ever spoken to Matt. Aoife dropped hints about Matt's affair. They all denied knowing anything about it, but Aoife was pretty sure they were lying. It was the following day before she managed to speak to Vicky.

'I don't remember mentioning it to Katie, but I definitely heard that Matt was having an affair.'

'Who mentioned it to you?'

'We have an informal arrangement that anybody who is free goes to the local pub on Friday nights. Usually at least four or five people turn up. One Friday they were all talking about Matt's affair when I arrived.'

'What exactly did they say?'

'Nobody had any details, but a few days ago I heard he was seen leaving a woman's apartment late at night.'

'The woman lives in this apartment block?'

'No, one of the other blocks in the complex.'

'Do you know her name?'

'Dearbhla.'

'Has anybody spoken to her?'

'Not that I know of. There wouldn't be much point now that Matt's dead.'

'What's her surname?'

'I don't know.'

'Where could I find her?'

'I've heard she owns a coffee shop in town. That's how I know her name. It's called Dearbhla's Dream Bean Brew.'

Aoife had just put Amy to bed when Nicole phoned.

'The Italian private investigators called me. They identified the man in the hotel.'

'Who is he?'

'Edgard something, I forget his surname. When they send their written report, I'll forward it to you. The important thing is they can't find any connection between him and Matt.'

'Why did he leave the hotel so abruptly?'

'We don't know yet. He's on holidays in New Zealand, so the detectives have to wait until he comes back to talk to him.'

'Where does he normally live?'

'London at the moment, although he moves around a lot.'

'When will he be back?'

'His office isn't expecting him until the end of the month.'

'Well, that's not too far away, Nicole.'

'I know, but apparently he's a middle-aged salesman. Why would a middle-aged salesman want to murder Matt?'

'I don't know. It's possible he was a witness to whatever happened to Matt. Something made him run away from the hotel.'

EIGHT

AOIFE WAS OFFERED a last-minute temping job, so she couldn't speak to Dearbhla that week. She didn't want to work that weekend as it was one of those rare occasions when Amy's weekend with her father coincided with Conor's weekend off.

'We could get a last-minute deal to somewhere dry and sunny,' Conor suggested as he shook the rain off his jacket.

'That sounds lovely, but I don't like to be too far away from Amy. What if she needed me?'

'She's never needed you yet, Aoife.'

'I know, but young kids get sick really quickly. I wouldn't trust Jason to take care of her properly.'

'When did Jason ever take care of her? Isn't that why he invites his mother to stay every weekend he has Amy? You trust Maura, don't you?'

'Yes, but—'

'Aoife, if you're not going to enjoy it, there's no point going away, but the first time doing most things is the hardest. Think of it as a trial run for the honeymoon.'

'Oh, alright, but somewhere close, okay?'

'Paris?'

The last flight to Paris on Friday left at 7.45. The earliest Jason ever collected Amy was 6 p.m., which didn't give Aoife time to get to the airport. There was no point in asking Jason to arrive early. If he even suspected Aoife was planning a trip, he probably wouldn't turn up at all. On Thursday night she texted him, *Can you collect Amy around 7? I'd like to say goodbye to her before she leaves and I'll be late home on Friday.* The reply came within seconds. *Can't. Have plans. Finishing work early and will collect her at 5.30 sharp. Important I leave immediately. Can't wait.*

On Friday Aoife had Amy packed and ready to go by 3 p.m. She parked her car in the garage. If Jason arrived early to catch her out, he would be furious to find she was already home. He might even drive away without stopping and who knew what time he'd return? At 4 p.m. her phone pinged. *Parked outside house. Where is Amy? Can't wait. Have to leave immediately.* Aoife was in the airport by 6 p.m.

Conor was going straight from work to the airport, so they agreed to meet at Bewley's. Aoife bought a coffee and was walking around looking for an empty seat when she spotted Katie at one of the tables.

'Hi, Katie.'

'Aoife, hi. This is my husband, Greg.'

Greg was in his early twenties, average height, slim with blonde hair, eyebrows that were too dark to be natural for somebody with such pale skin, and a perfect manicure. He pushed his fringe out of his eyes and gave her a bright smile.

'Katie tells me you're writing an article about Matt.'

'Yes, that's right. I've been meaning to set up an interview with you, actually.'

'Oh, I couldn't help you. I barely knew the guy. Where are you off to this weekend?'

'My fiancé and I are going to Paris.'

'That sounds lovely. Katie and I are flying to Romania. We're feeling very sorry for ourselves because we're working this weekend.'

Katie grinned. 'I'm so depressed, Greg even agreed to treat me to a coffee. Normally he has a fit if I set foot inside a coffee shop.'

'That stuff is poison, Katie.' He turned to Aoife. 'I should never have let her talk me into coming here, but I couldn't see any other way of getting her on the plane.'

'Do you always work weekends?'

Katie shook her head. 'Only once every two or three months. We're on a recruitment drive. Greg and I own a cleaning company. It's impossible to get Irish women to work as cleaners these days, but Eastern European women are more willing.'

'Really? My friend, Orla, has been trying to get someone to clean her house for months. Could you find her somebody?'

'Where does she live?'

'Malahide.'

'We don't have anybody in that area at the moment,' Greg said. 'Why don't you text Katie your friend's details? I'm doing another recruitment drive in Italy next month. Katie will let you know if we have any spare capacity.'

'Two recruitment drives. That sounds promising. My friend will be thrilled.'

'Greg shouldn't be giving you false hope, Aoife. I've a long waiting list already and it's not always easy to find suitable candidates.'

'Can't you recruit Eastern Europeans who already live in Ireland?'

Katie shook her head. 'If they can afford to come to Ireland on their own, they won't work as cleaners.'

'You have to go all the way to Romania to find staff?'

'We've tried other countries, but we've been most successful in Romania. Romanians are legally entitled to work in Ireland, but the girls from the poorer areas could never afford to get here. We pay their flight, they work for us for a few years, improve their English and move on to better jobs.'

'Do you have many employees?'

'About eighty,' Greg said.

'Eighty-two, actually,' Katie corrected him. 'We've only been in this business a couple of years, but we're growing all the time.' She smiled at her husband. 'We plan to have two hundred staff by the end of next year.'

'You must have a lot of clients.'

'Oh, we're inundated with people who are desperate for cleaners.'

'I've never been to Romania. What's it like?'

Katie was describing the Romanian countryside when they were joined by Conor.

'Hi, hon. This is Katie and her husband, Greg. They're friends of Nicole's.'

Katie smiled. 'Are you a reporter too?'

'No, Aoife's the one with the talent. My reports are bare facts. I've often been told they're mind-numbingly boring.'

'Conor's a detective. That's why I'm so excited we can get away for the weekend. He doesn't get many weekends off.'

'A detective?' Katie grinned. 'Wow! That must be an interesting job. What made you decide to work for the police?'

Greg looked at his watch. 'We'd better go, or we'll miss our flight.' He handed Katie her suitcase. 'It was nice meeting you both. I hope you have a great weekend.'

Katie looked surprised, but she smiled and hurried after him.

Conor kissed Aoife. 'Are they going to New York?'

'No. Romania.'

He grinned at her. 'See what happens when you tell people what I do for a living? You frighten them away.'

'They don't seem the kind that're easily scared.'

'Greg must just hate the police, then. I checked the departures board on my way in and the next flight is to New York, the following flight's to London and then there's our own flight to Paris.'

Aoife laughed. 'You sound like you want to take him in for questioning. Greg probably thought we'd like time to ourselves. Or maybe he wants time alone with Katie. Would you like to grab a coffee, or should we go straight to the departure gate?'

They rented an apartment with a view of the Eiffel Tower. It was a little basic but spotlessly clean and the view was to die for. They walked arm in arm down the Champs-Élysées, let a street artist do their portrait in Montmartre, bought crusty bread, pâté, grapes and wine in a local shop and had an impromptu picnic in the shadow of the Sacré-Coeur Basilica. That evening they took a boat ride down the Seine. Aoife hadn't been to Paris since her college days, and it felt almost like she'd stepped into an alternate reality. She existed in a shiny bubble that floated above her real life. In this bubble she had no ex-husband, no bills and no in-laws. She was a carefree student enjoying a city made for lovers with the man of her dreams.

The following morning, they opened the window in the main room and ate breakfast as they stared out at the Eiffel Tower.

Conor checked his watch. 'We'd need to be getting a move on if we're going to make the plane. It was a perfect weekend, wasn't it?'

'Glorious. Worth every cent.'

Conor's phone buzzed. He checked his messages. 'That's Mum. She says Dad has to go up north for work next week. He won't be back in time for the dinner.'

Aoife turned her face away to hide her relief, but the carefree bubble shimmered.

'That's okay. We can re-arrange it for another time.'

'No need. Mum said they'll come without him. Dad doesn't really care who they invite to the wedding. Mum's the one with lists of relatives and people they owe return invitations to.'

The bubble popped and Aoife landed in the real world with a thud. 'Conor, I wish you didn't have to work that Friday. Whatever happens, please don't be late. I don't care if there's a mass murderer on the loose. I need you there on time.'

'Have I ever let you down?'

'No. But if you're ever going to, this is not the time to start.'

Conor pulled her into a hug. 'I know my mother takes a bit of getting used to, Aoife, but she's one of the best people I've ever met. Once you get to know her, you'll see I'm right.'

'She doesn't like me, Conor.'

'I don't think that's true, but there's an easy way to find out. Ask her. Mum doesn't usually offer her opinion to people she doesn't know well, but she's very blunt. Ask her straight out "do you like me?" and you'll get a yes-or-no answer.'

He gave her a quick kiss, then went to pack his suitcase. *And when your mother tells me she doesn't like me, what do I do then?* Aoife wondered, but she kept her thoughts to herself.

NINE

MONDAY WAS DRY and bright, if a little chilly. Aoife figured she'd better grab her chance to catch Matt's father at the golf club. Irish weather was changeable at the best of times, but April was particularly unsettled. It could be weeks before she had another chance.

The golf club's website said they had recently relaxed the dress code to allow 'smart jeans' in the bar and restaurant, but a jacket had to be worn after 6 p.m. Aoife figured that wasn't really an issue as she would have to leave by four to be back in time to collect Amy from her grandmother's. Black jeans and a shirt would be fine. She dropped Amy at school and was pulling into the golf club car park by ten thirty.

To pass the time, Aoife worked her way through Wordle, Hardle and Hurdle. She was down to her last chance, but she filled in the blanks confident that the correct answer was 'elude'. It turned out to be 'etude.' She flung her phone on the passenger seat, picked it up again and texted furiously, *Etude is NOT an English word. Show me that word in an English dictionary!* A few seconds later Orla replied, *Hurdle again?* Followed by a laughing emoji. Aoife was about to reply when she spotted Matt's father entering the car park. He was a heavyset man, about the same age as his wife. Like his wife, he was slightly taller than average and he wore glasses on a chain around his neck. Aoife stuck the phone in her bag and watched as he said goodbye to his friends. When he opened the boot, she got out of the car. As he was putting his golf bag inside, she called out to him. 'Mr Gallagher, could I have a moment, please?'

He turned and smiled. 'What can I do for you, young lady?'

Okay, it was a bit patronising, but it was friendly, a far cry from his wife's frostiness.

'My name is Aoife Walsh. Your wife may have mentioned that we spoke last week.'

'I don't think so. You're a friend of my wife's?' He sounded doubtful. Aoife guessed not too many people described themselves as Mrs Gallagher's friend.

'I'm a reporter. I'm doing a story on your son. Nicole suggested I speak to you.'

The smile slipped but returned at full force within seconds.

'I'm afraid I can't help you, Aoife. Goodbye.'

He shut the boot and headed for the car door. Aoife didn't follow, but she raised her voice a little louder than necessary. 'Mr Gallagher, your wife told me she believes your son is still alive. Do you agree?'

Two middle-aged gentlemen had just walked past. As Aoife spoke, their heads swivelled in unison. Matt's father nodded at them. They returned the nod but didn't move. One bent down and fiddled with his laces. Matt's father hesitated before getting into the car and banging the door. Aoife heard the lock click.

She approached the two gentlemen. 'Hi.' Again, she raised her voice louder than necessary. 'Could I speak to you for a moment, please?'

In a normal tone, she explained that she was a reporter doing a feature on golf club membership and would they be interested in speaking to her? The men were so enthusiastic that Aoife wondered if interviewing them might actually be a good idea. They were clearly both sociable and nosy—a reporter's dream. Who knew what they could tell her about the Gallaghers? Aoife now had her back to Matt's father. As she wrote down the men's phone numbers, she listened carefully. Three minutes later she heard it—the bang of a car door. A few seconds later, a hand rested on her shoulder. 'Excuse me for interrupting, gentlemen.' Matt's father adopted a jovial tone. 'If I could just have a quick word with this young lady?' They nodded eagerly and he continued, 'Aoife, my plans for the afternoon have been cancelled. Would you like to join me for lunch? My treat, of course.'

⁂

They entered the golf club restaurant and the waiter led them to the only empty window table.

'Thank you,' Matt's father said. 'We'll sit over there.' He led Aoife to a corner table at the back of the room. He put the glasses on his nose and studied his menu in silence. Once the waiter had taken their order, he glanced around to make sure they couldn't be overheard before hissing, 'What did you say to those men?'

'The golfers? Nothing. I just asked if they would be willing to speak to me.'

'Why, for God's sake? Neither of them has ever even met Matt. It's taken almost a year for people to stop talking every time I enter a room. You're going to stir the whole thing up again.'

'I'm not trying to stir anything, Mr Gallagher. All I want to do is talk to people who knew Matt. But if you can't help me, I can always talk to your neighbours.'

'Matt left home when he was eighteen. That's the last time the neighbours saw him. There's nothing they can tell you.'

'Well, I have to start somewhere.'

'Are you determined to ruin our lives?'

'Mr Gallagher, I'm not your enemy and there would be no need for me to speak to your neighbours if you answered my questions. I'm just trying to find out what kind of person Matt was. What could be the harm in talking about your son?'

The old man picked up a fork and tapped his finger against the handle. 'If I speak to you, you'll stay away from my neighbours?'

'Agreed.' Aoife noticed there was no mention of the golf club members.

Mr Gallagher put down the fork, sat back in the seat and folded his arms. 'What do you want to know?'

'Tell me about Matt.'

'I don't know what you want me to say. Matt was like most young men in their twenties.'

'He was your only child?'

'Yes.'

'What was he like as a boy?'

'What's that got to do with anything?'

'This is a human-interest story. My readers expect to learn what kind of person Matt was. I can't write that until I understand it myself.' When Mr Gallagher looked sceptical, she said, 'Indulge me.'

'Matt was like any other boy. I was a bank manager before I retired. It was a very demanding role. I saw less of the boy than I would have liked.'

'Was Matt close to his mother?'

'Of course.'

'I got the impression from your wife that there were some difficulties.'

'Difficulties!' He looked around to check nobody was eavesdropping. 'Of course there weren't any difficulties. What are you talking about?'

'I understood that Matt might have been a difficult child.'

'Nonsense. He was a perfectly normal boy.'

'Would your wife agree?'

'Look, I don't know what my wife's been saying to you, but we were a perfectly normal family. Admittedly we had never envisaged ourselves as parents and the transition was difficult, but we did everything possible for that boy.'

'So Matt had no faults at all?'

'Of course he had faults. Nobody's perfect.'

'And what were those faults, Mr Gallagher?'

'Stubbornness. There was no talking to the boy once he made up his mind. It didn't help that his mother was stubborn too.' He caught himself and took another quick glance around the room. 'Stubborn is too strong. My wife only wanted what was best for our son. Matt didn't always appreciate that.' He shrugged. 'Like most boys, I imagine.'

'I understand both you and your wife objected to Matt's wedding.'

The waiter arrived with the starters. When he was well out of earshot, Matt's father said, 'That's a case in point. Matt was not stupid. If anybody else had pointed out that marrying a girl you've only known for three months was insanity, he would have agreed. But, of course, the fact that we objected was even more reason to go ahead.'

'Why did you dislike Nicole?'

'I didn't dislike her. I'd never even met her.'

'And yet you objected to the wedding.'

'She wasn't a suitable choice for Matt. People like her should marry their own kind.'

'What kind is that?'

'Criminals.'

'Your wife mentioned that Nicole's mother had been imprisoned for shoplifting. I didn't realise the family were criminals.'

'What family? The girl doesn't even know who her father is. How on earth could we be expected to explain that to people? Can you imagine what the wedding would have been like? My wife and I have a lot of influential friends. We've been invited to some of the highest-profile events in this country. For years we planned who we would invite to Matt's wedding. But how could we possibly explain that girl's family?'

Aoife made a sound she hoped would be interpreted as sympathy.

'My wife and I spent a considerable amount of time and money on raising our son. We deserved better.'

As Aoife finished her starter and the waiter cleared the table, Matt's father listed all the important people he had met during his career and how grateful each and every one had been for his expertise. 'Even after our shame has been spread all over the media, they still speak to me whenever we meet at social occasions.'

'I notice you speak about Matt in the past tense. You're convinced he's dead?'

'Of course.'

'But your wife disagrees.'

Mr Gallagher sighed. 'Their relationship may have been strained, but my wife was the boy's mother. She's not ready to accept that Matt is dead.'

'What do you think happened to him?'

'Isn't it obvious? The girl killed him.'

❧

The waiter arrived with the main course. Mr Gallagher commented on his steak while Aoife picked at her seafood pasta. When the waiter left, Aoife said, 'Why—'

Mr Gallagher put a finger to his lips. He waited a few seconds, then looked around to make sure the waiter was out of earshot. Turning back to Aoife, he said, 'Yes?'

'Why do you think Nicole murdered Matt?'

'I presume my wife told you about his inheritance.'

Aoife nodded.

'What other reason do you need?'

'Have you shared your suspicions with the police?'

'Of course not. The last thing we need is more people asking questions and, God forbid, a trial. I need people to forget we ever had any connection to that family.'

'Mr Gallagher, are you saying you believe Nicole is a murderer, but you want her to get away with it?'

'I've given this a great deal of thought, and I see no alternative. If reporting her to the police could bring Matt back, I'd have to consider our options, but Matt's gone and he won't return. Making my family notorious isn't going to change that.'

TEN

'WELL, THAT'S CERTAINLY taking what the neighbours think to extremes, right?'

'I missed that, Orla. What did you say?'

'I said do you—'

'The internet connection keeps dropping. Why are you phoning me on WhatsApp? Are you abroad?'

'I have a meeting in London. I'll be back tomorrow. Hang on a second and I'll move into the corridor.'

A few seconds later, Orla asked, 'Is that better?'

'Yes.'

'I said what will you do if Matt's father is right?'

'And Nicole's the murderer?'

'It would make an interesting angle to your story—"my interview with the billionaire butcher bride".'

Aoife laughed. 'Millionaire, not billionaire. It would be something if I found the murderer, though, wouldn't it? I bet none of the other journalists will think of an angle like that.'

'I'm sure they won't but, Aoife, if Nicole didn't do it, the chances of you finding the identity of the murderer are practically non-existent.'

'Why?'

'Because Matt died in Italy. What are the chances that somebody living here went all the way to Italy to murder him?'

'Most people are murdered by someone they know, Orla. And murdering Matt abroad would actually be quite a good idea. The Italian authorities don't want to frighten tourists, so they won't try very hard to find a body, and the Irish police are unlikely to get involved.'

'You're forgetting that murdering someone isn't easy and finding somewhere to dump the body is harder still. Whatever chance you have of getting away with it in your own country, how are you going to hide a body in a country where you don't know anybody, don't understand how things work and probably don't even speak the language?'

'I guess that depends on what the murderer did with the body.'

'What about the woman Matt was having an affair with? That gives Nicole another reason to kill her husband.'

'Dearbhla. She owns a café in Dublin. I'm going to drop in there tomorrow and see if I can find out anything.'

'Let me know what happens. I'd better get back to work. Oh, Aoife, I forgot why I rang. I've made our appointment at the bridal shop. It's two weeks from today. Don't forget.'

'Could we put it off until the following week? I've got to—'

'No, Aoife, we can't. You've put it off twice already. I told you I wouldn't accept any excuses. I'll be waiting outside the shop at ten on Tuesday morning. If you're not there, you'll have to find yourself another bridesmaid.'

'Okay, okay, I'll be there. Orla, could you do me a favour?'

'Sure, if I can.'

'You must know people in all the big law firms by now, right?'

'I suppose. The people I know are mostly at junior levels, though.'

'Could you find out which firm is managing Matt's trust?'

ELEVEN

IT WAS THE following week before Aoife got a chance to call to Dearbhla's café. It was ten thirty when she arrived and, as she'd hoped, the café was almost deserted. Aoife took one of the stools at the counter and ordered a cappuccino. Dearbhla appeared to be the only person on duty. She was older than she looked on her Instagram profile. Her hair was less blonde and she had considerably more lines. Aoife guessed she was about thirty.

'I think I recognise you,' Aoife said when Dearbhla handed her the coffee. 'You live in those apartments in Sandymount, don't you? The ones opposite the hospital?'

'Yes, that's right. I'm Dearbhla. I own this place. Are we neighbours?'

'No. I have a friend who lives there and I visit her sometimes. She lives in the same block as that guy who disappeared on his honeymoon, I've forgotten his name.'

'Oh yes, Matt.'

'You knew him?'

'He set up my website when I bought this place and he's helped me out a few times when I had IT issues.'

'That was kind of him.'

'Not really. He charged me an arm and a leg. Although I have to admit Matt was worth it. He did a great job.'

'I suppose that must be one of the problems with working in the city centre. He probably charged you for the time it took him to get here.'

'We don't have office space here. I do all the paperwork from home. There weren't any travelling costs. Matt only had to cross the apartment complex to get to my place.'

'I don't envy you owning your own business. It must be very hard working here all day and then going home to do office work.'

'Starting out is tough for everyone. I'm hoping to be able to hire full-time staff next year.'

'You were lucky Matt was willing to work around your schedule, Dearbhla.'

'Yeah, he was good like that. He didn't mind popping over at all hours.'

'I'm always looking for people who'll do small jobs around the house, but I'm afraid to hire anybody from the internet. Half of them are crooks. One flooded my friend's house recently. You're lucky Matt worked out.'

'Oh, I wouldn't hire anybody who wasn't recommended to me. Matt had done work for a few people in the building. Most of it was just small stuff like fixing a laptop that crashed, but I heard he does consultancy work for bigger organisations too.'

'I feel so sorry for his wife. Imagine being married a week and not knowing whether your husband has deserted you or you're a widow.'

Dearbhla nodded. 'It doesn't bear thinking about, does it?'

'Do you know his wife?'

'No, we never met. I saw her picture in the paper, though. Such a terrible thing to happen to a young woman.'

'Yes, and I'm sure it's made even worse by the rumours.'

Dearbhla looked away. She straightened a row of mugs that were already perfectly aligned. 'Rumours?'

'My friend heard people say the husband was having an affair.'

Dearbhla nodded. 'Well, to be honest, I'd heard those rumours myself. I'm not really surprised. Matt was a bit of a looker. It's like my mother always said—*find yourself a sensible, ordinary-looking guy you can rely on. The good-looking ones are more trouble than they're worth.*'

TWELVE

THE DAY AOIFE had been dreading for months arrived. She was tempted to tell Conor she wasn't feeling well and his family would have to come to dinner another day, but what would that achieve? It was only postponing the inevitable. She owed it to Conor to make his family feel welcome in her home, and anyway it was past time they finalised the wedding guest list. To cope with the stress, Aoife had her Friday planned out to the minute. She would drop Amy off at school, then she would clean the house until every inch of it sparkled. At noon, she would begin preparing the dinner. Maybe her culinary skills would impress Conor's mother. God knows, nothing else had.

At 9.20, Aoife's mobile rang. It was the recruitment agency.

'Aoife, it's Harriet. Are you working today?'

'No.'

'Brilliant. I've got a job for you. You need to be at the address I'm going to text you in an hour.'

'Sorry, Harriet. I'm not working today.'

'You have to. This is an emergency. The company are having their grand opening ceremony right now and their receptionist never showed up.'

'I'm sorry, but I'm really busy today.'

'Alright, look, the receptionist didn't just not show up, I forgot to book anybody. I've been phoning around since seven thirty this morning and you're the only person within travelling distance who's not working today.'

'I'd love to help you, but—'

'I'm going to lose the client, Aoife. This is the second time I've screwed up their booking. I might even lose my job. I'm desperate, Aoife. Please, don't let me down.'

As a compromise Aoife agreed to work until lunch, which would give Harriet time to find a replacement. At twelve minutes past two Harriet sent a text. *I tried, Aoife. Nobody else is available. Sorry to screw up your plans and thanks so much for helping me out.* All calls to Harriet's mobile went straight to voicemail and the receptionist at the office said she wasn't at her desk. Aoife considered walking out, but she couldn't be that irresponsible. The owners were so excited about their opening and prospective clients had been popping in all day. She would leave at the dot of five. An elaborate dinner was now out of the question, but she could still prepare something decent.

At four twenty, the owner came running out to reception. Could Aoife call the cleaning company and get them to send someone around immediately? The caterers had disappeared without cleaning out the boardroom, and the presentation was due to start at 5.30. And could she make sure that only people with invitations to the presentation were allowed upstairs? Oh, and the raffle winner had disappeared. She was an older woman with an orange outfit and long dark hair. Please find her. And the people who weren't invited to the presentation would be leaving soon, so could Aoife have taxis waiting?

'It's okay, Aoife. I'll leave now and get the five p.m. train. I'll pick up Amy and I'll be at your house by six thirty. Dinner will be ready by the time you get home. My family aren't fussy. They'd eat anything.'

Aoife was glad Conor couldn't see her expression. She knew very well his mother would start finding fault the second she entered the house.

THIRTEEN

It was 7.30 before Aoife pulled into her driveway. The smell of curry hit her as she opened the door and some of the tension left her body. Four seconds later a little voice screamed 'Mummy!' and Aoife knew the evening was not going to go well. She picked up Amy and hugged her.

'What are you doing here?'

'Daddy's late. Moaney's making chocolate dessert. He let me lick the spoon.'

Aoife laughed. 'Yes, I can see that. Let's get you washed up and then we'll check your bag. Did Conor help you pack?'

'Yes, and he found Supergirl. She was under the bed.'

'Well, you wouldn't want to be without Supergirl. How about we leave your bag and your coat in the hall and then you'll be ready to leave the minute Daddy arrives?'

Conor came to greet her, the sleeves of his sweatshirt rolled up and a bottle of wine in one hand. 'Dinner will be ready in about twenty minutes.'

'Thanks, hon. Did Jason phone?'

Conor shook his head.

'You promised I could have more chocolate, Moaney.'

Conor smiled at her. 'I put a big piece in your bag. You can eat it tonight in Daddy's house.' He raised an eyebrow at Aoife.

'He'll come,' Aoife mouthed over Amy's head.

Jason wasn't the most reliable of fathers, but it was no coincidence that he was late the very first time Aoife's future in-laws were visiting.

Yep, it was going to be that kind of night.

FOURTEEN

FIFTEEN MINUTES LATER, exactly at the agreed time, the doorbell rang. Aoife let Conor answer. She patted her hair, straightened Amy's top and tried to look welcoming. As Grainne entered the hall, Aoife heard her say, 'Your brother's text says he'll be here in ten minutes. I haven't heard from that sister of yours. Unreliable as usual!'

'Sarah isn't unreliable, Mum. She's trying to settle into college life. That's her priority at the moment.'

Grainne sniffed. 'How many times have I told you all that family comes first? Nothing is more important.'

'Sarah will be here, Mum. Come inside.'

Grainne followed Conor into the room, acknowledged Aoife's greeting with a nod and thrust a bottle of wine into her arms.

Although they had only met on a handful of occasions, Aoife had already figured out that her future mother-in-law's limited wardrobe consisted of two outfits: blue jeans for everyday wear and black jeans for special occasions. Today had been designated a black jeans day. Aoife guessed she should be flattered. The jeans were paired with a white-and-black top.

Grainne had also taken the trouble to get her hair done. Gone were the familiar grey streaks that featured in about half of Conor's family photos. Grainne's hair was now the exact shade of Conor's. Aoife thought the grey streaks suited her better. Jet black might be Grainne's natural colour, but few women in their sixties could carry it off. Especially if, like Grainne, they rarely wore make-up. Aoife gave herself a mental shake. Finding fault with everything Grainne did was not going to help the situation.

'Mum, this is Aoife's daughter, Amy.'

Grainne looked at the child, her brow furrowed. 'Hi, Amy.'

Amy ducked behind Aoife. Aoife wished there was someone she could hide behind.

Grainne sniffed. 'Oh, we're having curry. Did Conor tell you it's my favourite?'

'Conor made it, actually.'

Grainne's eyebrows shot up and the frown returned. 'You made dinner, Conor?'

'Aoife got delayed at work.'

'I see.' Grainne pursed her lips and cast a scathing glance at Aoife that clearly said *What kind of woman invites her future in-laws to her home and then doesn't even bother to cook for them?*

'Can I get you a drink, Grainne?' Aoife asked.

'No, thank you. I'm not much of a drinker. A glass of wine with my dinner is enough for me.'

'Have some sherry, Mum. I got a bottle in especially for you.'

Grainne hesitated, then smiled at her son. 'Okay, then. You talked me into it.'

Aoife saw a ray of light on the horizon. If they plied Grainne with drink all night, it might make the dinner more bearable.

The doorbell rang. Conor went to answer it, but Aoife motioned that she would get it. She wasn't spending a moment on her own with that woman if she could help it. Amy ran after her. It was a relief to see Sarah on the doorstep. The more people Grainne had to distract her, the better.

'Hi, Sarah.' She hugged the girl, who was a female version of her brothers. 'You cut your hair!'

Sarah ran her fingers through the dark layers which barely reached her chin. 'I was sick of long straight hair. Half the world wears their hair like that now. It's so boring.'

Aoife fingered her own long straight hair and grinned.

'Oh, Aoife, I'm so sorry. Your hair is beautiful. I just wanted to stand out, that's all.'

'At your height, you're going to stand out whatever you do with your hair.'

'Don't I know it! Height is the curse of the Moloneys. It's alright for the guys, but have you any idea how hard it is to find clothes to fit this?' She pointed at her tall, lanky frame.

'You're very big!'

Sarah crouched down on her knees. 'You must be Amy. Look what I got you.' She handed the child a brightly wrapped present. Amy's face lit up.

'You got me a present?' She ripped the paper apart, revealing a Playfoam set.

'You can make shapes with it,' Sarah said.

'I'm going to play with it now.'

Aoife put a hand out to stop her. 'What do you say to Sarah?'

'Thank you, Sarah.'

Good girl! Take it into the kitchen and I'll be with you in a minute.'

Amy ran off, clutching her present.

'You shouldn't have, Sarah, but thank you. That's a great present. It will keep her occupied until her dad arrives.'

They followed Amy into the kitchen, dumped all the Playfoam on the table and spent a few minutes making shapes. Then they joined Conor and Grainne in the dining room.

'Hi, Mum!'

'You made it, Sarah. I thought we'd be having dessert by the time you got here.'

'Ha, ha, very funny. I said I'd be here before Rory and I am, aren't I?'

'At least your brother told me he'd be late. I had no idea where you were.'

'I didn't phone because I wasn't late.'

'You were seven minutes late exactly. Your brother was kind enough to invite us here tonight.' She glanced at Aoife. 'And he was good enough to make us dinner. The least you two could do is show up on time.'

'Seven minutes past is perfect timing, Mum. What are you having, Sarah?'

'Wine would be great.'

Grainne frowned.

Sarah gave her a hug. 'Relax, Mum. I'm not your baby anymore.'

Grainne shook her head. 'God only knows what you're up to in that college.'

'Least said about that the better, I think, Mum. The rest of us survived college life. Sarah will too. And that must be Rory,' Conor said as the doorbell rang again.

A few seconds later he returned with Rory and a girl in her early twenties who was so tiny that from behind she could easily be mistaken for a child. She was the very definition of 'petite';

barely five foot with a waist Aoife was certain she could span with two hands. Her skirt barely covered her behind, and her breasts were almost popping out of her skintight top. Everything about her was false, from her eyebrows to her fingernails to the generous breasts that were a physiological impossibility on someone so tiny. Beneath all the make-up, she wasn't beautiful, Aoife realised. Her tiny mouth and huge eyes gave her face an unbalanced look, and her nose was slightly hooked, but all that was saved by her hair. Her thick waist-length auburn hair distracted you from her imperfections. Rory smiled proudly as he introduced her.

'This is Tatiana.'

Tatiana gave a tiny wave. 'Hi, everyone.'

'Now we're all here, why don't you take a seat and I'll bring in dinner?' Conor said.

'I'll help.'

'It's okay, Aoife. I can manage.' He gave Aoife a meaningful look and she glared at him. She needed him as a buffer and he damn well knew that.

Fortunately, Grainne was distracted by Tatiana and was anxious to find out how long she and Rory had known each other. When she discovered they had only met the previous week, she visibly relaxed.

Conor returned, placed a large dish of scallop and tomato salad on the table and told everyone to help themselves. Amy had followed him into the room. She tugged at Aoife's arm.

'I'm hungry.'

They hadn't set a place for her, so Aoife pulled Amy onto her lap and handed her a bread roll.

'This is lovely, Conor.' Grainne smiled at him. 'If you ever get sick of being a detective, you'd make a great chef.'

'I helped Moaney make the dessert,' Amy piped up as the others agreed the salad was exceptional.

'Really! That's—' Sarah began, but her mother interrupted.

'My son's name is Conor. I do not want you calling him Moaney again.'

Amy's lip quivered. Aoife pulled her closer. Conor began, 'Mum,' as Amy took a big breath and shouted, 'He's my Moaney!'

'That is not—'

'Conor and I have discussed this, Grainne. Moaney is Amy's nickname for Conor and he's okay with that.'

'How could he possibly be happy with such a ridiculous name? He's just agreeing to keep the peace. Well, I'm not having it.'

'Mum!' The coldness in Conor's voice made her pause.

'I just—'

Conor's tone softened. 'I know you mean well, but I like Amy calling me Moaney.' He winked at the little girl, who glared at Grainne and said, 'See!'

'Shh,' Aoife whispered in her ear.

'You're not Amy's father?' Tatiana asked.

'No. He is not,' Grainne replied, her voice thick with disapproval.

Tatiana's eyes lit up. 'And when are you and Aoife planning to marry?'

'July,' Aoife replied.

Tatiana nodded. 'Rory, you and Conor are very alike. Are you twins?'

Rory, who was two inches shorter and six years younger, looked startled.

'No! Conor's the old man of the family.'

'Your brother is not old. He's barely in his thirties.'

'Like I said, old.'

'Nonsense,' Tatiana murmured. She tossed her hair and smiled. 'I would have guessed you were the younger brother, Conor.'

Grainne sniffed. 'You said you thought they were twins.'

Tatiana was unfazed. 'Now I know they're not the same age, I think Conor looks younger.' Tatiana flicked her hair again. 'Conor's hair is darker and his eyes are bluer and he's at least five inches taller than Rory.'

Rory stared at her. 'What has the colour of his hair and his eyes got to do with his age? And he isn't five inches taller!'

Tatiana ignored him. 'Rory tells me you're a detective inspector. That's very impressive for one so young.'

Sarah suppressed a giggle. Amy looked questioningly at Aoife, then, half-eaten bread roll clasped in one hand, she ran out to the kitchen to play with her new toy. Tatiana didn't acknowledge Sarah's interruption, but her eyes hardened.

'You should follow your brother's example, Rory. You've been in the same company now for three years and you haven't been promoted once. Conor must have been promoted several times.'

'Conor had to concentrate on his career. He had a son to support. I have no intention of settling down for years yet.'

'You have a son?' Tatiana's eyes were wide with astonishment. Far too wide for the gesture to be natural. How often had she practised that in the mirror?

Conor tried to hide his amusement. 'Yes, Blaine. He's sixteen now. He lives in England with his mother.'

'Sixteen! You must have been a child when he was born.'

Grainne pursed her lips. 'Conor was a child. My sons do not make very good choices where women are concerned, I'm afraid.'

She looked straight at Conor as she spoke and Aoife knew it was a dig at her.

'I didn't choose to be a teenage father, Mum. But I don't regret it. I can't imagine my life without Blaine.'

Tatiana sipped her wine. 'Being a father so young has obviously done you the world of good, Conor. You have a great job and a lovely home.'

'It's my home, actually,' Aoife said.

Tatiana looked a little taken aback. 'You both live here?'

'No. I have my own house in Dublin.'

Tatiana looked at Aoife for the first time. 'It must be difficult for you to get time together.'

'We manage.'

'I never thought of that,' Sarah said. 'You both work. Conor has such weird shifts and there's Amy to take care of. How do you manage?'

'Conor comes here most evenings for dinner and Jason takes Amy every second weekend.'

Right on cue, the doorbell rang. Aoife excused herself. Amy came running down the hallway and reached the door just as Aoife opened it.

'Hi, Daddy.'

'Hi, sweetheart.' He gave her a hug. Amy ran off to the bathroom. Aoife picked up the overnight bag and handed it to him.

'Are you going to make me wait on the doorstep?'

'No, I'll walk you out to the car. Amy won't be lon—'

The door to the dining room opened and Sarah came out with her mobile to her ear. 'I just have to take this. I'll be back in a sec,' she whispered to Aoife.

Aoife moved aside to let her leave. Jason moved to the opposite side and opened the door to the dining room.

'Oh, hi, sorry to interrupt. I'm looking for Supergirl. Amy won't move without it.'

'I put it in her overnight bag,' Conor replied.

Jason ignored him. 'You must be Aoife's future in-laws. I'm Amy's dad.'

Rory and Sarah said hi. Grainne scowled at him. Tatiana gave him a wide smile and flicked her hair over her shoulder again. Aoife wanted to scream at her, 'Yes, we can all see you have beautiful hair. For God's sake, leave it alone!' Instead she called, 'Amy!'

Amy came running down the corridor. 'I'm ready, Daddy.'

Jason picked her up and hugged her, throwing a triumphant look at Conor.

'What a beautiful little girl,' Tatiana, who had barely glanced at the child until now, almost purred. 'She looks just like her daddy.'

'You must be Aoife's future sister-in-law.'

Tatiana giggled. 'Oh no, I'm Tatiana. Rory's friend.'

'Friend!' Rory stared at her, but Tatiana ignored him.

'It's very nice to meet you, Tatiana.'

Amy pulled at his sleeve. 'Daddy! Come on!'

As they were walking out the door, she whispered, 'Conor's mummy is very cross. I don't like her.'

Jason's entire face lit up. 'You like Nana, though, don't you?'

'I love Nana.'

'And Mummy loved Nana once too.'

Amy looked up at him, her brow creased. 'Mummy doesn't love Nana anymore?'

Aoife gave her a hug. 'Of course I love Nana. Now why don't you race Daddy to the car, sweetie?'

Amy ran down the path towards the car. 'Come on, Daddy! I'm going to win.'

When she was out of earshot Jason said, 'Pretty girl, that Tatiana. Not stunning like Orla, but almost as pretty as you were when we married. You know, before your skin got blotchy and you got those bags under your eyes.'

Despite herself, Aoife laughed out loud.

Conor came into the hall. 'Mum sent me to find Sarah. What's so funny?'

'Jason was just telling me I've become quite ugly in my old age.'

Conor put an arm around her. 'Yep, he's right. I don't know how I put up with you at all.'

Jason scowled. For a moment Aoife thought he might reply, but he maintained his policy of pretending Conor didn't exist, turned his back on them and walked away.

Aoife waited in the hall until Conor returned with Sarah.

'Sarah, would you turn that phone off, please? It's downright rude walking out like that.'

'Sorry, Mum. I didn't mean to be long.'

Grainne tutted but said nothing.

Tatiana smiled at Conor, and one hand headed for her hair.

'Watch out,' Sarah said.

'Excuse me?'

'You hit me in the face last time you did that.'

Rory chuckled and Tatiana glared at him. She turned to Aoife. 'Your husband is a good-looking man. You obviously have a type.'

'What do you mean?'

'They're both dark and slim, and although your husband isn't nearly as tall as Conor, he's a bit taller than average. He's not half as good looking as Conor, of course.'

'Jason's her ex,' Sarah said. 'I thought he was pretty good looking myself. What's wrong with him?'

'Nothing's wrong with him. He's just not quite as manly as Conor.'

Rory spluttered and Sarah laughed out loud.

Tatiana didn't even glance in their direction. 'What does Jason do for a living, Aoife?'

'He's an accountant.'

Tatiana nodded. 'Yes, that makes sense. He has a slightly nerdy look to him. A little delicate, maybe?'

Aoife laughed. 'I don't think he would appreciate being described as delicate.'

'Does he live nearby?'

'A short car drive.'

'How does he feel about you moving to Dublin after the marriage?'

'We're not moving. Conor and I are going to live here.'

'What?' Grainne dropped her fork and it bounced off the wooden floor. 'Conor! How can you live in Kildare? You work in Dublin.'

'Kildare is a commuter town, Mum. Lots of people travel to Dublin every day.'

'Yes, people who can't afford to live in Dublin. You already have a house there.'

'True,' Conor said, picking up his mother's fork. 'But this is Amy's home. Her grandmother is nearby, and so is her school and her friends.'

'The child is barely five years old. She'll make new friends.'

'We don't want her to make new friends. She's going to have enough change in her life. We think living in this house will give her a sense of stability.'

Grainne sat back in her chair and folded her arms. 'We?'

'Yes, Mum. That is what I think and that is what Aoife thinks.'

Grainne opened her mouth, then clamped it shut.

'Time for the curry, I think.' Conor went out to the kitchen and Aoife followed. She rested her back against the closed door and sighed. 'Well, the evening's certainly been a success so far. How many new reasons does your mother have to hate me?'

Conor threw the fork into the dishwasher. 'Mum doesn't hate you, Aoife. She distrusts you because she doesn't know you. What you both need is to spend a little time together.' His hand hovering above a drawer of clean forks, he paused. 'I've just had a brilliant idea.'

'What idea?'

Conor grinned at her as he pushed open the door to the dining room. 'Mum, Aoife and her friend Orla are going wedding dress shopping next week. Why don't you join them?'

'I—I'm very busy next week and I'm sure Aoife would rather—'

'Please, Mum. This is really important to me.'

'But—'

'That sounds like such fun,' Sarah said. 'Can I come too? We can have a champagne breakfast and make a day of it. It will be like that programme about the dress. What's it called?'

'*Say Yes to the Dress*,' Tatiana muttered.

'That's it. We'll be like the people on that show.'

Aoife had no doubt she was right. They would be exactly like the people on the programme. Bickering and making digs at each other the entire time.

ൠ

As they stood at the door waving goodbye to his family, Conor put his arm around Aoife and gave her a 'there, it's all sorted' smile. She could have throttled him.

ൠ

'But this is great, Aoife.' Orla sounded genuinely thrilled. 'You said Grainne is very direct. This is our opportunity to confront her about her attitude to you. It will be two against one. She won't stand a chance.'

'Two against two. Sarah is coming.'

'Even so. Can you imagine any other scenario where I could help you confront your future mother-in-law? It's perfect.'

'It will be a disaster.'

'You're such a worrier. Everything's going to be fine. Oh, by the way, I'll text you the name of the legal firm handling Matt's inheritance. You realise they won't talk to you, don't you?'

'Yeah, I'm going to ask Nicole to set up an appointment and bring me along as her friend.'

'That might work. What happened about the café owner who was having an affair with Matt? Did you speak to her?'

'I think that was just gossip. Matt helped her with some IT issues. Dearbhla works in the café all day and does the paperwork in the evenings. She said Matt had called to her apartment when she had issues.'

'So Matt wasn't having an affair?'

'I'm not certain. Dearbhla had heard the rumours too. Matt might have been having an affair with somebody else.'

FIFTEEN

AOIFE PUT ALL thoughts of wedding dress shopping out of her mind. As she waited on a park bench for Luke, Matt's best man, she tried to figure out how to get information from Matt's solicitor. Ten minutes later she still had no idea how to approach him. Her thoughts kept drifting to the black clouds above her head. It had been Luke's suggestion that they meet in the Phoenix Park. At the time, it had seemed like a good idea, but now Aoife worried the weather was conspiring against her. People weren't generally at their most talkative when they were soaking wet.

A few minutes later, a young man strolled towards her. He wore a black Adidas tracksuit with white stripes down the arms and legs and black-and-white runners.

'Thanks for agreeing to meet me at such short notice, Luke,' Aoife said when he joined her on the bench.

'No problem. I always go for a run at this time on my days off. I don't mind delaying it a little, especially if it will get more attention for Matt's disappearance.'

'Great. I'm writing a human-interest story, so I need to know more about Matt, his childhood and his family. You know, the sort of thing that makes people feel they care what happened to him.'

Luke nodded. 'Yup. Makes sense.'

'How long have you known Matt?'

'We grew up on the same street. I was supposed to go travelling with him after college, but I failed my final year exams and had to repeat them. Then I was offered an internship, so it never worked out.'

'But you stayed in touch?'

'Not really. We sent each other the occasional WhatsApp message, but I hadn't seen him in years until he phoned me a few months after he returned to Ireland.'

'That's when he asked you to be his best man?'

'Yeah, we've played squash most weeks since then.'

'How well do you know Nicole?'

'We met a few times, but we mostly discussed wedding stuff. I can't say I really know her.'

'You must know Matt's parents quite well.'

Luke shrugged. 'I'd say hello if we met in the street, but I couldn't really tell you much about them.'

'I met them recently. Their attitude to Matt's disappearance struck me as odd.'

'Their attitude to most things is pretty odd.'

'In what way?'

'They were never like normal parents. Somehow, they managed to do most of the things the other parents did without really having any interaction with Matt.'

'How do you mean?'

'Well, take birthday parties, for instance. How many parents can throw a little kid's birthday party where they never see their own child?'

'How did they manage that?'

'They invited the entire street, hosted a sit-down meal for the parents and left us in the garden with the au pair. We didn't mind at all at the time, but looking back, I can see it was pretty odd.'

'What was Matt's relationship with them like?'

'When he was a kid, it seemed like the au pair was his mother. As a teenager he didn't want to have anything to do with them.'

'That's pretty normal for teenagers, isn't it?'

'It's not that normal for parents to be okay with it. Matt told me they barely spoke to him until they found out how much he was going to inherit.'

'Matt told you about the inheritance?'

'Oh yeah, he didn't find out about it until he turned eighteen. We spent a lot of time together back then, so, of course, I knew all about it.'

'And the inheritance made Matt's parents more interested in him?'

'I wouldn't say that, but they never shut up talking about it. According to Matt, they said "how could somebody as irresponsible as you manage a fortune?" about a hundred times a day. They said it when he slept late, failed French, played his music too loud, all the time basically.'

'They envied him?'

'Yes. Well, envied and resented, I'd say.'

'They resented him because he would inherit a lot of money?'

'That too.'

'What do you mean?'

'They resented Matt's existence.' Luke's phone rang. He glanced at the screen then rejected the call. 'It was obvious neither of them wanted to be parents. They shipped Matt off to boarding school when he was eight.'

'I didn't know that. I wonder why they had a kid if they never wanted them. Not many people get pregnant by accident in their fifties.'

'Well…' Luke grinned. 'This is just gossip, but the way I heard it is the Gallaghers split up before they became parents. They got back together and a little over a year later, Matt was born. The locals claim Mrs Gallagher got pregnant deliberately to make sure he couldn't leave her again.'

'At her age, that wouldn't be an easy thing to arrange.'

'Which is why the gossips claim she went to a fertility clinic. Some people even say Mr Gallagher found out about it and has never forgiven her.'

'How long did Matt spend in boarding school?'

'Not very long. His parents couldn't afford it, so he was back in the local school by the time he was ten, but they packed him off again a few years later. That's how they prioritised their money. First on the list was always getting Matt out of their way.'

'How long was he a boarder?'

'Two years when he was eight, the year he turned twelve, and they tried to send him off again when he was fifteen, but he refused to go. They had huge fights about it. Matt told me they actually said straight to his face that they didn't want him around.'

'That must have been terrible for him.'

'I'm sure it was.'

'Did he ever talk about it, Luke?'

'No. You know what young guys are like. They never admit to their feelings. Matt used to shrug it off. He'd say in some ways he was lucky.'

'Lucky?'

'Other parents expected a lot of their kids. Matt said all his parents wanted was for him to disappear off the face of the earth.' Luke shrugged. 'I guess they got their wish.'

SIXTEEN

Aoife tossed and turned all night. She tried reading, counting sheep and listening to music, but all she could think about was wedding dress shopping with Grainne. She was so wound up she didn't even feel tired the following morning as they waited in the Shelbourne hotel. The table covered with a thick white linen tablecloth and set with china and sterling silver barely registered with her. When the waiter placed a glass of champagne in front of her, she almost jumped out of her chair. Orla touched her arm. 'This is going to be a good day, Aoife. Think what a relief it will be not to have to go into a panic every time Conor's family visit.'

'Orla, I don't see how we're going to…' She stopped as Grainne entered the room in blue jeans and a white T-shirt. Was that her way of saying this day wasn't even worth her good jeans?

Orla stood up and held out her hand. 'Grainne, hi, I'm Orla.' She pointed at the three glasses of champagne. 'I hope you like champagne. The waiter will be back in a minute to take our order.'

Grainne's mouth fell open. Her eyes ran up and down Orla, taking in her naturally blonde curls, the slate-grey dress whose simplicity and cut practically screamed designer, the killer heels and her perfect body. Aoife grimaced. She could almost hear Grainne wondering why Conor gave someone as dull as Aoife a second glance when a breathtaking beauty like Orla was on the sidelines.

Grainne snapped her mouth shut, blushed slightly and took the hand Orla offered. She nodded at Aoife. 'Sarah won't be joining us. I asked her not to. I'll have a quick cup of coffee with you and then I'll leave you to your shopping. Conor means well, but… well, men can be insensitive sometimes. It's bad enough you can't have your own mother with you today. The last thing you need is someone you barely know taking her place.'

It was the first time Grainne had addressed Aoife without getting in some kind of a dig. Aoife was lost for words. It hadn't occurred to anybody else that she didn't want somebody else's mother helping her choose her dress. Was it possible Grainne had a sensitive side?

Orla filled the silence. 'That's very thoughtful of you, Grainne. But please, don't rush away. Have you had breakfast?'

'I had a cup of tea before I came out.'

'Check out the menu. They do great French toast here, or if you'd rather something light, you could get a fruit plate.'

They discussed the weather and the traffic while Orla gave Aoife meaningful glances and at one stage kicked her under the table. Eventually she lost her patience and blurted out, 'Why don't you like Aoife?'

Grainne, who had been showing signs of relaxing, stiffened. 'I don't dislike her.' She turned to Aoife. 'I don't dislike you, Aoife.'

'But you don't want her to marry your son?'

'I don't have any say in that. Conor makes his own decisions.'

'But you would rather he didn't decide to marry Aoife, wouldn't you?'

Grainne put her cup down on the saucer, turned to face Aoife and said, 'Yes, I would.'

Aoife really didn't want to know, but Orla wasn't going to let the subject drop, so she said, 'Why?'

'Because you have a child, an ex-husband and an ex-mother-in-law. It's a lot of baggage.'

Aoife nodded. 'It is. But there's nothing I can do about that.'

'I know, but that's why I would rather Conor found somebody else. It's nothing personal, Aoife. If Conor had met you when you were still single, I'm sure I would have been delighted to welcome you into our family.'

When Aoife didn't reply, Orla said, 'Conor could have chosen somebody with no baggage. He chose Aoife. And he has a son too, doesn't he?'

'It's not the same. Blaine lives in England. He won't be part of Aoife's daily life. Conor will have to raise another man's child.'

Aoife shook her head. 'He doesn't have to, Grainne. He chooses to.'

'Yes, he does, and now everything revolves around you and your daughter. It's the same with Blaine. Conor always goes out of his way to make that relationship work, and everything centres around Blaine's mother and stepfather. Conor's needs are never even considered.'

Aoife kept her voice steady. 'That's not fair, Grainne. I consider Conor's needs all the time.'

'Do you? Is that why he'll be commuting from Kildare every day?'

'Conor and I discussed that in detail and we made the decision together.'

Grainne scoffed. 'You made the decision and Conor agreed.'

'Conor can make up his own—' Orla began, but Aoife interrupted.

'No, Grainne has a point. The decision to live in Kildare was made for Amy's benefit. I would not put my needs above Conor's, but I will always put Amy's needs above both of ours.'

Grainne sat back in her seat and nodded. 'That is exactly my point.'

'And the fact that Conor is willing to put my child's needs above his own shows me that my decision to marry him is the right one.'

'For you, maybe.'

'It's the right decision for all of us, Grainne. Would you prefer to have a daughter-in-law who put her child last? Is that the kind of mother you want for your own grandchildren?'

'I would like the mother of my grandchildren to be childless when she married my son.'

Before Aoife could reply, Orla said, 'What if Conor and Aoife broke up and Conor chose to marry someone like that red-haired girl Aoife told me about? Would that make you happy?'

Grainne snorted. 'That one has no interest in anybody but herself.'

'Exactly. In fact, you could never be sure what type of mother any future girlfriend would make unless she already had children. At least with Aoife you know what you're getting.'

'Someone who left her husband before her child was even two years old. The last thing Conor needs is another child he hardly ever gets a chance to see.'

'Aoife's gone out of her way to keep Amy's father involved in his child's life. That's one of the reasons she wants to live in Kildare.'

Grainne looked unconvinced. Orla gave Aoife a look that said *I tried. It's up to you now.*

'Do you think Sarah is ready to get married?' Aoife asked.

'Sarah? No, of course not. She's just a kid.'

'She's eighteen. The age I was when I married Jason. Kids make mistakes, Grainne. Jason was not a good choice for me.'

'Or any woman,' Orla added. 'And Aoife had just lost her parents. She wasn't thinking straight.'

'I'm not a kid now, Grainne. This time I chose a good man. I can't promise our marriage will last forever, but I know Conor and I will work to make that happen.'

'And because he's her child's father, Aoife won't badmouth Jason, but I can tell you he was a terrible husband. The worst mistake Aoife made in that marriage was not leaving sooner.'

Grainne sighed. 'I'm not blaming you for having a kid, Aoife. I'm just saying—'

'That it's not the ideal situation. We get that, Grainne, but the decision has already been made. Aoife will be your daughter-in-law. And if you give her a chance, I'm sure you'll really like her.'

Grainne shrugged. 'I don't know what to say. I can't change how I feel.'

'It's okay to worry, Grainne. Just give Aoife a chance. You know it would make Conor happy if you two were friends. Isn't that what you want?'

Grainne looked from one to the other. 'Okay, I'll try. Aoife, I'm sorry if I seemed unfriendly. I was just disappointed.' She hesitated. 'Well, mainly I was disappointed, I was also mad as hell, but it's possible I was unfair. Truce?'

'I'd like that.'

SEVENTEEN

Aoife was surprised to discover she could think of Grainne now without her stomach churning. From the day she and Conor had become engaged, Aoife had pictured herself as part of a loving extended family. A family that would come to think of Amy as one of their own. Her first meeting with Grainne had killed the dream, but now Aoife began to wonder if it might be a possibility. Her thoughts were interrupted by the receptionist asking them to follow her. Ciaran Burke would see them now.

Nicole had been reluctant to visit Burke & Sons Solicitors. 'I can't ask straight out if I'm going to inherit Matt's money. They'll think I'm a terrible person.'

'You don't have to. Tell them I'm a friend and I'll ask the awkward questions.'

The receptionist opened the door to a large office. A slight man in his forties with thick glasses rose to greet them. 'Ciaran Burke, Mrs Gallagher.' They shook hands. 'We were all so sorry to hear of your husband's disappearance.' He looked questioningly at Aoife.

'Please call me Nicole. This is my friend, Aoife.'

When they were seated and the receptionist had offered

them tea or coffee, Ciaran tapped the manilla folder on his desk. 'I understand you want to know the terms of the trust set up for your husband.

'Yes. Matt never mentioned it, I had no idea his grandparents were rich.'

'They weren't. I believe one owned a grocery shop and the other worked in the civil service.'

'How did they end up with so much money?'

'They bought homes in Howth, within a few streets of each other, I understand. In those days Howth was considered to be almost the countryside. Houses there sold for less than three thousand. A similar house on that street sold for six million last year.'

'Six million!'

'Well, of course Matt's grandparents died long before the houses reached that value, but the money has been very well managed and it's grown considerably over the years.'

Nicole nodded at Aoife, who asked, 'Can you tell us what happens to that money if Matt is legally declared dead?'

The manilla folder was at an angle on his desk and Ciaran spent several seconds straightening it before making eye contact with Nicole.

'I'm sorry to have to tell you this, but under the terms of Matt's grandparents' will, the money is held in trust. Matt has use of the trust while he is alive, but it doesn't belong to him, so it can never be part of his estate. He has no control over who inherits the trust after he dies.'

Nicole didn't reply, so Aoife asked, 'So who does inherit it?'

'It goes to his parents.'

'Isn't that a little unusual?'

'I've come across situations like this before. Matt's grandparents wanted the money to stay in the family. They were elderly when divorce was made legal in Ireland, and they didn't approve of it. They worried that Matt would divorce and lose half of his inheritance. Our firm set up the trust so that couldn't happen.'

'I see. Are Matt's parents aware of this?' Aoife asked.

'Yes, of course. When Matt reached eighteen, I met with the family and explained the will in detail.'

'What was their reaction?'

'Matt's parents were astonished the fund had grown so much. Of course, Matt was delighted, although he wasn't too happy about having to wait until he was thirty.'

Aoife looked at Nicole, who was staring into space. She didn't appear to be listening to the conversation, so Aoife continued, 'Why did Matt have to wait that long?'

'It was important to Matt's grandparents that he made his own way in life. They felt that was unlikely to happen if he inherited at a young age.'

'Has Matt…?' Nicole cleared her throat. 'Has Matt been in contact with you recently?'

'We met five weeks before you went on your honeymoon.'

'Why?'

'Nicole, Matt is still legally alive, so he's still legally my client. I can't discuss our conversation with you.'

&

As they left the solicitor's office, Nicole grabbed Aoife's arm. 'Why would Matt go to see the solicitor before he disappeared? Why, Aoife? Why would he do that?'

'Maybe he wanted to make sure you'd receive the inheritance if he died.'

'Then why didn't he make a will?' The desperation in her voice caused several passers-by to stare.

'I guess there wasn't much point once he found out he couldn't leave you his inheritance. Why does it bother you that Matt met with his solicitor?'

Nicole's lip trembled. 'What if Matt ran away? What if he met with the solicitor to find out how he could access his inheritance from abroad?'

'I thought you were certain Matt would never leave you without a word.'

'I was certain Matt and I were completely honest with each other. Now I discover he was about to become a millionaire and he didn't bother to mention it. What else was he hiding from me?'

EIGHTEEN

AOIFE DROVE NICOLE back to her apartment. They talked over coffee, but Nicole was still upset and Aoife needed to leave. She always collected Amy at 5.30 and she would only change that in an emergency, but she didn't like leaving Nicole alone when she was so upset. Maybe Katie could spend some time with her.

Katie's door was answered by a pretty girl in her late teens balancing her phone, a dish of ice cream and a spoon in one hand.

'Hi, is Katie in?'

The girl smiled and shook her head. 'No English. Katie!' She said a few words in an Eastern European language.

The bathroom door opened. 'Aoife, I wasn't expecting you today. Is everything okay?'

'Nicole and I are just back from seeing Matt's solicitor. She's a bit upset and I have to go home. I wondered if you could spend some time with her.'

Katie glanced at the teenager, who was now curled up on the sofa, punching buttons on her phone.

'It's a little difficult. This is Gabriela's first day in Ireland. Gabriela!' They exchanged a few sentences in the foreign language and Katie said, 'I'll go down to Nicole now and I'll text Vicky to drop in when she gets home. Gabriela will be alright on her own for a half hour.'

They walked down the corridor together.

'Is Gabriela one of the Romanian girls you hired? I didn't realise you invited them into your home.'

'I don't always, but Gabriela is one of my younger recruits. She's only just gone seventeen, so I'm keeping her with me for a few days until I find someplace suitable for her to stay. Greg's in Italy this week, so the timing worked out well.'

'Do many Italians want to work as cleaners here?'

'No. We don't hire Italians. It's reasonably easy for Romanians to get to Italy, but they often find they can't afford to go any further. When they realise there isn't much work in Italy, they often agree to work for us.'

Katie punched the lift button and they were still talking when it opened.

'Hi, Katie!'

'Sadhbh, hi.' She smiled at a slim woman in her mid-twenties with shoulder-length brown hair. 'Have you met Aoife?' Without giving either of them time to reply, she continued, 'I'm really glad I ran into you, Sadhbh. I was about to call up to Nicole, but if you're free, could you spend some time with her? She's a little upset.'

'Sure. Just let me drop off my stuff and I'll go straight there.' She smiled at Aoife. 'You must be the reporter. I'm Nicole's next-door neighbour.'

'And she's one of the best neighbours imaginable, Aoife. Sadhbh's spent more evenings with Nicole than anyone else.' Katie stepped away from the lift, but Sadhbh didn't follow. She grinned at Aoife.

'What are neighbours for? I don't want people comparing me to the Fergusons, do I?'

'The Fergusons?'

'They used to live in my apartment, but they moved out last year. Apparently they were the worst neighbours ever and they never stopped gossiping about—'

'Aoife, I'm sorry to interrupt, but I really have to rush. Sadhbh, would you mind coming back to my place? I have a houseguest and I'd rather not leave her alone for too long. I can fill you in on why Nicole is upset.'

Katie put an arm around Sadhbh's shoulder and waved at Aoife as she led Sadhbh away.

The following day Aoife called to Sadhbh's apartment on the pretext of checking up on Nicole. When there was no answer, she tried Vicky's. After learning that Nicole was now feeling a little better, Aoife mentioned running into Sadhbh.

'You haven't interviewed her yet?'

'I tried twice, but she wasn't in.'

'Yeah, she spends a lot of time at her boyfriend's place. Sadhbh's the best. You should see her in the pub on Friday nights. I've never known anybody who could drink that much without showing any signs of being drunk.'

'Sadhbh mentioned the Fergusons.'

Vicky froze, mug midway to her mouth. 'Who?'

'The Fergusons. They used to be Nicole's neighbours.'

'Really? I didn't know them.'

'I understood they only moved out last year. You've lived here longer than Nicole, haven't you?'

'Yes, but people in this block didn't become friends until after Matt disappeared.'

'Sadhbh said the Fergusons were terrible gossips. I got the impression Nicole was one of the people they gossiped about.'

'I wouldn't know. I never met them.'

'Vicky, I've spoken to almost all your neighbours, and it was obvious that every one of them considered you a friend. Are you saying they didn't tell you what the Fergusons were gossiping about?'

'They probably didn't think it was important.'

When Aoife raised an eyebrow, she said, 'I can't tell you about the Fergusons, okay? Katie would kill me.'

'Why?'

'She said the Fergusons are liars and we don't want any of their lies appearing in your article. Besides, I don't think Nicole's ever heard the rumours. She'd be really upset. Especially if they appeared in the papers and other people believed them.'

'What did the Fergusons say, Vicky?'

'Look, everyone calls me a gossip and I know they're right. I just can't seem to stop everything in my head popping out of my mouth, but I would never deliberately hurt anyone, especially Nicole.'

'What if I promised not to repeat anything you say in my article?'

Vicky's eyes darted around the room as if searching for an escape route, then she blurted out, 'The Fergusons said Matt was abusive.'

NINETEEN

CONOR WAS ON the night shift that week. When he called to say goodnight, Aoife filled him in on what she had learned.

'Matt was abusive?'

'Apparently. I suppose it wasn't surprising, really. Nobody had ever shown him any love. His parents are probably glad he's out of the way. Especially as they'll get his money when he's declared legally dead.'

'Aoife, you're not suggesting Matt's parents killed him, are you?'

'Don't you think it's possible?'

There was a pause and Aoife could picture his frown as he considered her question. 'No,' he said at last. 'If the Gallaghers were capable of killing their own son, they'd have done it when he was a kid. Then they would have had immediate access to the money.'

'Wouldn't that be too risky? A child's murder would be a priority. The police wouldn't give up until they found the culprit.'

'True, but kids die in accidents all the time. It wouldn't be that hard to set one up. Killing an adult would be a whole different ball game. From the sound of it, Matt rarely visited his parents and he wasn't comfortable enough around them to relax. They'd never have the strength to overpower him.'

'Conor, you tell me all the time how little it costs to hire a junkie to kill somebody. They'd do anything for money.'

'Yes, but you couldn't trust junkies to get on a plane to Italy to murder somebody. God only knows where they'd end up. Besides, you can't stop these guys on the street and ask them to kill somebody. You'd need to have some connection with their world.'

'I suppose you have a point. But the Gallaghers are the only people who benefit from Matt's death. That makes them the most likely murderers, even if I can't yet figure out how they did it.'

'That's one possibility, Aoife. The other is that Nicole found out about the inheritance. It would have been natural to assume that, as Matt's wife, she'd inherit his money when he died. There's a reason the spouse is always the most likely suspect.'

Aoife needed to speak to the Fergusons, but Vicky claimed not to know where they lived and Aoife felt she would be betraying a confidence if she asked Katie. It was possible Sadhbh would have a forwarding address for them, but Aoife was unable to get in touch with her. No matter what time she called to the apartment, Sadhbh was never there. In the meantime, Aoife continued working her way through the list of relatives Matt had invited to his wedding. Most of them had little to say. They met Matt and his family at weddings and funerals. Other than that, they had virtually no contact. Aoife was beginning to think she was wasting her time. Then she spoke to Stephen.

'Matt's father and my mother were cousins. I'm eleven years

older than Matt, so we never hung out together when he was a kid, but I turned up to all the big events in his life: twenty-first, graduation and, of course, his wedding.'

'Did Matt tell you when he decided to marry Nicole?'

'Of course.'

'Do you know Nicole well?'

'The first time I met her was the day of the wedding.'

'Did you think it strange Matt hadn't introduced you earlier?'

'There wasn't much opportunity for us to meet. I travel a lot for business, so our contact was mostly by phone.'

'Did you and Matt ever discuss his inheritance?'

'Occasionally.'

'When was the last time you discussed it, Stephen?'

'A few weeks before Matt disappeared. His parents hadn't reacted well to news of his wedding. They said they'd make sure Matt never saw a cent of his inheritance if the wedding went ahead. He was quite upset about it.'

'Did you discuss the argument with Matt's parents?'

'No. I don't have much contact with them. They never liked me.' He laughed. 'Their opinion of me was formed when I was a teenager. Back then I rode a motorbike and they decided I was a disgrace to the family. I think that's partly why Matt and I stayed in touch. He liked annoying his parents.'

'Did you know that a few weeks before he disappeared, Matt contacted the legal firm that handles his inheritance?'

'No, but I'm glad he did. It was my suggestion.'

'Why did you suggest it?'

'I told Matt he needed to find out what control his parents had over his inheritance. I didn't think it was likely they could stop him inheriting, but if there was the slightest loophole, you can be sure they'd take advantage of it. Matt believed they hated Nicole, but I think that was just an excuse to cause trouble. Those two practically worship money. There's not much they wouldn't do to get their hands on a few quid, let alone five million.'

TWENTY

It took another two days to finish the wedding guest list, but Aoife didn't discover anything else of interest. She dropped Amy at school on Monday morning and, after a quick breakfast, settled down to work through the bank statements Nicole had given her. She started with Matt's credit card statements, but there was nothing unusual there. His bank account didn't show any major payouts. Most of the money paid into the account seemed to be from customers. There were a few limited companies, Dearbhla's coffee shop amongst them. Matt's main customers were a local charity and a company called Nooks & Crannies Ireland. Aoife googled them and found a gift shop in Portlaoise. Their website was well laid out. If Matt had set it up, he'd done a great job. She was about to phone the shop when her mobile rang.

'Hi, Aoife, it's Vicky. I thought you should know that the police visited Nicole last night. Matt's body's been found.'

TWENTY-ONE

WHEN CONOR DIDN'T answer his phone, Aoife called Orla.

'Where did they find the body?'

'Some hikers came across it in a ravine in the mountains, about an hour's drive from Matt's hotel.'

'How did he die?'

'A bullet in the back of the head. It looks like he might have been kept prisoner for a while. His hands and feet were bound with zip ties and his mouth was gagged. Nicole's devastated, but at least it rules her out as a murder suspect. Several hotel staff saw Matt at breakfast the morning he disappeared, and Nicole spent the afternoon on the beach. She hardly left his dead body in the hotel room. How would she get rid of it? Besides, where would she get her hands on a gun?'

'I wouldn't say it rules her out, Aoife. If Nicole's the murderer, my guess is she hired a professional to do the job.'

'Conor says it's not that easy to hire a professional. You'd have to know somebody in their circle.'

'It might not have been an Irish hitman. Nicole travelled the world. Who knows what kind of people she met on her travels? Some of them might have had connections to criminal gangs.

And if the Fergusons are right and Matt was abusive, Nicole now has three reasons to kill her husband.'

'Three?'

'One, she thought she'd inherit a fortune. Two, Matt was cheating on her. Three, he was beating her up. If you ask me, the third one is justification enough to kill anybody.'

Aoife would have liked to judge for herself if Nicole was devastated by the news of Matt's death, but she couldn't just drop by at a time like this. She waited a week before phoning. Nicole didn't answer. Aoife was now reliant on Vicky for updates. Katie was a second option, but Aoife felt she was too guarded. Vicky could always be relied on to relay all the latest news.

The next time Aoife visited her apartment, Vicky had guests.

'We were just talking about Nicole,' Vicky explained as she invited her inside. 'She's so upset, we want to make sure somebody is with her as much as possible over the next few weeks.'

'Nicole was right. You are very good to her,' Aoife said, smiling at Katie and Sadhbh. 'If there's an award for best neighbours, you three would be a shoo-in.'

Vicky had ordered pizza, and she offered Aoife a slice. They discussed Nicole's reaction to Matt's death and what they could do to help her. Aoife was hoping for a chance to speak to Sadhbh privately, but it looked like the meeting wasn't going to end any time soon. They had moved on to discussing all the tragic women they had ever known when Sadhbh suggested going to the pub.

Aoife checked her watch. 'I can't, I'm afraid. I have to get home to my daughter and my friend Orla is coming over later. Katie, remember you said you might be able to find somebody to clean Orla's house? Have you had any luck?'

'No, Aoife, I'm sorry. My waiting list is still a mile long and Gabriela's fully booked.'

'What about the girl Greg brought back from Italy?' Vicky suggested. 'I met them this morning in the lift. Florina, isn't it?'

'No, Florina's not ready. We haven't trained her yet.'

'Orla's not particular, Katie. Anybody who can run a hoover will do.'

'It wouldn't work, Aoife. Florina doesn't speak any English. How would your friend tell her what needs to be done?'

'Orla is very resourceful. She'd probably have photos pasted all over the house.'

'I think Aoife's suggestion is brilliant,' Sadhbh said. 'It would be on-the-job training, Katie. And Florina would hardly expect full pay when she has no experience. Maybe she could do a few hours for me too, and I'm sure Nicole would like some help. Let's go to your place now and talk to Florina.'

She jumped up and headed for the door.

'Sadhbh! Where are you going? I didn't agree to anything yet. And how are you going to speak to Florina? She hasn't a word of English.'

'I speak a little Italian. Vicky said Florina lived in Italy for over a year. She must have picked up some of the language.'

'Okay, ladies, this is getting out of hand. I have a very in-depth induction Florina has to go through. Now, I will make an exception for Aoife's friend as she was the first to ask, but that's it. Aoife, does Orla speak Italian?'

'No.'

'Well, then, she'll have to make do as best she can.'

'I'm sure Orla will manage.'

Sadhbh returned to the couch. 'Okay, I'll take the next girl, then.'

'There will be no "next girl". We've finished our recruitment for the year.' Katie stood up. 'I have to get back to Florina. I shouldn't have left her alone this long.'

'I thought Greg was with her.'

'He has to go out soon. Call me tomorrow.'

Now all Aoife had to do was get Vicky out of the room for a few minutes.

'Are you two still going to the pub?' she asked.

'Definitely,' Sadhbh said, and Vicky elbowed her in the ribs.

'You can't keep this one out of a pub once the idea gets into her head. Are you sure you won't come with us, Aoife?'

'No, thanks. It's time I was leaving.'

Vicky looked at her tracksuit bottoms. 'Right, Sadhbh, give me two minutes to pull on a pair of jeans and I'll be with you.'

'I'd better get changed too,' Sadhbh said.

Aoife walked out with her. 'Sadhbh, did the Fergusons leave a forwarding address?'

'Yeah, but I haven't seen it in ages. I don't think there would be much point in interviewing them. As far as I know, they didn't mix with any of the neighbours.'

'I'd better talk to them anyway. I don't want my editor asking why I didn't speak to Matt and Nicole's closest neighbours.'

'Okay, I'll have a look around at the weekend. If I find it, I'll text you.'

Aoife worried that Sadhbh would forget her promise after a few drinks, but two days later the text arrived. The Fergusons lived in Finglas. Aoife put the address into the sat nav on her phone and was on her way to their house within the hour.

TWENTY-TWO

MRS FERGUSON WAS an elegant woman in her fifties with a smile that lit up her entire face.

'Abusive? That poor girl. I never would have guessed. Matt seemed like such a nice lad.'

'I'm not saying Matt was abusive. I understood you and your husband were the ones who said it.'

'Oh, no! It definitely wasn't us.'

'What did you think of Matt?'

'We didn't really know him. Most of the people in those apartments were in their twenties. They had no time for old fogies like us.'

'Matt and Nicole ignored you?'

'Not at all. Any time we met in the corridor, they said hello. Once or twice we discussed the weather, but we were never likely to have much in common.'

'Did you ever hear noises coming from Matt and Nicole's apartment?'

'Sometimes I could hear their music. It wasn't loud enough that I felt the need to complain, but the stuff they like sounds more like noise to me.'

'You never heard arguments of any sort?'

'Never. Maybe there's another couple in the complex with a similar name? All I can say is Matt and Nicole seemed like a perfectly normal young couple to us.'

Aoife paid a second visit to the other three apartments on Nicole's floor. Some looked uncomfortable when she raised the issue of domestic violence. Two eventually admitted to being aware of the rumours, but none had heard or seen anything suspicious.

Conor always flew to London for Blaine's parent–teacher meetings. Whenever possible, he took a few days' holiday and he and Blaine spent some time together. That evening he phoned Aoife from London.

'Nicole's apartment complex is rife with rumours. Matt was having an affair, Matt was violent. How am I supposed to prove any of it, Conor?'

'Maybe none of it is true.'

'Why would somebody spread malicious rumours about Matt?'

'They might be spreading malicious rumours about everybody. You just haven't heard the rest of them yet.'

'You might be right. Well, I'm out of ideas. What would you do next if you were me?'

'You could try talking to the cousin. What was his name?'

'Stephen.'

'Yes, he seems to be the only person who kept in regular contact with Matt.'

'Okay, I'll give it a shot.'

'Aoife, Mam phoned me this morning. She's getting really excited about the wedding. She asked if we could go around to her place tomorrow to discuss it. I can't, obviously, but could you go?'

❧

As she settled down to work the following morning, Aoife told herself not to think about Grainne. She had planned to avoid her until the day of the wedding. It had seemed the safest way to protect their fragile truce. But refusing to meet her obviously wasn't an option, so there was no point thinking about it.

Stephen had given Aoife his mobile and landline number. When he didn't answer his phone, she tried his home. A woman answered.

'Hi, could I speak to Stephen, please?'

'He's not here at the moment. This is Penny, his wife. Can I take a message?'

'It's Aoife. Stephen may have mentioned me. I'm investigating his cousin Matt's death. Could you ask Stephen to phone me?'

'Okay, but I don't really see how Stephen could help you. He and Matt haven't spoken in years.'

'Are you sure? I thought he was at Matt's wedding.'

'Oh yeah, Stephen was there alright. He sent them a wedding present, so they could hardly refuse to invite him. He is family after all.'

'Were you at the wedding, Penny?'

'No, I've no time for that lot. Stephen insists on inviting them to all our family occasions, but they never show up. I really don't understand why he makes such an effort with them. They're not worth it.'

'You're quite sure that it's been years since Stephen and Matt spoke?'

'Oh yes. Stephen said he congratulated them at the wedding, but Matt barely acknowledged him. When we heard Matt had disappeared, Stephen said what a pity it was that they were practically strangers.'

TWENTY-THREE

AOIFE CHANGED HER outfit three times before heading to Grainne's house. On the way she phoned Orla.

'Stop worrying, Aoife. Grainne is onside now. Offer to help her pick out an outfit for the wedding, let her decide the seating plan for her relatives and if she wants to add a few extra wedding guests, smile and agree. Everything will be fine. How's the investigation going?'

'Not well. There's no proof Matt was violent. That might have been another rumour. And now I've found out that everything Stephen told me was a lie.'

'Who's Stephen?'

'Matt's cousin. He said Matt spoke to him regularly. Stephen's wife says they hadn't spoken in years.'

'Maybe they spoke but Stephen lied to his wife about it.'

'It's possible, I suppose, but why would he do that?'

'Some people lie about everything. They don't seem to be able to help themselves. There are also people who need to be at the centre of any drama. That causes them to lie too.'

'Maybe, but which is Stephen? And Stephen knew about

the inheritance and that Matt's parents were opposed to his marriage. How did he know those things?'

'It sounds like somebody is keeping him informed. Maybe he's in touch with Matt's parents.'

'He said they hated him.'

'Maybe they do, but I'll bet they're not above using him. People that obsessed with what others think of them would be dying to know who was at the wedding, what was said at the speeches and if their names were mentioned.'

'So they used Stephen to keep tabs on Matt?'

'It's possible, at least as far as the wedding is concerned. Stephen obviously wanted to be involved in their lives. All the Gallaghers would need to do is drop a few hints and they'd have a very willing spy.'

Aoife raised her hand to ring Grainne's doorbell, but she couldn't bring herself to do it. Just as she was telling herself to get a grip, the door opened.

'Aoife! Great, you're here. Come on in. I can't wait to show you everything.'

Without giving her a chance to reply, Grainne led her through to the large dining room, where every inch of the highly polished table was covered in magazines.

'I know your generation are all about the internet, but I need to see things properly, so I bought these.'

'Oh!' Aoife picked up one of the magazines and read the title. '*Blushing Bride*. What are you looking for, Grainne?'

'I want to help. I know you have your investigation to worry about and Conor works all hours, so I've hired you a wedding planner. Tatiana!'

Aoife felt her heart sink. It couldn't be.

Tatiana sauntered into the room carrying a bottle of champagne in one hand and an iPad in the other. Aoife figured she was aiming for a professional look. She wore a black trouser suit and had tied her hair into a bun. It was quite a nice suit, but the jacket had a very deep V and Tatiana wore nothing inside it, which made the outfit more appropriate for the catwalk than the boardroom.

'Hi, Aoife. I arrived early to set up. I've spoken to Grainne and we've agreed a budget.' She put a finger to her lips and adopted a stage whisper. 'Top secret. Nobody but Grainne and I know the figure.'

'I didn't realise you were a wedding planner, Tatiana.'

Tatiana avoided eye contact as she filled three glasses with champagne. 'I organised some family weddings. I plan to set up my own business soon. This will be good experience for me.'

'I see.'

'I hope you don't mind.'

Aoife could hear the tension in Grainne's voice, and she felt dreadful for being so ungrateful.

'Aoife, I can understand if you would prefer to choose your own wedding planner, but Rory suggested Tatiana and she's worked wonders already. And we'll have more money to spend on the actual wedding because she'll give us a friends and family discount.'

'It was kind of you to find a wedding planner, and offering to pay for the wedding is an extremely generous gift. And, Tatiana, it's good of you to give us a special rate but we really don't need a wedding planner. It's just going to be a small family affair. I can easily organise it myself.'

Tatiana's face fell, but Grainne was having none of it.

'Nonsense, Aoife. You clearly don't have the time or the plans would already be finalised. Now, Tatiana had a brilliant idea. Did you know you could have your wedding in Powerscourt?'

'Yes, but I'm sure you'd have to book it years in advance.'

'I thought that too, but Tatiana phoned them and they can fit you in. Isn't that marvellous?'

'There must be some mistake, Grainne.'

'We've booked it already.' Grainne beamed, eyes bright with excitement. 'The Powerscourt Hotel is booked way in advance but the estate can only cater for one hundred and eighty guests and that's way too small for most Irish weddings. You said you want a small wedding. It's perfect.'

'It would cost a fortune, Grainne. No, I won't hear of it and I'm sure Conor won't either.'

'You leave Conor to me. Now, could we see a picture of the wedding dress? We want to get the theme just right.'

'But—' Aoife had been about to say she'd already done the big white wedding thing and she didn't want to go through that again. She remembered just in time that this would be a further reminder of her unsuitability in Grainne's eyes, so she rooted in her bag, took out her phone and found the pictures Orla had taken of her wearing the dress they had chosen.

Tatiana's mouth fell open. 'Oh no! That's totally wrong.'

'It's very beautiful, Aoife,' Grainne said. 'It certainly suits your trim figure, but I wonder if it's a little plain. Now that you're having a more formal wedding, do you think something more elaborate would be appropriate?'

'I've already paid a deposit and I really like this dress. I agree it's plain, but isn't that fashionable these days? You couldn't get much plainer than Meghan Markle's dress.'

'That thing is nothing like Meghan's dress.' Tatiana's voice rose. 'There isn't a train. It isn't even full-length!'

'That's because the reception is in the garden. Something too formal would be completely wrong.'

'The garden? In your own house!' Tatiana turned to Grainne. 'Is she serious?'

Grainne gave her a warning look. 'Meghan had two wedding dresses, didn't she? Maybe you could use this one for dancing and have a more elaborate one for the ceremony?'

'Two dresses! It's not a royal wedding, Grainne, and taxpayers aren't funding the bill.'

'I'll pay, of course. It's my idea.'

'No, Grainne. I can't let you waste your money like that. All Conor and I need is a small ceremony and a marquee in the back garden. We're really looking forward to it.'

Grainne's eyes hardened. 'You're sure that's what Conor wants?'

'Yes, I am. Why don't you phone him right now and ask?'

Grainne went out to the kitchen to make the call. It took longer than Aoife expected. When she returned, Grainne's hostility had vanished and she gave Aoife a friendly grin.

'You're quite right. Conor did want a simple wedding, but I've convinced him you deserve better.'

'But—'

'I won't hear a word about the cost. Conor wanted to contribute, but I finally convinced him that this is my right as his mother. He's had second best in all his relationships so far. Well, not anymore. Tatiana and I are going to make sure his wedding is quite spectacular.'

ණ

The second she was out of sight of Grainne's house, Aoife pulled over and phoned Conor.

'Mum's right, Aoife. You do deserve better than a marquee.'

'I don't want anything better. Having the wedding in the garden would have been perfect. Even thinking of Powerscourt brings me out in chills.'

'I thought you loved the place.'

'Yes, for a coffee and an afternoon stroll, not for my wedding.'

'Okay. I'll tell Mum we're having it in the garden like we planned.'

'No. It's too late now. Grainne will think I'm stopping you from having the perfect wedding and we'll be at loggerheads again.'

'Are you sure? I can tell Mum it's all my idea.'

'She won't believe you. No, Conor, it'll be fine. You're right, I do love Powerscourt and the fancier the wedding is, the happier Amy will be.'

'True. And it will make it much easier for us. We won't have to do any organising at all. You can concentrate on your investigation and I can spend a bit more time with Blaine. Mum and Tatiana will do all the hard work. All we have to do is turn up on the day.'

TWENTY-FOUR

As SHE HEADED for the golf club the following morning, Aoife decided Conor was right. She no longer had any control over the wedding, so why worry about it?

She drove slowly through the golf club car park until she found Matt's father's car and pulled into a space opposite. The morning was warm and sunny, so she leaned against the car, scrolling through Insta reels while she waited. He was a few feet away when he spotted her.

'What now?'

'Mr Gallagher, I'm sorry for your loss.'

'You didn't come all this way to say that. What do you want?'

'Have you a moment to talk about Matt's cousin, Stephen?'

'They're second cousins.'

'Okay. Do you and Stephen keep in touch?'

'No. Why?'

'I got the impression from him that he was close to your family.'

Mr Gallagher shoved his golf clubs into the boot. 'He sends Christmas cards. When Matt disappeared, he called to the house. He claimed he wanted to express his condolences.'

'You didn't believe him?'

'No, I did not. He watched us closely the entire time and tried to draw us into a conversation about his parents' health.'

'His parents are ill?'

'They never had a sick day in their lives. He was trying to get us to talk about our own health.'

'Why?'

'Obviously he wanted to figure out how long we were likely to live.'

'I'm sorry, Mr Gallagher. I'm not following this conversation.'

'I thought you were supposed to be a hotshot reporter. Haven't you figured out yet what Matt's death means to Stephen?'

Aoife shook her head.

'Matt's grandparents wanted their money to stay in the family. Nobody owns the inheritance outright, we just have use of it while we're alive.'

'You have no say in who receives the money after you die? You can't will it to your wife?'

'My wife already has access to the entire trust, as do I. The money came from both our parents, so we are joint heirs. But as you say, we have no control over who receives the money after we die.'

'So the money goes—'

'To Stephen, yes.'

⁂

Mr Gallagher drove away, but Aoife stayed in her car, trying to work out the significance of what she had just heard. Her phone buzzed.

'Grainne phoned me. Why didn't you tell me you're having your wedding in Powerscourt?'

'I'm trying not to think about it, Orla.'

'Why not? It sounds brilliant.'

'I wanted a small wedding with you, Amy and Conor's family. Now we're going to have one hundred and eighty guests, most of whom I'm sure will be Grainne's neighbours and distant relatives Conor hasn't seen in years.'

'What's so strange about that? Everyone knows weddings are really family reunions in disguise. The bride and groom are just the excuse for a party.'

'That's what I was trying to avoid.'

'I heard about the second wedding dress.'

'What? I never agreed to a second dress.'

'Grainne thinks you have. She asked me to help you choose it.'

'I'm not buying a second dress, Orla.'

'Grainne says she'll pay for it.'

'She can pay for anything she likes. I have chosen my dress and that is the one I'm going to wear.'

'Grainne has a point, Aoife. The dress we chose is completely unsuitable for a formal wedding, and if you're going through this entire thing to keep her happy, why not go the whole hog?'

Aoife sighed. 'I know you're right, but that would be the third wedding dress I've chosen. I'm not setting foot inside another bridal shop.'

'I thought you'd say that, so I worked out a compromise.'

'What compromise?'

'Grainne was so sympathetic about your mother that I said wedding dress shopping is hard for you and you wouldn't be able to do it a second time.'

'She bought that?'

'Sort of. She offered to choose the dress for you. I said that would be fine.'

'You said what! No! Grainne never wears anything but jeans. She'd probably let Tatiana pick the dress, and I don't even want to think what that one would consider suitable.'

'Which is why I'm going shopping with them. The shop already has your measurements and I know your style.'

'But—'

'Don't worry, Aoife. Chief bridesmaid to the rescue. I have everything under control.'

ɷ

When Conor phoned Aoife from London that evening, he asked, 'Did you speak to Matt's cousin? Stephen, isn't it?'

'I talked to his wife. It seems Stephen and Matt had barely spoken in years.'

'So Stephen lied when he said they were great friends?'

'Yep, but how did he know Matt and his parents had argued?'

'Everybody at the wedding would have noticed Matt's parents weren't there. It wouldn't be hard to guess there had been an argument or that the most likely reason was that the Gallaghers didn't like Nicole.'

'But would they guess Matt's parents had threatened to prevent Matt accessing his inheritance if the wedding went ahead?'

'You only have Stephen's word that ever happened. He probably made it up. It always seemed odd to me that Matt would have taken a threat like that seriously.'

'I don't know, Conor. I think they must have threatened him. It explains why he never told Nicole about the money. He didn't want to get her hopes up.'

'Or maybe there's a much simpler answer. Matt wanted to

surprise her. I'd love to be able to do that. Imagine if I could buy you a mansion, hand you the deeds and say, "Hey, guess what? As of today, we're millionaires." It would make for one hell of a thirtieth birthday party.'

Aoife laughed. 'I can just see your face. Oh well, we can dream.'

'Even if it's too late for me to have an unforgettable thirtieth birthday party.'

'Don't worry, old man. We'll do something special for your fortieth.'

'You're going to become a millionaire by then?'

'I'll try, although I can't make any promises. But, Conor, Stephen knew Matt had been to see his solicitor.'

'Aoife, you're the one who told him that. All Stephen said was that he recommended Matt get legal advice. I'm guessing Stephen wanted to sound like he was involved in everything, so he said visiting the solicitor was his suggestion.'

'But why would Matt go to see his solicitor?'

'He was getting married. He wanted to get his finances in order. That's perfectly normal. We're going to change our wills after we're married, aren't we?'

'Yes, but we have kids. Childless guys in their twenties don't normally bother about wills.'

'But Matt wasn't any ordinary guy. He was only three years from becoming a millionaire. The last time the will had been explained to him, he was eighteen. I'm guessing at that age the only thing that concerned him was how soon he could get his hands on the money. Now he's about to become a husband, he wants to make provision for his wife. Either that or he wanted her to sign a prenup.'

'And once the lawyer explained that one wasn't possible, so

the other wasn't necessary, there was no point in mentioning the visit to Nicole. The longer I think about it, Conor, the more convinced I am that you're right.'

'It isn't possible for Matt to leave his wife money?'

'Didn't I tell you, Conor? Matt wouldn't actually have inherited millions. His grandparents' will entitled him to the use of the family trust fund once he turned thirty. He never had the option to leave the money to Nicole, so a prenup or a will would have been pointless.'

'That explains why Stephen is desperate to give the impression that he and Matt were close.'

'So the police won't think he had reason to want Matt dead? But the money didn't go to Stephen. It went to Matt's parents.'

'For now, yes, but they're both in their eighties. How long are they likely to live?'

'I thought of that, but the Gallaghers could live another ten years. Would Stephen really kill his cousin so he could inherit money ten years from now?'

'True. Aoife, maybe you should advise the Gallaghers to invest some of their new-found wealth in a good security system. It sounds like they might need it.'

TWENTY-FIVE

WEDNESDAY AFTERNOONS WERE Aoife and Amy's alone time. As the weather was getting warmer, they spent that afternoon on the beach building sandcastles and splashing around in the waves. When they got home, Amy wanted to call to her friend's house and show her the shells she had found on the beach. Aoife had just dropped her off when Vicky phoned.

'Aoife, I was with Nicole this afternoon when the Italian investigators phoned her. They've spoken to that man who checked out of the Italian hotel.'

'What did they find out?'

'Nothing. At first he said they were mistaken and he hadn't been in Italy in years. When that didn't work, he flatly refused to say another word.'

'What are they going to do now?'

'They suggested Nicole should phone him. He might be more inclined to feel sympathy for her. She won't. She's too depressed to care.'

'Do you want me to phone him?'

'Could you? I'll text you the number. You will follow up on it, Aoife, won't you? Ever since we heard about Matt's money, we've all been worried sick the police will think Nicole killed him. The wife is always the main suspect, isn't she?'

'Yes, but didn't Nicole tell you that the money doesn't go to her? Matt's parents inherit it.'

'I know, but they're elderly, aren't they? The police might think Nicole figures she can influence them into leaving the money to her.'

'I don't think that's likely, Vicky. If Matt had lived, Nicole would have access to his money. Why throw away a certain fortune in the hope that you'll inherit one? Besides, Matt's parents don't have the option to leave the money to anybody. Under the terms of the trust, it goes directly to Matt's cousin.'

Vicky seemed intent on talking for hours, but Aoife eventually managed to get off the line. She had just started to prepare dinner when the doorbell rang.

'Hi, Aoife.' Grainne was practically glowing with excitement. 'Tat and I were in Kildare Village. I bought the most beautiful outfit and I just had to show it to you.'

Tat? Too stunned to reply, Aoife opened the door and they walked ahead of her to the sitting room. Grainne flung seven shopping bags on the floor. Her eyes danced as she rooted through them.

Tatiana winced as the beautifully wrapped packages piled on top of each other in a crumpled heap. 'Let me do that, Grainne.' She carefully removed a lilac coat and dress and held it against the older woman.

'That's beautiful, Grainne,' Aoife said, a little astonished to find she didn't need to lie.

'Thank you. Tat helped me choose it. Now, we won't stay. I

really only dropped in to let you know that we chose your dress. It needs slight alterations, but it will be ready in a few days.'

'There are wedding dresses in the outlet centre?'

'No. We bought it in Dublin yesterday.'

'It isn't the dress either of us chose,' Tatiana added with a slight pout. 'But your friend insisted she knew best.' Her lip curled. 'We thought she was a bit pushy, didn't we, Grainne?'

Jealous cow, Aoife thought, but before she could reply, Grainne said, 'Orla wasn't pushy, Tat. She was determined to choose a dress Aoife would love. They've known each other since they were kids. Naturally Orla has a much better understanding of Aoife's taste.'

'She let Aoife buy that other short thing. What does that tell you about her taste, Grainne?'

Grainne frowned at her. 'Anyway, Aoife, I know you didn't want a second dress, but I'm sure you'll love the one we chose, won't she, Tat?'

Tatiana shrugged. 'It wouldn't be my choice, but at least it looks like a proper wedding dress.'

'Tat means the new dress is more formal than your other dress, Aoife. But the dress you chose is no less beautiful.'

'Yeah, sure.' Tatiana sniffed. 'Formal.'

'I'll pay for it, of course, Grainne.'

'You will not. We already agreed I'm paying for everything and that includes your dress.'

'But—'

'For heaven's sake, Aoife.' Tatiana put a hand to her head as if to ward off a headache. 'Do you have to make everything an argument? I'd be so grateful if somebody wanted to pay for my wedding.'

Grainne patted her arm. 'It's alright, Tat. Aoife doesn't mean—'

'When Rory and I get married, Grainne, you won't get anything but gratitude from me if you want to pay for our wedding.'

'Married!' Grainne paled and Aoife had to bite her lip to hide a smile.

'Not yet, of course. We're both too young. But I am looking forward to being an official member of the Moloney family.' Tatiana's lips formed a smile, but there was more defiance than happiness in her eyes. 'We'll be sisters soon, Aoife.'

'Right.' Grainne gathered up her bags. 'Come on, Tatiana. It's time we left. We want to get to Dublin before rush hour.'

Vicky forwarded the information the Italian investigators had discovered about the mysterious man in the Italian hotel. Edgard was a sales manager with a well-known international organisation that had branches throughout western Europe, the USA and Canada. Aoife tried his phone number several times over the next few days. It went to voicemail every time. Maybe he wouldn't accept calls from Irish numbers. Aoife blocked her phone number and tried again. On the third ring it answered.

'Hello, Edgard speaking.' His tone was brisk and business-like with the slightest hint of a foreign accent.

'Hi, my name is Aoife Walsh. I wonder if you can help me.'

'I can certainly try, Aoife.' His tone was now light and slightly flirtatious.

'I understand you have been contacted by investigators looking into the murder of Matt Gallagh—'

All traces of flirtation gone, Edgard interrupted. 'I'm a very busy man, Miss Walsh. I have already made it perfectly clear that I know nothing about that man's disappearance and I do not intend to waste another second discussing it. Goodbye.'

Over the next few days, Aoife tried calling him from her landline and from Conor's phone, but the calls went straight to voicemail.

She sent a short note to his work email explaining her background and her role in investigating Matt's disappearance, but she wasn't surprised when there was no reply.

Aoife had a hospital appointment in Dublin on Monday afternoon. Orla suggested they meet outside her workplace. She would take a half-day, they'd go to lunch and then to Orla's house to try on the second wedding dress. It had been almost three weeks since Aoife had been offered temp work, so she decided to save money by taking the bus. The bus was late as usual and Aoife was hurrying across O'Connell Bridge when she saw a young couple in front of her, walking arm in arm. Aoife could only see the backs of their heads, but she recognised them immediately. Tatiana's hair was unmistakable and, although she wished it was no longer the case, even after almost three years of separation, Aoife would recognise Jason anywhere.

TWENTY-SIX

'WHAT DO YOU think I should do?' Aoife asked as they walked from the train station to Orla's house in Malahide. 'I should tell Conor, but you know how he feels about Jason. I don't want to cause any trouble.'

'I suppose it depends on how serious Rory is about Tatiana. Could they have broken up?'

'I don't know. Conor's still in England with Blaine. He phones every night, but we haven't talked about his family. But even if Tatiana and Rory are still together, they might not be exclusive. Tatiana and Jason…' Aoife stopped suddenly, both hands covering her mouth. 'Oh my God, Orla. What if Tatiana becomes Amy's stepmother?'

'Wasn't she talking about marrying Rory last week? She and Jason couldn't be going out together that long. I wouldn't worry about it.' Orla stuck her key in the door. 'They're a long way from—' Her words were drowned by the hum of a hoover.

'Florina!'

When there was no answer, Orla went into the kitchen and tapped a young girl on the shoulder. She was slim, with long dark hair tied up in a bun. She wore a pink tunic over fitted black cargo pants. The girl jumped, swung around, and put her hand to her throat. Removing her headphones she said something in a foreign language. To Aoife's surprise, Orla answered her.

'This is the girl who works for Katie?'

'Yep. Florina.'

'You speak Romanian?'

'You didn't know? I must have told you about Cosmin. The guy I went out with for about a year after college?'

'I remember you mentioning him, but I didn't know he was Romanian.'

'That's why we split up. He got a job back home. He taught me a little Romanian and I've been brushing up on it since Florina arrived. We can't manage anything too complicated, and I have to give Florina a chance to practise her English, but we do okay.' She said something else in Romanian.

'Hi.' Florina smiled at Aoife. 'I make coffee now.'

When they were alone, Orla poured two glasses of wine and they went to her bedroom to try on the dress.

'I saw Nooks & Crannies embroidered on Florina's top. Is that the name of Katie's company?'

'Yes. Good name, isn't it?'

'Mmm.'

'What's wrong?'

'I've heard that name before, but I can't remember where.'

'There are probably lots of companies by that name.' Orla opened the large white box she had left on the bed. Before removing the dress, she said, 'If you give this a chance, Aoife, you'll love it. It's not exactly what you wanted. Grainne would never have accepted anything that wasn't full-length, and it has a tiny train. But it's really beautiful.'

Aoife had never doubted she would love the dress. Nobody

could fault Orla's style. The dress had a V-neck that wasn't too revealing and lace straps.

'It's what they call a trumpet fit. It's not as fitted as a mermaid shape and not as wide as an A-line.'

'It's beautiful. I hope it didn't cost too much.'

'Grainne wouldn't let me look at the price tags. As mothers-in-law go, she's not the worst.'

'I know. She's very protective of Conor. If I didn't have Amy to think of and I could devote all my time to her son, I'm sure we'd get on famously.'

Florina arrived with a tray on which were two mugs and a coffee pot. 'We'd better have that downstairs, Florina. We don't want to risk spilling it on the dress.' When Florina looked confused, Orla translated.

'What does she think of the dress?' Aoife asked.

Orla translated again and Florina said 'Beautiful,' then added something in rapid Romanian.

'Florina says she'll have a dress like that some day.'

Aoife changed back into her jeans and all three of them had coffee downstairs. Florina said that she was using Duolingo to learn English. 'Greg promise he and Katie pay for English lessons but not yet.'

She and Aoife tried to have a conversation. Orla listened and waited until they were completely lost before translating. All three dissolved into giggles at some of their misunderstandings.

Orla had taken a photo of Aoife in the new dress and she sent it on to Grainne. A few minutes later, she got a reply—'thank you.' They assumed Grainne was busy and would phone or text them when she had a chance, but two hours later they still hadn't heard from her. Aoife tried not to worry, but she couldn't reconcile the silence with Grainne's excitement the previous week when she had chosen her 'mother of the bride' outfit. Aoife had an uncomfortable feeling that she and Grainne were at odds again, although she couldn't imagine why.

ණ

A few days later, Conor returned from England. After Amy had gone to bed, Aoife asked him if he had seen Rory recently.

'We spoke yesterday. Why?'

'I was wondering if he and Tatiana are still an item?'

Conor laughed. 'You're not going to get rid of your wedding planner that easily. Rory says she's working non-stop on it. It seems to be her full-time job these days.'

'What does she normally do?'

'I think Rory said she's a dancer. I suppose there aren't a lot of options for dancers in Ireland.'

'Probably not. Do you think they're serious?'

'No. At least Rory isn't. I'm not sure about Tatiana. You don't like her?'

'Not much. She flirted with you right in front of me.'

'You don't need to worry about Tatiana, my love.' He pulled her close. 'You're the only woman for me. Besides, I'm the one who should be worried. When I'm forty, you'll only be thirty-five. You'll have no use for an old man like me.'

'Yeah, you're right. Make the best of me while you have me, old man,' Aoife said, giving him a kiss. 'Conor, do you ever wonder what we'll be like when we're the Gallaghers' age? I see us hobbling down the street, arms wrapped around each other because neither of us is steady on our feet.'

'Sounds good to me.' They kissed again until Conor pulled away. 'That reminds me, someone forced an elderly man off the road this morning. I heard about it on the news. The man's car was pretty banged up, but he only suffered minor injuries.'

'Thank God for that. I swear you take your life in your hands every time you get in a car these days. Did they catch the guy who did it?'

'No, but they mentioned the name of the victim. It was Matt's father.'

ꕥ

Aoife phoned the main Dublin hospitals, but Matt's father wasn't registered at any of them. Conor got in touch with the local police station. They confirmed the victim had no serious injuries and had been released from hospital that afternoon.

'It was Stephen, wasn't it? Oh God, Conor. You were right. I should have warned them Stephen might try to kill them.'

'It wasn't Stephen. When I heard about the incident, I had some of the guys check him out. Stephen flew to New York last week and he hasn't returned.'

'He could have paid someone to do it.'

'I doubt he would have the connections. It was probably just a coincidence, Aoife. There're a lot of lunatics on the road these days. The driver was probably drunk or stoned out of his mind.'

'Was Matt's mother in the car when the accident happened?'

'No.'

'If Stephen was trying to get his hands on their fortune, he'd have made sure both of them died at the same time, wouldn't he? Killing one wouldn't be any use to him. He still wouldn't get the inheritance, and two deaths close together would be very suspicious.'

Conor nodded. 'Unless of course it was Matt's mother who

arranged the accident. Then nobody else would have to die. She'd have all the money to herself once her husband was dead.'

'Because two and a half million isn't enough for her?'

'You'd be surprised what wealthy people would do for money, Aoife. It's like a drug to most of them. They can never have enough.'

'Mrs Gallagher struck me as an awful woman, but I can't see her hiring somebody to kill both her husband and her son.'

'No, probably not. She's even less likely than Stephen to know any hitmen.'

'Although…' Aoife paused. 'When she was trying to discourage me from writing about Matt, she said she was certain Matt was alive. I thought it was a bit odd that she was so convinced. She didn't seem to care much about her son. Why would she find it so hard to accept his death?'

'And you said she told the police the same thing. She seems determined to put an end to all investigations into her son's disappearance.'

TWENTY-SEVEN

THE FOLLOWING DAY, Aoife was again going through Matt's bank statements when Conor phoned.

'Aoife, did something happen between you and Mum while I was away?'

'No. The last time I saw her was when she bought her wedding outfit in the outlet. She was really excited. We haven't spoken since. Why? What's wrong?'

'She asked me to meet her for lunch today and then proceeded to explain that you had been lying to me all these years and marrying you would be a disaster.'

'What!'

'She claims you had several affairs while you were married to Jason and you almost drove him to suicide. Apparently, you only pretend to be a good mother and Jason had to drag you off Amy a few times when you lost your temper with her.'

'Well, no prizes for guessing where all that came from.'

'I know, but she swears she's never spoken to Jason and that they don't have any mutual friends.'

'Did she say who told her that crap?'

'All she would say was that it was told to her in confidence.'

'It was Tatiana. When I was in Dublin last week, I saw her with Jason. They were walking down the street arm in arm.'

'What? She's cheating on Rory? Why didn't you tell me?'

'I know how you feel about Jason. As long as Rory wasn't serious about Tatiana, I felt it was better to let the affair play itself out.'

'Rory's my brother, Aoife. You should have told me.'

'Sorry. It's hard to know what to do sometimes. You've kept things about Jason from me too.'

'True. Okay, I'll call Mum back. I've been telling her about Jason for years. She won't believe any stories that came from him.'

'I guess that will be the end of our wedding planner.'

'Maybe. I'll tell Rory first and let him decide if he wants to break it off with Tatiana. Then Mum can make up her own mind about keeping Tatiana as the wedding planner.'

Aoife rang Orla to tell her Jason's latest antics. They talked for so long she was almost late arriving at Maura's house to pick up Amy. While Amy was in the bathroom, Aoife said, 'I saw Jason with a girl last week. Tatiana, isn't it?'

'Oh, Aoife, I'm so glad you know. I've been going on at Jason about it ever since I found out.'

'Jason doesn't need to tell me he's dating somebody, Maura.'

'But surely you agree that Amy and Tatiana have to meet as soon as possible? It's not fair to wait until the wedding to introduce them.'

'Wedding! Jason and Tatiana are getting married?'

'What? No! They barely know each other.'

'But you just said… Maura, what wedding were you talking about?'

'Yours, of course. Jason made me promise not to tell you

about Tatiana. He says everybody will expect him to be pining for you and there he'll be with a beautiful girl on his arm. He's so excited, he can't see that he's not being fair to Amy. He can't just spring Tatiana on the child. They need to be introduced gradually.'

'I'm sorry, Maura, I'm confused. Jason isn't coming to my wedding. You know he hasn't accepted that we'll never get back together. Having him at the wedding wouldn't be fair to Amy, Conor or me.'

Maura frowned. 'That's all behind you now, isn't it? I mean, Jason has Tatiana after all. Obviously he's accepted that you both have to move on.'

'I hope you're right. If Jason settles down with somebody else, maybe we can start building bridges. But not yet, Maura. It's far too soon. And definitely not at my wedding.'

'You're going to cancel his invitation?'

'Jason never received any invitation.'

'Yes, he did, Aoife. He showed it to me.'

'He showed you an invit—never mind, Maura. It must be a mistake. I'll sort it out.'

'So we're not invited?'

'Of course you're invited, Maura. You're Amy's grandmother. You'll always be a part of my fam—'

'I'm ready, Mummy,' Amy called, giving Aoife the perfect excuse to end the conversation.

⁂

'You're going to have to talk to Tatiana,' Orla said. 'She must be the one who gave Jason the invitation.'

'I know, but there's no point arguing with her if she won't be our wedding planner for much longer.'

'Thank God you found out before the wedding day. Can you imagine Jason standing by quietly while you and Conor say your vows? Oh my God!'

'What?'

'Remember that movie we watched years ago about Betty Broderick?'

'The woman who murdered her ex and his new wife?'

'Exactly. Jason's the male version of Betty, isn't he? He's only one step away from murdering you all.'

'Don't exaggerate, Orla. Jason's sense of self-preservation would never allow him to murder any—'

'Hang on!' Aoife heard Orla open the door and say something in Romanian. 'Florina's here, Aoife. We're going to the movies.'

'You two go out together?'

'Not much. I've tried introducing her to my friends, but they're too old for her.'

'She doesn't have friends of her own?'

'No. The people in her apartment block are really standoffish. None of them say more than hello. I have to go or we'll be late. Talk to you tomorrow, Aoife.'

Aoife sat at her desk, phone still in her hand. She'd tell Jason he wasn't welcome at the reception, but the marriage ceremony would have to be public. How could she stop Jason attending? Could she ask Maura to get Jason's brothers to keep him busy that day? While Aoife was rehearsing her conversation with Maura, she glanced down at her desk, which was still strewn with Matt's bank statements. One of the names caught her attention—Nooks and Crannies. Of course! She knew she'd seen that name somewhere.

TWENTY-EIGHT

Aoife dropped Amy at school and went straight to Katie's apartment.

'Hi, Aoife, what are you doing here so earl—'

'Matt worked for you. You were one of his biggest clients. Why did you pretend you didn't know him?'

'What? Who said—'

'I saw it on his bank statement. Your company—Nooks and Crannies—paid money into Matt's account every month for five months before he disappeared. You lied to me.'

'I didn't lie.'

'You both did. Greg said he didn't know Matt either.'

'Greg knows nothing about the admin side of the company. That's my job. Matt provided an online service. Neither of us ever met him. We didn't know he lived in this building.'

'You just said you handle the admin. Nicole said Matt invoiced all his clients. His address must have been at the top of the invoice. It's a legal requirement.'

'He used a post box number.'

'Really? Funny Nicole didn't mention it.' Aoife took out her phone. 'I'll just check that with her now.'

'Oh God! End that call.' Katie opened a cupboard, removed a bottle of whiskey, poured herself a generous amount and downed it in two gulps. She held out the bottle to Aoife.

'No, thank you. Why did you lie to me?'

'This is really awkward. Aoife, you have to promise me you won't repeat it to anybody.'

'That depends on what it is.'

'It's nothing to do with Matt's death.'

'If that's true, I won't have any reason to put it in my article.'

'It was me. I was the person Matt was having an affair with.'

TWENTY-NINE

THE NEXT TEN minutes were taken up with Katie justifying her actions. She hadn't known Nicole back then. The affair meant nothing to either of them. It was a moment of madness they both regretted.

'Why did you tell me about the affair?'

'It was only a matter of time before you heard about it. I figured if I was the one to mention it, you'd never suspect Matt and I were involved.'

'How did Matt's affair become common knowledge?'

'I've no idea. Aoife, don't mention the affair to Nicole, please. She doesn't need to know. It will only hurt her. Our friendship means so much to her.'

'But it's not really friendship, is it?'

'Of course it is.'

'You think so? It was you who arranged for everyone in the building to look out for Nicole, wasn't it? Everything you've done is out of guilt, not friendship.'

'Maybe at first. It's true I felt terrible when Matt disappeared. I thought he ran away because he couldn't cope with the guilt of what we'd done. I couldn't bear the thought of Nicole up in that apartment without a single friend to help her. Whatever you might think of me, Aoife, I got Nicole through the worst time of her life.'

'You did. But how would you feel if you were Nicole? How would you feel if you discovered Nicole had been having an affair with Greg?'

Katie got up and walked to the patio doors. For a few minutes she stared out at the balcony, then, without turning her head, she said, 'Would one more make much of a difference?'

'Greg is cheating on you?'

'Why do you think we hire teenage cleaners? Why do you think they have to stay in this apartment for the first two weeks?' She turned to face Aoife. 'I was so stupid. Greg said teenagers were easier to train and that letting them stay with us was a good recruitment tactic. The girls' parents would be happier to let them go abroad if they knew they would be taken care of. I should have known he was lying. It was Matt who told me what was really going on.'

'That Greg was having affairs with them?'

'Yeah. He's put two of them up in apartments in town. He told me they'd been sent home for stealing.'

'Is Greg having an affair with Florina?'

'Probably. He brought her all the way from Italy, so I'm sure he tried it on.'

'Is that why you didn't want Florina working for Orla?'

'I didn't want anyone I knew to even speak to her. It's one thing to have my husband cheating on me, it's quite another when everyone knows about it. When Sadhbh said she spoke some Italian, I panicked. No way was I letting any of those girls speak to my friends. I couldn't bear it if I was an object of pity.'

'Have you spoken to Greg about the affairs?'

Katie shook her head. 'When Matt told me, I got really drunk. He did too. That's when we slept together. How could I say anything to Greg after that? I was just as guilty as he was.'

'Not quite. He cheated on you first.'

'That wouldn't make any difference to him. Greg is king of the double standard. If he found out I'd cheated on him, he'd leave me. No second chances.'

'I see.'

'I hope you do, Aoife, because if you tell Nicole, she'll tell everyone. There won't be a person in this apartment block who'll speak to me and my marriage will be over.'

'Could Greg have found out about the affair?'

'And said nothing? No way. If I even look at another man, Greg sulks for a week. If he'd found out about me and Matt, I'd know about it.' When Aoife looked doubtful, she added, 'And I wouldn't be the only one. The entire block would hear the screaming.'

THIRTY

AMY SQUEALED, 'HIGHER, Moaney. Higher!'

Conor gave the swing another push.

'That's enough, Amy. Conor needs a rest. He's been pushing you for a half hour now.'

'But I can't swing that high by myself.'

'Keep practising. You'll manage.'

'But I want—'

'Push yourself or get off the swing, Amy.' Aoife's tone was harsher than she intended, and Amy's face puckered. Aoife kissed her, then gave her one shove on the swing before returning to the park bench. Conor joined her.

'What's wrong?'

'Nothing.'

'Come on, tell me.'

'It's just a lot of little things. I'm worried Jason will try to ruin our wedding. My investigation is going nowhere. Your mother hates me again. Everything is getting on top of me.'

'Mum doesn't hate you. Ever since she found out Jason spread those lies, you've become "that poor girl who was married to a psycho".'

'Jason will try something else. You know he will.'

'And we'll put an end to it, just like we put an end to those stupid lies. We can handle Jason and you can handle the investigation. You always do.'

'I don't know, Conor. I was so sure I was getting someplace when I found out Katie and Matt had an affair.'

'Maybe you were. It gives Katie's husband a reason to kill Matt.'

'It would if he knew about it. Katie says he doesn't.'

'She could be wrong.'

'I don't think so. She says Greg's the jealous type. He'd scream the place down if he found out.'

'What if he found another outlet for his anger?'

'You mean murder?'

THIRTY-ONE

AOIFE DIDN'T KNOW Greg well enough to guess if he was capable of murder. The one person who might be able to shed light on his personality was Vicky.

A couple of days later, Aoife found an excuse to visit Vicky. They drank coffee while Vicky filled her in on the latest gossip in the complex. When she mentioned an argument that had taken place in the pub a few weeks earlier, Aoife had her opening.

'It must be worrying when people in the group argue.'

'A little, but we talked about it afterwards, so I don't think it will happen again. Car parks always cause issues in apartment complexes, but the pub isn't the place to discuss them.'

'You're right, Vicky. It would be so easy for a group like yours to fall apart. All you would need is one person thinking their partner was interested in someone else and it would only be a matter of time before everyone was at loggerheads.'

Vicky smiled. 'I don't see that happening. It's not like we're at an office Christmas do. We only have a few drinks. We're not all legless.'

'Oh, those office do's are awful, aren't they? I was at one where a guy thought someone was paying too much attention to his wife. It wouldn't have been so bad if he'd fought with the guy, but he literally dragged his wife from the room. We were all so worried about her.'

'Was she okay?'

'She said she was, but who knows what really goes on in somebody else's relationship? I definitely saw fear in her eyes that night. I'm guessing it wasn't the first time her husband scared her.'

Vicky launched into a story of a celebrity couple she read about who were both ferociously possessive and the public brawl and arrest that followed.

'I read about that,' Aoife interrupted, trying to steer the conversation back to Katie and Greg. 'You're lucky none of the men in your group are like that. Although, statistically speaking, it's more than likely that at least two or three of them are the controlling type.'

'No way. All the guys in this complex are lovely.'

'But how lovely would they be if they thought their relationship was threatened? What if a new guy joined the group and Sadhbh or Katie were attracted to him? Imagine how their partners would react. That could break up any group.'

Vicky laughed. 'I can't see that happening. Sadhbh would have to take her eyes off that boyfriend of hers long enough to notice another man, and Katie and Greg are rock solid.'

'Rock solid? I love that. It's such a great description of a happy couple.'

'It's an accurate one. I can't imagine either of them having the slightest interest in another person.'

'That's good. I wonder if anybody in the group is already having an affair.'

Vicky frowned. 'I'm sure nothing like that is going on. I'd have noticed.'

'Would you? Nobody knew Matt was having an affair.'

'But we barely knew Matt or Nicole back then. If someone in our group was having an affair, I'm sure I'd notice.'

'You're probably right. If there was tension in the group, it would be hard to miss.'

'Of course it would. And there isn't anything like that going on. Everybody is very relaxed. People aren't watching each other all the time or being aggressive to their partners. I think your work is getting to you, Aoife. You come across too many weird people. Normal people don't act that way. Certainly nobody I know does.'

THIRTY-TWO

AOIFE WROTE UP the notes of her conversation with Vicky. Greg obviously hid his controlling side well. She needed to speak to someone closer to him. If Greg was having an affair with Florina, she might be able to shed more light on his character. Aoife checked her watch. It was Jason's weekend with Amy. If he wasn't too late, Aoife might have the chance to drive to Orla's house and speak to Florina tonight.

Six p.m. came and went and there was no sign of Jason. By the time Conor phoned her at midnight, Jason still hadn't turned up and he hadn't gotten in touch.

'I could murder him, Conor. Even if he'd told me he couldn't have her this weekend, I could have come up with some explanation, but he'd promised Amy a special surprise today and she was devastated when he didn't show up. I phoned Maura, but she hadn't heard from him either.'

'This is payback, isn't it?'

'Yep. We scuppered his plans to ruin our wedding and he's making Amy pay.'

'Poor kid. Is she still upset?'

'She's fine now. At eight I said Daddy must have been

delayed, let's go to the movies. She'd never been to the cinema at night before. She was thrilled.'

'You'll have to think up something special to do with her tomorrow.'

'Yeah. I'm taking her to Tayto Park. One of her friends at school told her about the Superhero Climbing Wall and she's been begging me to go ever since. I know we agreed to meet tomorrow afternoon, but—'

'Don't worry about it, Aoife. I finish at three, so I'll pick up takeaway and bring it over to your place. Amy will like that.'

'Thanks, hon.'

'There's nothing to thank me for. What are you going to say if Jason phones?'

'I've been thinking about it all evening. At first I was going to scream at him, then I thought I'd try appealing to his better nature.'

'I'm not sure he has one.'

'Neither am I. Maybe I'll say Amy had a marvellous evening and it might be better if he collected her on Saturdays in future.'

Conor chuckled. 'That should do it.'

ॐ

Aoife was packing the car while Amy ran in circles around her, singing a three-note song she'd made up about superheroes, when Jason arrived.

Amy ran to him. 'Daddy! Daddy! Me and Mummy are going to Tayto Park. I'm going to put Supergirl in my pocket and climb to the top of the Superhero Wall.'

'It's your weekend with Daddy, sweetie.'

Amy folded her arms and scowled. 'I want to go to Tayto Park!'

Aoife left them to it. As she closed the front door, she heard Amy wail, 'Mummy promised I could climb the Super Wall. It's not fair!'

Aoife was checking her phone when Jason joined her in the kitchen. She could see he had opened the Google Maps app.

'Two hours!' He held the phone inches from her face. 'It's a two-hour round trip! This is your fault, Aoife. You had no right to promise her you'd take her to Tayto Park. You know I detest amusement parks.'

Aoife took a step back and kept her head down as she continued scrolling. 'If you'd told me you were turning up today, I wouldn't have made any promises. I'd no reason to assume you'd come.'

'You're trying to keep me from my daughter.'

Aoife was tempted to scream at him, but she took a deep breath. Although she could no longer concentrate on the screen, she continued scrolling as she said, 'Why would I do that?'

'So the great detective could step into my shoes. He can't wait to replace me as Amy's father.'

Aoife glanced at him but looked down at her phone immediately. 'If you tell me you're coming to collect Amy, she'll be here waiting for you. If you tell me you'll be late, she'll be here waiting for you.' She looked him straight in the eyes. 'If you don't turn up and don't contact me, I'll do whatever is necessary to make my daughter forget how unhappy she is when her father ignores her.'

'How dare you! I do not ignore my daughter. I—'

'Jason, I thought we agreed years ago that you wouldn't come into this house without an invitation. Now, if you don't want to take Amy this weekend, I'll take her to Tayto Park. If you want to keep her for the weekend, that's fine too. Just let me know your decis—'

Amy came running into the kitchen, face screwed up and eyes red from crying.

'You promised we'd go to Tayto Park, Mummy.'

'That's right, sweetie. I did. If you stay here, we'll go to Tayto Park. I don't know what Daddy has planned.'

'Alright, Amy. I'll take you to the amusement park.'

Amy jumped up and down. 'I'm going to climb the Superhero Wall. Daddy, can we go to the night movies afterwards? Mummy took me to the night movies yesterday. I saw two new superheroes and we had popcorn and ice cream and Mummy even let me have a big bar of chocolate and I was up way, way, way, past my bedtime.'

Jason glared at Aoife. 'We'll see, sweetie. Help me get your things from Mummy's car.'

&

Aoife wasn't in the mood to interview anyone and she was pretty sure Florina didn't work at the weekend. As Conor's shift didn't end until 3 p.m., she phoned Orla. When there was no reply, Aoife decided to drive to Dublin. There was a free exhibition in the art gallery, and although she wasn't a huge fan of art, truly famous paintings rarely made it to Ireland. It would be a shame to miss it.

The exhibition was even better than she had expected and it was 3.30 before Aoife left the art gallery. Conor would be on his way home now, so she decided to surprise him there. As Aoife drove down his street, she could see two cars in his driveway. If Grainne was visiting, she'd come back later. As she drew closer, she recognised the car. Conor's visitor wasn't his mother. It was Orla.

❧

Aoife drove past the house and pulled over. Why hadn't she stopped? What did she think would happen if she joined them? She sat in the car for several minutes, then took out her phone and called Conor.

'Hi, hon. Jason collected Amy, so I'm free. Do you want to meet me in town?'

'Sorry, Aoife, I'm tied up. Can you give me a few hours? How about I come around to your place like we agreed?'

'Okay. Are you still at work?'

'What was that? Sorry, my love, I have to go. See you later.'

Aoife waited a few minutes, then texted Orla. *Find myself at a loose end this afternoon. Want to meet?* Within a few seconds, her phone pinged. *Can't, Aoife, sorry. Lot on this afternoon. Talk later.*

THIRTY-THREE

AOIFE TURNED AROUND and drove past Conor's house again. She parked at the top of the street, where she could see anyone entering or leaving his house. Groups of kids were playing on a green area opposite the houses. After a while, some came over to stare at Aoife. She smiled but didn't engage and they eventually wandered off. What was she doing here? She trusted Conor, didn't she? Whatever he and Orla were doing, he was not cheating on her. She was certain of that. So why couldn't she go home? It was almost three hours before Orla came out of the house alone and drove away. Fifteen minutes later, Conor got into his car.

Aoife texted him. *Migraine coming on. Going to bed. Sorry to ruin your evening.*

She turned her phone off before he could call her.

Aoife spent the evening walking around her house in circles, the same thoughts going round and round in her head. She trusted Conor. She trusted Orla. Neither had ever shown the slightest interest in the other. There had to be a rational explanation for this. They were planning a surprise for her. Something to do with the wedding? It would explain why they'd lied. It didn't explain why they'd spent three hours together. What surprise took that long to plan? And who knows how long they'd been together before she arrived. Could Conor have lied about working today? Could he and Orla have spent last night together? She shivered. Was it possible they'd been in bed together when she'd phoned?

The following morning, Aoife decided she had overreacted. Conor and Orla were planning a surprise for the wedding. A surprise that took three hours to plan would be spectacular. She wouldn't ruin it for them. She would never mention having seen them together. Yesterday never happened.

Aoife continued seeing Conor as normal and meeting up with Orla regularly. Neither had changed in the slightest. When Conor had his arms around her or she and Orla were laughing about old times, Aoife had absolutely no doubt she had nothing to worry about. Neither Conor nor Orla were capable of the level of duplicity she had suspected them of. It was when she was alone that the doubts started.

THIRTY-FOUR

NOW SHE HAD decided there was nothing going on between Conor and Orla, Aoife was able to concentrate on the investigation again. She needed to speak to Florina about Greg. There was no point arriving at Orla's house too early. Florina wouldn't relax if she had hours of work waiting. Better to call in the afternoon. In the meantime, she'd see what she could find out about Edgard.

Vicky had sent her on the bio constructed by the Italian private investigators. Edgard was fifty-two. He lived in London with his wife and two teenage daughters. His eldest daughter was in college abroad. Edgard worked as a salesman for a well-known multinational. Aoife checked out their website and read his bio. He'd joined the organisation three years earlier. He'd spent the first year in their San Francisco office and the second in Paris. Aoife zoomed into his photo to get a good look. Edgard was tall and broad with sandy-brown hair. His suit looked expensive and his thinning hair was strategically arranged to cover his entire scalp. Beneath the expertly cut suit jacket, she could detect a slight paunch. Not a fitness nut, then. Edgard's company regularly hosted conferences throughout Europe. Photos of the delegates were posted on the company's Facebook page. Edgard appeared in most but not all. Aoife checked their website for upcoming conferences. She ran her finger down the list. The last Thursday of the month they were holding a conference in Dublin. The conference was free, but attendees were asked to register online. Aoife set up a fake email address and used Orla's name and address to register herself as an attendee.

Feeling like she was finally getting somewhere, Aoife drove to Orla's house. When Florina answered the door, headphones in her ears, Aoife said she was looking for Katie.

'Katie not here. Work.'

'Can I wait?'

Florina nodded and Aoife followed her into the kitchen. Florina was in the middle of cleaning out the fridge. She moved some of its contents off the table to make room for Aoife and she switched on the coffee machine.

When she handed Aoife a mug, Aoife pulled out a second seat and pointed to it. She gave Florina the coffee and poured another mug for herself.

'Do you like living in Ireland?'

'Yes, yes, I like very much.'

'Do you miss Italy?'

Florina shook her head. 'Good weather, good food, little work.'

'How did you find out about this job?'

'I work sometimes in hotel in Italy. Greg talk. He say much more work in Ireland and much money.'

'Was he right? Is the money better?'

'No. Greg promise he find me good work. Much money. He

say work for Orla first, then other work. Now he say soon do other work. I want work for Orla. Orla say she give me airfare to pay Greg and I work for her always. I work for her friends too and earn much money.'

'You want to work for yourself?'

'Yes. I boss.'

'Have you told Greg?'

'No. First need new apartment.'

'You can't stay where you are?'

'No. Katie rent apartment. Very nice apartment. Big. Five bedrooms. Katie say other girls come but not yet.'

'Do you see much of Greg?'

Florina shook her head. 'He phone.'

'Do you like him?'

Florina shrugged. 'Angry I want work for Orla.'

'He'll be angry when you tell him?'

The young girl nodded.

'He'll be annoyed, Florina, but that kind of thing happens all the time. As long as you pay him back for the airfare, he'll get over it.'

'Get over it?'

'He'll understand.'

'No. Very angry.'

'Why do you think that?'

'In Katie's house I hear Greg on phone. He shout very much at Romanian girl on phone. She cry. I not hear all, but she say "home". Greg very angry she want go home.'

'Did you tell Katie?'

'Katie come home. Greg shout about Romanian girl. I not understand, but he very angry.'

'How did Katie react?'

'React?'

'What did Katie say?'

'She say nothing. Katie scared.'

As she read over her interview notes that evening, Aoife felt some of her stress dissipate. Conor had been right. Her investigations often seemed hopeless, but they always worked out in the end. It was looking more and more like the murderer was Greg. Florina had confirmed he was aggressive and that Katie was scared of him. It was quite possible he'd been so enraged when he found out his wife was cheating on him that he'd murdered her lover. He had motive. Now she needed to find out if he'd had the opportunity.

Aoife opened her Instagram account and checked for Greg or Katie. Both had accounts although neither posted regularly. She flicked through Greg's posts, checking the dates. Her heart sank when she found one on the day of Matt's murder. Greg was sitting at a table covered with half-empty pint glasses. She checked the comments. He'd been at a stag night in Dublin when Matt was murdered. Aoife checked out the groom's page. There were several photos taken that weekend, and Greg was in most of them. Aoife clicked on the bride's page. Dozens of posts were labelled 'my hen weekend in Dublin'. Aoife flicked through them until she found Katie. Damn! Greg was in Dublin the night Matt was killed and his wife and about a hundred friends were witnesses. She was right back where she'd started.

THIRTY-FIVE

ONCE EVERY WEEK since his accident, Aoife had phoned Mr Gallagher's golf club. It was three weeks before she was told he was on the golf course. Aoife drove straight there. When Matt's father saw her leaning against her car, he just sighed wearily. His face was bruised and the spring had gone from his step. He now had a golf cart, which he dragged behind him. When he opened the car boot to stow away his golf clubs, Aoife rushed to help him.

'I can do it,' he snapped.

'You don't look well. I was sorry to hear about your accident.'

'Who said it was an accident?' Some of the energy had returned to his voice. 'A young hooligan tried to kill me and the police haven't done a dammed thing about it.'

'What exactly happened, Mr Gallagher?'

'I was driving home from the golf club when this car appeared out of nowhere. It drove right up behind me and hit my bumper.' He shut the boot and leaned heavily against it. 'I couldn't believe it. It was like something out of a movie.'

'It sounds terrible.'

'He kept hitting the bumper and pushing me forward and

then we came to a corner and he bumped me right off the road. Another mile down the road and I might have gone over a cliff.'

'What did the man look like?'

'Young. He wore a baseball cap, so I couldn't see his face.'

'What did the police say?'

'They said it was a miracle I wasn't seriously injured, and wasn't it bad luck that I was attacked on one of the few stretches of road in the area that isn't covered by CCTV?'

'That was unfortunate.'

'Unfortunate my eye! That hooligan knew exactly what he was doing.'

'You think he deliberately targeted you?'

'Me, any elderly person. It doesn't matter to that type. They go looking for vulnerable people who can't fight back. Bloody cowards, the lot of them. I tell you if I was twenty years younger…' He paused. 'Why are you here, Aoife? Are you planning to write about my accident? "Bereaved father attacked by hooligans"?' A flush rose to his cheeks. 'For the love of God, would you leave us the hell alone?' He got into the driver's seat, banged the door and drove at breakneck speed from the car park. Then, as if remembering his ordeal, he slammed on the brake and barely crawled out the long driveway.

As she was in the golf club anyway, Aoife decided it would be a good time to speak to the golfers she had met on her first visit there. She checked her notebook for their phone numbers. Neither was in the golf club at the time, but one, Clement Smyth, offered to meet her in a local coffee shop.

Clement was middle-aged, with thinning brown hair. He sat very erect, hands resting in his lap when he wasn't drinking his coffee. It came as a surprise when he wanted to discuss golf membership. Aoife had completely forgotten she'd used that as an excuse to speak to them. She pretended to take notes as they spoke, waiting for an opportunity to bring the conversation back to the Gallaghers.

'Would you say your social life revolves around the golf club?'

'Yes, indeed. We play at least twice a week during the summer and always at the weekend.'

'We?'

'My wife's a member too. We always meet up for a few drinks after a game. That's how we get to know the new members.'

'How well do you know the Gallaghers?'

Clement picked up his coffee mug. He seemed to be choosing his words carefully. 'Mrs Gallagher's been a member of the club for years. We attend the same meetings and functions, but I couldn't say I know her. I don't even know her first name.'

'But your opinion of her is unfavourable?'

'My wife said she had too much to drink after one game and spent the night badmouthing her husband and son. There's no excuse for washing your dirty linen in public.'

'What did she say?'

'Something about her husband being useless and if she'd married a better man, she might have the type of son she deserved and not the useless, ungrateful brat she was lumbered with.'

'Why did she think Matt was ungrateful?'

'She said he was due to inherit money shortly, so she asked him to invest in some project of hers. He refused. She said he was just like his father, timid and risk-averse, and that she was the only person in the family with any guts.'

'Do you know what investment she was talking about?'

'Something to do with vulture funds.'

'The companies that buy up underperforming mortgages?'

'Yes. She told my wife that the economy will crash soon and the people she wanted to invest with would be able to buy up homes for practically nothing and sell them when the market recovers.'

'How could Matt help her? As I understand it, he wasn't due to come into any money for another three years.'

'She needed funds. She planned to use Matt's involvement as collateral to get a loan. She wanted to put their house up too, but her husband wouldn't agree.'

'It sounds very risky.'

'That's what her husband and son said. After she'd had a few drinks, Mrs Gallagher told my wife and her friends that getting married was the biggest mistake of her life and that she wished there was some way she could undo it.'

THIRTY-SIX

'BUT THAT WASN'T a threat, Aoife. It was a drunk woman moaning about her family.'

'She thought they were stopping her from getting rich, Conor. Only yesterday you said rich people would do anything to get more money.'

'I didn't mean they'd kill for it.'

'People kill for money all the time.'

'True, but that's no reason to suppose Mrs Gallagher killed Matt or tried to have her husband murdered.'

'She strikes me as the kind of woman who would do exactly that.'

'Be careful of bias, Aoife. Don't immediately assume that people you dislike must be guilty.'

ᘛ

'What do you think, Orla? Conor says I'm prejudiced.'

'It could just have been a lunatic driver. He might not have intended to hurt Matt's father.'

'That's always a possibility, I suppose, but isn't it a bit of a coincidence? Matt was about to become a millionaire and he's murdered. Then his father inherits the money and he is almost killed. It's a pity Stephen was out of the country. He seems the most likely suspect.'

'I don't know about that, Aoife. What about his wife?'

'Stephen's wife? Does she even know about the money? She said she couldn't understand why Stephen tries to keep up contact with his family. If she knew about the money, she'd understand.'

'Why? Keeping in touch with Matt's family won't do anything for Stephen. He won't get his hands on that money until the Gallaghers die, and then he'll get it irrespective of the Gallaghers' opinion of him.'

'It's easier to ask your relatives for money if you keep in touch.'

'Does Stephen need money?'

'Everybody needs money. But you're right, Orla. I should have checked to see if he has any immediate financial problems.'

The next morning Aoife made her weekly phone call to Nicole. For the first time since Matt's body had been discovered, Nicole answered.

'Hi, Aoife. Sorry I didn't return any of your calls. My mind's been on other things lately.'

'Of course. I understand, Nicole, and I'm so sorry about Matt.'

'Thanks. Actually, I'd like to speak to you. I'm about to go for a walk. Can you call around in an hour?'

Aoife pulled into Nicole's apartment block fifteen minutes before they were due to meet. While she was waiting, she phoned Stephen's landline number. As she had hoped, his wife answered it.

'Hi, Penny, this is Aoife. We spoke recently.'

'Oh yes, you were looking for Stephen. Did you not get him? He's out of the country at the moment, but you should be able to reach him on his mobile.'

'That's why I phoned, actually. I accidentally deleted his number. Would you be able to give it to me?'

'Sure.'

Aoife pretended to take a note of the number she called out.

'Thanks. It must be difficult having him out of the country so much. My husband used to travel a lot, and at times I felt like a single parent.'

Penny laughed. 'Tell me about it. But those credit card bills won't pay themselves.'

'Don't I know it? My husband's always saying, "your credit limit is not a sales target". I dread those bills. It's like having a tax audit every month. I swear he makes me justify every single purchase.'

'Tell him he doesn't know how lucky he is. If I could get my husband to stick to the credit limit on just one card, I'd die a happy woman.'

THIRTY-SEVEN

Aoife knocked on Nicole's door. Nicole had lost weight since they had last met, but she seemed calmer, less on edge.

'At least I know Matt's dead,' she said, handing Aoife a coffee. 'I thought I always knew that, but somehow it's a relief to find out for certain. Whatever happened to him, nobody can hurt him now.'

They talked about Matt for a while and eventually Aoife said, 'I've been thinking about the hotel you and Matt stayed in. The Colonnina, wasn't it? Why did you choose that particular hotel?'

'I suggested Italy. We both love it. Matt even lived there for six months. Matt said one of his clients had an account in the Colonnina and we'd get a discount if we used their name.'

They talked about Nicole and her plans for the future. She was going to find a new place to live. She'd miss her friends, but she could always visit. It was time to put her life with Matt behind her and try to move on.

'I'm not really interested in the article anymore, Aoife. I'd hoped media attention would help me find out what happened to Matt. Now I know, there doesn't seem much point.'

'You don't know who murdered him, Nicole.'

'I'm not sure I care. Finding the murderer won't bring Matt back.'

'No, but is it right that his murderer should be living as if nothing had happened? What if they murder someone else?'

'The Italian police will continue the investigation.'

'What do you think happened to Matt?'

Nicole shrugged. 'He probably got bored waiting for me to wake up. He must have wandered down some alley and got mugged.'

'Muggers don't usually shoot their victims in the back of the head or hide their bodies in a ravine. And Italy isn't much different from Ireland where guns are concerned. It's almost unheard of for petty criminals to be armed.'

'The Mafia are armed. Maybe Matt came across a drug deal or something like that.'

'The Mafia don't normally attack tourists.'

'Well, that's for the Italian police to worry about. Your article isn't going to find some Italian murderer. I understand you have to write it, Aoife. You have deadlines to meet. Just leave me out of it from now on, okay?'

Aoife went straight to Katie's apartment. She wanted to confirm her suspicion that Katie's company had an account in the Colonnina. She knocked three times before the door was swung open. Katie's hair had come loose from its customary ponytail, and strands trailed down her face. Her mascara was smudged, and from the whiff of sweat, Aoife guessed she hadn't showered that morning.

'What the hell are you doing here?'

As Aoife gaped at her, Greg charged out of the bedroom, pulling a suitcase behind him.

'Greg, don't!'

Greg pushed past her, knocking against Aoife's arm in his rush to leave.

'Are you happy now?' Katie hissed at Aoife. 'You promised you wouldn't say anything, you bitch.'

'About the affair? I didn't tell anybody.'

'So less than three weeks after you found out, Greg just guessed. Is that it?'

'I have no idea how he found—'

'Oh, get out.'

'Katie, I promise you I never told anyb—' Aoife's voice trailed off as the realisation hit her.

Katie pounced on it immediately. 'I knew you were lying. You told somebody, didn't you?'

'Only my fiancé.'

'The detective?'

'Yes.'

'Who did he tell?'

'There's a slight chance he told Orla and I suppose it's possible Orla might have said something to Florina.'

The anger seemed to drain out of Katie. She flopped down on the couch.

'Orla speaks Romanian?'

'A little, yes. But that may not be what happened at all. Conor might not have said anything, and even if he did, Florina told me her only contact with Greg is by phone.'

'Yeah, sure.'

'I believed her. She didn't talk about Greg as if she knew him. She even said she was scared to tell him she was leaving.'

'Leaving?'

'Florina wants to go out on her own. Orla's going to lend her the airfare to pay back Greg so she can be her own boss.'

The colour drained from Katie's face. For a few seconds, there was silence, then she said, 'You were the only person who knew I was having an affair with Matt. Thanks to you, not only is my marriage destroyed but I now know for certain Greg was cheating on me with another of the maids.' When Aoife didn't reply, she looked at her and through gritted teeth hissed, 'Get out of here.'

Aoife drove home conscious that she had handled the situation very badly. She should never have mentioned Conor. There was no reason at all to assume Conor had told Orla or, indeed, that Orla would say anything to Florina. Aoife often discussed her cases with Orla and she'd never blabbed before. Then again, Orla had never had private meetings with Conor before either. Had she?

'Conor, did you mention to anybody that Matt and Katie were having an affair?'

They were walking through the Curragh, Amy riding ahead on her tricycle. 'Of course not. Why would I tell anybody?'

'There's no chance you could have mentioned it to Orla?'

'Orla?' He turned his head to one side so she couldn't see his expression. 'I definitely never mentioned Matt's affair to Orla or to anybody else. Why do you ask?'

'Greg found out about it and he's left Katie. She says I was the only person who knew about her and Matt. She thinks Orla told Florina and Florina told Greg.'

'But you didn't say anything to Orla?'

'No, it never came up.'

'Then Greg found out some other way. Maybe the neighbours saw them together.'

'They're all friends of Nicole's. That building is alive with rumours, and they're all talking about Matt's affair. If they had known he was sleeping with Katie, somebody would have told me about it by now.'

'Well, you figured it out from Matt's bank statements. Nicole could have found out the same way. Actually, she could have found out long before Matt was killed. I told you there's a reason the wife is always the main suspect.'

'And you definitely never mentioned it to Orla?'

'Definitely not.' Again he turned his face away. 'Amy, I'm going to race you home,' he called, running ahead and leaving Aoife staring after him.

THIRTY-EIGHT

Aoife tossed and turned all night. She trusted Conor, but she needed to know what was going on. She'd have to ask him straight out. But then he'd think she didn't trust him, and how could their relationship survive that? It would be easier to build bridges with Orla. A thought struck her. Maybe she didn't need to speak to either of them. Florina might know what was going on.

Florina seemed surprised to see Aoife again. Aoife said she had left her sunglasses behind on her last visit. Florina clearly didn't understand. When she went into the kitchen to switch on the coffee machine, Aoife stuck her sunglasses under the sofa cushion. When Florina returned with the coffee, Aoife sat down, got up again, put her hand under the cushion and withdrew the sunglasses with a flourish. The slight crease between Florina's eyebrows disappeared, and she grinned.

As they sipped their coffee, they discussed Duolingo, and Florina showed Aoife all she had learned.

Aoife brought the conversation around to Romania and asked Florina if she missed her family and friends. She encouraged Florina to share her family photos, then she took out her own phone. The first photo she showed was a group shot of herself, Jason and Orla when they were in college. Florina jabbed at the phone and said, 'Orla!'

'Yes, that's when we were teenagers.'

They looked at other photos of Orla and Aoife, then came to a group photo taken at Amy's fourth birthday party. There were a number of adults and kids in the picture. Aoife pointed at Amy. 'My daughter.' She held her breath, waiting for Florina's response.

Florina smiled. 'Pretty girl.' Then she pointed at Conor. 'Conor!'

'You know Conor?'

'Yes, Orla friend.'

'Do you see him much?'

Florina nodded. 'He here when I come to work. Sometimes here when I go home. Here very often.'

As Aoife drove home, she came to a decision. It was clear that either Conor and Orla were having an affair, something she still couldn't believe either was capable of, or they were planning a surprise for her, most probably something to do with the wedding. Conor had told her that Rory and Tatiana had broken up, so Grainne must know everything there was to know about the wedding preparations. Grainne wasn't the type to keep secrets. Even if Conor had asked her not to mention the surprise he was planning, Aoife would know from Grainne's expression that something was up. She was sure of it.

THIRTY-NINE

Aoife was barely in the door when her phone rang.

'Hi, Stephen.'

'Did you tell the police I had reason to want Matt's parents dead?'

'Why would I think that?'

'When the police left, I visited Matt's parents. They told me you know I'm in line to inherit if anything happens to them.'

'Why didn't you tell me that?'

'Because the fewer people who know, the better.'

'So you pretended you and Matt were friends?'

'We were friendly.'

'Not according to your wife.'

'You spoke to Penny? She never mentioned it. What did she say?'

'That you and Matt have barely spoken in years.'

'I don't tell her every time we speak. She says I'm an idiot hoping I'll get my hands on that money some day.'

'Why does she think that? The money will come to you automatically, won't it?'

'Penny thinks it will go to our kids. She says we'll be in our dotage or in our graves by the time those two pop it.'

'So you're saying that you and Matt really were close?'

'Well... maybe not as close as I pretended. I figured there was a good chance you'd find out about my inheritance if you dug deep enough. If you thought Matt and I were friends, you were unlikely to write an article suggesting I was a murderer.'

'How often exactly did you speak to Matt?'

'Rarely.'

'And he never told you his parents would have him disinherited if he married Nicole?'

'No.'

'He never mentioned going to see a solicitor?'

'No.'

'When the police spoke to you, did they ask about your finances?'

'No. Why?'

'Credit card debts can be a serious problem, can't they?'

'What?'

'If something were to happen to the Gallaghers, I imagine it would be a real relief to be debt-free again.'

'So it was you. I knew it. You listen to me, you malicious bitch. I may not be able to get my hands on that money yet, but I can borrow against it. I'll never be desperate for money. I certainly would never kill for it. And if you don't keep your interfering nose out of my business, you might find out exactly what would drive me to murder.'

Grainne had often mentioned going to an exercise class in Dundrum every Thursday. The gym was opposite the Dundrum

Shopping Centre, and as it was almost impossible to find parking in the town, Aoife guessed Grainne would park there.

Aoife arrived at the shopping centre an hour before Grainne's class and started searching the huge car park. It took her fifty minutes to find the car. Aoife went back to her own car and parked opposite the lift. Twenty minutes later, Grainne appeared. Aoife walked towards her.

'Hi, Grainne.'

'Aoife, hi. I didn't expect to see you here.'

'Oh, I often come to Dundrum. They do great bargains at Harvey Nicks.'

'I'm not much of a shopper myself. I was just at my exercise class.'

'How are the plans for the wedding coming along?'

Something flashed across Grainne's face, but it was gone so fast Aoife couldn't identify it.

'Oh, fine. I'm leaving all that to Tatiana.'

'Tatiana is still involved? Conor said she and Rory split up.'

'Yes, but they were never serious and Rory doesn't seem to care, so why would I hold a grudge?'

'You're probably right, although Conor seemed a bit shocked when I told him.'

'Conor's very protective of his family. Aoife, I really must rush. It was lovely seeing you. We must meet up again sometime soon.'

She took a few steps towards her car.

'That's a great idea, Grainne. Maybe we could meet next week and discuss the wedding plans.'

Grainne gave a dismissive wave of her hand. 'Don't worry about that. Leave it all to Tatiana. She's more than capable of managing everything. I've a lot on these days, but I'll phone you in a few weeks and we'll get together then. Got to rush, Aoife. Bye.'

ക

What the hell was going on? Grainne knew something, that was clear. She was so anxious not to let anything slip that she wouldn't even speak to Aoife. Okay, well, if Grainne wouldn't say anything, Aoife was pretty sure Tatiana wouldn't need much persuading.

FORTY

THE FOLLOWING DAY Aoife phoned Rory. 'I just remembered Tatiana still has the shoes I plan to wear to the wedding. Do you have her number?' When Rory gave her the number, Aoife said, 'I'll phone her and arrange to drop around and collect them. Where does Tatiana live?'

Aoife wasn't that familiar with the north side, but her sat nav brought her to a large grey concrete apartment block in a pretty rough part of town. This didn't seem like the kind of place Tatiana would choose to live. Aoife parked as close as she could get to the entrance and waited. She didn't like having to ask Maura to keep Amy late, but she couldn't put off sorting this out any longer. It was evening before Tatiana emerged. She wore a long black coat that reached her ankles and spotlessly white runners. Over one shoulder, she carried a large gym bag. She got into a red Mini. Aoife could tell from the licence plate that the car was almost twenty years old, but it was polished to a high shine, the windows were spotless, even the hubcaps gleamed.

Tatiana drove to a hotel outside the city centre and parked

in the driveway. Aoife caught up with her a few yards from the hotel entrance. She had assumed Tatiana was on her way to the gym. Clearly she had been wrong. Tatiana had changed into red stiletto shoes with an impossibly high heel that was so pointed it could probably double as an effective weapon.

'Tatiana!'

The girl turned, a wide smile on her face. When she saw Aoife, the smile vanished.

'What do you want?'

Aoife was a little taken aback. She had never seen Tatiana without a full face of make-up, but even for Tatiana, this was a bit over the top. Her false eyelashes were ridiculously thick and curled, her lips appeared swollen and her make-up was so thick, Aoife was tempted to draw a nail down her cheek to see how deep she could go before touching skin.

'I... I can see you're busy, Tatiana. Could we meet sometime to talk about the wedding plans?'

'What!'

'I'd like to discuss the wedding plans. Maybe we could meet some day next week?'

'What the hell is wrong with you? You have so little interest in your own wedding that you don't even know I'm not your wedding planner anymore? God! Could you be any more of a princess?'

'Princess?'

'You just sit around while everybody waits on you. Poor Aoife. We all have to organise her wedding because she has no mother. What a load of bull!'

'It wasn't my suggestion that you organise our wedding, Tatiana.'

'No, of course it wasn't. You're far too precious to bother

about boring things like wedding plans. You really play up the "Orphan Annie" bit, don't you?'

'Forget it, Tatiana. Bye.'

As she turned to leave, Tatiana grabbed her wrist. 'I'm not finished with you.'

'Let go of me!'

'No, I won't.' For a small girl her grip was surprisingly strong. 'Do you know the very first thing Rory told me about you was that your parents died when you were eighteen? He told me that even before he mentioned your name, and then he waited for me to be suitably shocked.'

'So it annoys you that my parents are dead. That must be really difficult for you. Now let go of my arm.'

'It annoys me that you have no idea how frigging lucky you are. You were in college when your parents died, for God's sake! You were a bloody adult. And Rory said their insurance policy paid for your college and that lovely house you live in.'

'You think I'd rather have an insurance policy than my parents?'

'I think you're so bloody lucky that what would be a tragedy for most people only ends up making your life better.'

'Better! Let go of me right now!' Aoife raised her hand so it was level with her eyes. Tatiana tightened her grip. Using a technique she had learned years ago in a self-defence class, Aoife brought her hand downwards in a sudden sharp movement and broke free. As she made to grab Aoife again, Tatiana's coat fell open, revealing a red one-piece outfit and black fishnet tights. The material was a shiny see-through fabric with two holes that revealed Tatiana's nipples.

Tatiana froze when she saw Aoife's expression. She grabbed her coat and pulled it around her.

'Have I shocked the little princess?' Her tone was mocking, but embarrassment was written all over her face.

'I—'

'Don't you dare look at me like that, you bitch. It's your fault I have to do this. I had a good thing going with that wedding planning until you ruined it.'

'You have to—'

'I'm not a hooker if that's what you're thinking. At least not anymore.' Her features contorted into a sneer. 'Not all of us are as lucky as you. My parents didn't have the decency to die. They just threw me out on the streets when I was fourteen. And that was the nicest thing they ever did to me.'

'That's awful. I didn't know.'

'Of course you didn't. You live in your own perfect little world where two men love you and want to take care of you. I was fourteen when I met the first man who said he wanted to take care of me. Three weeks later he pimped me out.'

'Tatiana, I—'

'You think you have the right to feel sorry for me, bitch? I'm worth ten of you. I've got more guts than you could dream of. By the time I was twenty-one, I had gotten myself away from that scumbag and off the drugs he had me hooked on. Of course, I didn't have a life insurance policy to put me through college.' Her voice turned wistful. 'Not that it would have done me much good if I had. I was thirteen the last time I sat in a classroom.'

'I—'

Anger flared in Tatiana's eyes. 'Will you stop saying that! You're like a bloody goldfish. I, I, I,' she mocked. 'What a shock! The princess can't talk about anything but herself. Well, this is what happens to the rest of the world when they don't have family to fall back on.' She pointed at her outfit. 'I'm a lap dancer. And a bloody good one. Nobody touches me unless I want them to and nobody controls me.'

A young woman walked by. Like Tatiana, she wore a long coat and stilettos. She tapped her watch. 'Showtime, Tat.'

'I'm coming,' Tatiana said without moving her eyes from Aoife's. 'When I'm not here, I hang around clubs looking for guys who can afford to keep me in the style I intend to become accustomed to.'

'Like Rory?'

'Rory was a stepping-stone. He took me places where I met other guys with a bit of money. I figure I have about ten years to find someone seriously rich, but in the meantime, if some guy lets me move in with him, I can save a bit of money on rent until I find someone better.'

'Didn't you even like Rory?'

'He was okay. I've known a lot worse.'

'But—'

'Oh, don't get all self-righteous. It's not as if Rory ever loved me, or Jason either, for that matter. But I would have moved in with one of them, at least for a while. I'd have had a decent place to live and I'd have kept him happy. But no, the little princess couldn't stand it that one of her castoffs liked me. You just had to ruin everything, didn't you? So now I'm off to another fun-filled stag do. Thanks a lot, bitch!'

Poor Tatiana, Aoife thought as she walked back to her car. She would have to find some way to help her. Maybe she could use Tatiana as a source for an article on prostitution in Ireland. If she could sell the idea to an editor, she might be able to get the paper to pay Tatiana. That should help her a little. Aoife's face broke into a grin. How could she ever have doubted Conor? He and Orla had obviously taken over planning the wedding. That was why Grainne wouldn't talk to her. She didn't have anything to say because she was no longer involved, and she didn't want to ruin the surprise. Why it had to be a secret that Conor and Orla were planning the wedding was something Aoife didn't quite understand, but she didn't care. Orla hadn't betrayed her and Conor loved her. That was all that mattered.

FORTY-ONE

On her way home, Aoife phoned Orla.

'Hi, what are you up to tomorrow?'

'Nothing. I was supposed to be going to a nightclub, but I'm wrecked. I think I might be coming down with something. All I want to do is curl up on the sofa.'

'How about a girl's night in?'

'Sounds good. It's Amy's weekend with Jason?'

'Yep, and Conor's working nights.'

'Why not stay over?'

'That would be nice. I need to leave early, though. I want to have breakfast waiting for Conor when he gets home from work.'

'You're getting up at seven a.m. on a Saturday? Sounds like you're trying to make up for something.'

'Maybe.'

'You seem in a really good mood.'

'I certainly am. See you later.'

❧

For once Jason collected Amy on time. Aoife wondered if this was a sign she should buy a Lotto ticket. It seemed to be her lucky day.

She pulled up outside Orla's house at 7.30. There was no answer when she rang the doorbell. Orla's car was in the driveway, but she rarely took it to work. Aoife pulled out her phone.

'I'm at your house. Where are you?'

'On the train. I'll be there in about twenty minutes.'

'Okay, I'll...' Aoife was turning away when she noticed a slight crack. She pushed the door and it opened easily. 'Orla, your door isn't fully shut.'

'That's not like Florina. Maybe she hasn't left yet.'

'I'll try the kitchen. She might have her earphones in.'

'Florina!' Aoife called as she pushed open the kitchen door. It didn't budge. She put all her weight behind it. It moved a little, but Aoife couldn't see what was causing the obstruction. 'Florina!' she bellowed loud enough to be heard over any headphones. No answer.

'I can't get in. Something's blocking the door.'

'Florina often pushes the table against it when she's washing the floor. Go through the sitting room.'

'Okay.' Aoife headed for the sitting room. 'You know it's really not safe, her wearing those headphones all the time. An entire army could break in and she'd never know.'

'She'll be fine. It's a very safe area and I think what Florina loves most about the job is the chance to learn English while she works.'

'Her English has certainly come a long way in a few weeks,' Aoife said as she opened the adjoining door to the kitchen. 'I think...'

Aoife froze.

'You think what?'

The phone crashed onto the tiled floor as Aoife stared at what had been obstructing the doorway.

It was Florina.

FORTY-TWO

For several minutes Aoife couldn't take her eyes from Florina. The young girl was lying face-down, her body stretched out inches from the kitchen door, face buried in her own blood.

'Oh dear God!' Aoife muttered to herself. She took a few steps closer, then stopped. There was nothing anybody could do for Florina now.

She picked up the phone and checked it was still working. The screen was cracked, but it still had a dial tone. The phone rang.

'What happened? Did you get cut off?'

Aoife opened her mouth, but no words emerged. She tried again. 'I…I…'

'What? Is something wrong? Have I been burgled?'

Aoife swallowed. 'I'll meet you at the train station, Orla.'

Without waiting for a reply, Aoife disconnected the call and dialled 999.

⁂

When the police had finished questioning them, Aoife drove Orla to her parents' house. As they pulled up, they could see

Orla's mother standing at the window, one hand covering her mouth. Before Aoife had turned off the engine, she was tottering down the driveway in her four-inch heels, her short golden bob swaying from side to side. She yanked the passenger door open and almost dragged Orla from the car.

'My poor girl!' she wailed, enveloping Orla in a tight hug. 'Darling, are you okay? I can't believe this has happened to you.'

'I'm fine, Mum.' Orla disengaged herself from her mother's arms. 'I didn't see anything. Aoife was the one who found Florina.'

'But it must have been such a shock, my darling. I know how fond you were of that girl. What a thing to happen. If the girl had to get herself killed, couldn't she have done it in her own home? You can't go back to that house. You're staying with your father and me and that's final.'

'Just for a week or so, Mum, until the house is cleaned up and I can go home.'

'You are never living there again, Orla. I won't hear of it. What if that murderer comes back?' She shivered and threw her arms around her daughter again. 'When I think how close you came to being killed,' she muttered into Orla's ear. 'If you'd come home a half hour earlier, you'd be lying there dead like that poor girl.'

'The police think the murderer must have known Florina,' Aoife said. 'It's unlikely a stranger would have shot her in the back of the head. They think she might have been mixed up with organised crime.'

'Wasn't she a teenager? Orla said she's only been in the country a few weeks. How could she have become involved with criminals?'

'We don't know, Mum. Aoife's a bit shaken up by the whole thing. I think she needs—'

'Yes, of course. I'm sorry, Aoife. Please, come inside. I'll make you both a cup of tea myself. You girls need lots of sugar for the shock. That will keep you going until Margaret has dinner ready.'

'Margaret!' she called as they entered the house. 'Have you made up Orla's bed?'

'Yes, I'm just about to start dinner.'

'I need you to make up the spare bedroom first. Orla's friend will be staying here tonight.'

'Thank you, but I'll just have a cup of tea and then I'll go home.'

'You are not driving home after a shock like that, Aoife. Imagine if you were in an accident. Orla would be so upset, and she's been through enough for one day. You'll spend the night here and that's an end to it. That fiancé of yours can collect you in the morning.'

ර

'I'm not sick,' Aoife said, pushing aside the fifth cup of coffee Conor had brought her since they arrived at his house. 'Let's go to the beach. It's a lovely day.'

'You need to rest, Aoife. You've had a terrible shock.'

'I'm fine. I can't lie here on the couch all day. I'm not an invalid.'

'Okay, if you must, but just a short walk. The beach is too far away.'

'Conor, if you keep treating me like a character in a Jane Austen novel, I'm going home.' She pulled on her shoes.

'Where's my jacket?'

Conor pointed at the chair behind her.

'Great. Now, I am going to the beach. Are you coming?'

ණ

'Do you think they're connected?' Aoife asked as they walked barefoot along the beach.

'Florina and Matt's murders?'

'Yeah.'

'I don't see how they could be. Matt and Florina never met.'

'They were both shot in the back of the head. Orla says that's execution-style. Even the police said Florina was probably murdered by organised criminals.'

'Matt was murdered in Italy. We have no idea who killed him, but it's unlikely to be the same people who killed Florina.'

'Is it? I googled murders in Ireland earlier. Did you know that twenty-two people were murdered here last year? When you take out women who were killed by their partners, you're left with fifteen.'

'Aoife, I know where you're going with this and—'

'No, let me finish. I couldn't find recent figures for gun homicides, but six years ago, seven men were killed by guns. Do you know how many women died that way?'

'No.'

'One. That's one woman in the entire country. So the fact that I know two people who were shot this year is unlikely enough. What are the chances that the deaths are unrelated?'

'Aoife, there is no way Florina's death is your fault.'

'How can you be sure? Orla and I were the only people Florina knew in this country. And I'm the one investigating a murder. It has to be my fault.'

'You weren't the only people Florina knew. She knew Katie and Greg. Katie and Matt had an affair. And you said Florina might have had an affair with Greg. There's your connection.'

'Katie thinks Florina and Greg had an affair, but I don't believe it. Florina spoke about him as if he was a stranger.'

'If Katie believes Florina was having an affair with her husband, doesn't that give her a motive for murder?'

ꙮ

Aoife didn't believe Conor's theory about Katie being a murderer. She didn't think Conor really believed it either. He was just trying to find a way to stop Aoife from blaming herself. Even if Katie could get her hands on a gun, there was no way she was capable of blowing a hole in Florina's skull. But investigators have to follow any theory, however outlandish, so Monday morning saw Aoife knocking on Vicky's door. She'd already checked Instagram, but neither Katie nor Greg had posted on Friday. If anybody knew where Katie had been that day, it would be Vicky.

'Come in, come in.' Vicky put a hand on Aoife's arm and hurried her inside. She shut the door, leaned against it and, almost breathless with excitement, adopted a stage whisper.

'You won't believe what's happened. Katie and Greg have split up.'

'Really? Why is that?'

'I haven't found out yet. Around lunchtime on Friday I heard screaming coming from the car park. When I went to have a look, there was Katie throwing things at Greg.'

'What things?'

'Her keys, for one. They caught him on the side of the ear. She threw her shoes as well, but they missed. Then she jumped on him. We had to pull her off. And then'—Vicky's eyes were as wide as saucers—'I can't imagine who would have done it, but somebody called the police.'

'Were Katie and Greg arrested?'

'Greg was. Katie stormed back to their apartment. I followed, but she locked herself in the bedroom. About an hour later, she came out and demanded I drive her to the police station.'

'Why?'

'She said it would ruin their business if Greg had a criminal record.'

'Did the police release him?'

'Eventually, but it took forever. It must have been nearly nine before they let him go. As soon as Katie heard the police weren't going to charge Greg, she insisted on leaving. She said she never wants to set eyes on him again.'

FORTY-THREE

'WELL, THAT'S FAIRLY conclusive evidence. If Greg and Katie were both in the police station, somebody else killed Florina.'

'Looks like it. How are you, Orla? Are you feeling better?'

'Yeah, I'm fine. I had a bit of a cold, but I'm over it now.'

'How are you coping with what happened?'

'It's not like there's anything I can do about it. The police contacted Florina's family. When the autopsy has been completed, they're taking her home. I won't even be able to go to the funeral.'

'I'm sure the police could find out the funeral details for you. If you want to fly over for the day, I'll go with you.'

'Thanks, Aoife, but I just want to forget it ever happened. I've got a few big work things coming up, but as soon as I can, I'm going away for a week.'

'Are you finding it hard living with your mum?'

'Yeah. I mean, Mum's the best. She really is. Nobody could do more for their family. But all the attention gets a bit overwhelming after a while. I hope I'll be able to move back to my own place soon.'

'Your mum won't like that.'

'She won't like it wherever I go. She keeps talking about my lucky escape. On Sunday I had a lie-in and she came running into the bedroom to make sure the murderer hadn't killed me in my sleep. I can't cope with the dramatics.'

'Can we be sure your mum isn't right, Orla?'

'In what way?'

'Maybe you did have a lucky escape. Florina was killed in your house. Isn't it possible the murderer thought she was you?'

'We don't look anything alike. Florina was dark, I'm blonde. She was a much slighter build too. I can't see anybody mixing us up.'

'She was executed, Orla. Maybe the murderer had no idea what she looked like. They could have been told to go to your address and kill the person who lived there.'

'If whoever gives the orders is that vague, innocent people would be murdered all the time.'

'Remember the guy in one of those gangs who shot himself in the head a few years back? I don't think we're dealing with the brightest of God's creatures.'

'They can't all be dumb or the police would have shut them down years ago. Anyway, I'm working on industrial espionage at the moment. Everyone involved is a crook, but they would barely recognise a gun if it was waved in front of them. Whoever killed Florina knew what they were doing. I wasn't the target.'

At the crack of dawn, Aoife woke and couldn't get back to sleep. Ever since she'd discovered Florina's body, she'd had a recurring dream where she was in Orla's kitchen chatting with Florina. Out of nowhere a man in a dark hoodie materialised, gun pointed at Florina's head. Florina's entire body exploded into tiny pieces and the man pointed his gun at Aoife. He pulled the trigger with one hand and lowered his hoodie with the other. Aoife's eyes flicked between the bullet that was moving in slow motion towards her skull and the murderer's face, which was slowly being revealed. As the bullet hit her skull with the force of a speeding train, Aoife woke panting and drowned in sweat. She switched on the lamp and worked on slowing her breathing. After going out to the bathroom and checking on Amy, she closed her eyes and tried to concentrate on happy thoughts. It was useless. Florina was all she could think of. Why would anybody want to murder her? How could Florina have come in contact with criminals? Hours later, Aoife admitted defeat. She reached for her phone.

'Orla, do you know where Florina lived?'

'Huh!' There was a shuffling sound and then a crash. 'Damn! Aoife?'

'Yeah, do you know Florina's address?'

'Are you out of your mind? It's five a.m.'

'Is it? I'm sorry, Orla. I've been awake for hours. I thought it was later. But now you're awake, do you have Florina's address?'

'No. Why would I have her address?'

'I thought she might have given it to you. She lived in Drumcondra, didn't she?'

'Yeah, why?'

'I'd like to talk to her neighbours.'

'She said they never spoke to her.'

'I know, but they might be nosy. Nicole's neighbours spend half their time gossiping about each other. Who knows what Florina's neighbours might have seen?'

Orla sighed. 'Okay, I have the detective's number. I'll phone him later and let you know.'

'Thanks.'

'And, Aoife, don't ever ring me at this hour again unless it's an emergency.'

❧

By noon, Aoife was standing outside the building where Florina had lived. It was nicer than she had expected. The car park was to one side of the building, tucked away behind mature trees. The apartments looked out on a reasonably sized walled garden. Red and yellow roses climbed the walls. Green shrubs were mixed with purple flowers Aoife couldn't identify. In the centre of the garden there was a tiny fountain. Aoife checked the apartment numbers. Florina's apartment was on the ground floor, almost directly opposite the fountain. Aoife was standing on tiptoes, trying to see between the slats of the closed blinds, when a voice behind her said, 'Can I help you?'

A small woman with white hair glared at her. Her words were polite, but her tone implied she had no doubt Aoife was planning to rob the place.

'Hello, I'm a friend of Florina's. She used to live in this apartment. You may have heard that she died recently.'

'Indeed.'

Clearly being a friend of Florina's was not going to earn her any brownie points. 'Well, to be honest, Florina was my friend's maid.'

'Oh!' The woman's tone lightened. 'I had no idea. How could she afford to live here?'

'The apartment came with the job.'

'Really? These apartments are not cheap. Florina was a maid? Well, isn't that interesting.'

'You didn't know her very well?'

'No. We all try to steer clear of the people in that apartment. We've had a lot of trouble with the residents over the years.'

'Florina caused you trouble?'

'To be fair, she seemed fine, but we figured it was only a matter of time before her friends came back.'

'Friends?'

'The people she shared with. Is your friend planning to keep the lease? I presume she'll want a new maid.'

'I don't know.'

'Well, I hope she does. A corporation owns that apartment and they don't care who rents the place. We've been plagued by gaggles of young girls for years now. We're never sure how many people live there.'

'Florina said there were five bedrooms. Her English wasn't great, so I'm assuming she meant five rooms.'

'No. It's five bedrooms. I managed to get a look in once when the place was being renovated. The sitting room has been turned into two bedrooms.'

'So originally it was a three-bedroom apartment?'

'Yes.'

'Five girls in one apartment must have been noisy.'

'It's not so much the girls themselves that were the problem, it was the men that came with them. I'm pretty sure they were drug dealers.'

'Men?'

'There were four men who were always around the place.' The woman shuddered. 'Not the type you'd want to meet in a dark alley, I can tell you. There used to be a bench under this window, and at least two of them sat there day and night smoking God knows what.'

'Why do you think they were drug dealers?'

The woman pointed at a full-length window. 'They turned the kitchen window into a door so they could carry out their business in private. We never knew who was coming or going, but there was a constant flow of people in and out of that place at all hours.'

'And you're certain these people were buying drugs?'

'Oh, yes. I read an article in the paper a while back about the drug trade in Dublin. It mentioned a house in one of the rougher parts of the city where the residents sell drugs from their kitchen window. Half of Dublin knows about it. They interviewed taxi drivers who said people ask to be taken to the "drug house". The minute I read it, I knew. I rang the management company and said that's exactly what's going on here.'

'Did the management company call the police?'

'Several times, but the police weren't in the slightest bit interested. All they said was they were looking into it.'

'Did people call to the house when Florina was here?'

'No. The apartment's been very quiet since she moved in. I wish I'd gotten to know her. She was obviously a decent, hard-working girl, but we didn't know your friend had taken over the lease. And when we saw those men coming out of the apartment, we thought it was only a matter of time before the whole thing started up again.'

'What men?'

'Two of those hooligans who lived with the girls.'

'You saw them coming out of the apartment while Florina was there?'

'Not me. Sheila in Number 56 saw them. We don't think Florina was there at the time. She usually went out in the mornings.'

'When was this?'

'About a month ago.'

'When did the other girls move out?'

'About a week before Florina arrived.'

'You've no idea where they went?'

'No. We didn't see them pack up or anything. One day they were here, the next they were gone. We assumed they'd gone home and it was only a matter of time before they came back again.'

'They weren't Irish?'

'Most of them sounded East European, although at least one of the boyfriends had a very strong Dublin accent.'

'Did the girls come and go or was it always the same ones?'

'I think they were the same ones. I mean, we rarely saw the girls and it was pretty hard to tell them apart anyway. They were all tall, young, skinny things. And, as I said, we were never sure how many girls lived there at any one time, but at least four of them were always the same because the four boyfriends never left.'

'You said one of the boyfriends was Irish. Did you speak to him?'

'Good Lord, no. Every one of them looked like they'd kill you as soon as look at you. Des in Number 63 heard one of them on the phone the last time they were here.'

'That was the time they went into the apartment when Florina was out?'

'Yes.'

'Did your neighbour hear any of the conversation?'

'He said the Irish guy was yelling into the phone. There was a lot of effin' this and effin' that. Des only heard two sentences. The first was "Maybe you want to tell Jacko that, but I certainly don't".' And the second was "How long does she think we're going to put up with this crap? You tell that stupid bitch if she goes on like this she's going to get herself killed".'

FORTY-FOUR

'DID THE OTHER girls work for Katie or has she recently taken over the lease?' Orla had been sniffy when Aoife phoned, the memory of the 5 a.m. call still fresh in her mind, but Aoife's news made her completely forget the incident.

'Yeah, I wondered that too.'

'So these girls hung out with guys who might be criminals. The guys still have a key to the apartment, and they seemed mad at Florina for some reason.'

'They called her a bitch and said they weren't going to put up with "it" for much longer. Orla, did Florina ever mention any guys?'

'Never, and she didn't own anything of value. Why would they sneak into the apartment when she wasn't there?'

'Maybe they stored their drugs there. What if the owners got sick of listening to the residents' complaints? Or what if the police told the owners they were investigating complaints made against their tenants and the owners felt they had to take action? They might have packed up the girls' belongings while they were still abroad and rented the apartment to Katie. If the drugs were hidden in the apartment, the men would have to break in to get them back.'

'It's possible, I suppose, but it doesn't explain why they were threatening to kill Florina.'

'Yeah, you're right.' Aoife was absent-mindedly twirling her hair around her finger when inspiration struck. 'What if Florina came back unexpectedly and found the men with drugs? She might have threatened to tell the police.'

'I can't see her doing that. If she was planning to involve the police, I'm sure she'd have told me first. I am a lawyer, after all.'

'She wouldn't tell you if she was planning to do something illegal.'

'Like what?'

'Bribe them.'

'No, Aoife. She'd never be that stupid. Florina was one tiny girl. They'd beat her up for just suggesting it.'

'Yeah, you're probably right. Okay, what if she offered to store the drugs for them?'

'That would make her an ally. It wouldn't give them any reason to call her a bitch or to kill her.'

'It would if she stole from them.'

'Stole drugs from criminals? Who in their right mind would do that?'

'Florina needed money, Orla. And she might not have stolen much. Imagine she's sitting in the apartment when an old customer knocks on the door. How tempting would it be to take a few pills, or whatever else they are selling, and keep the money for herself?'

'Okay, that might explain why the men called her a bitch, but what did "How long does she think we're going to put up with this crap?" mean?'

'I don't know.'

'Put up with her stealing from them, maybe?'

'You know that type, Orla. They wouldn't tolerate stealing for a second. But if Florina had evidence she was threatening to bring to the police, they might have to put up with the bribery for a while until they worked out how to get the evidence back.'

'Oh God! Maybe they couldn't find the evidence because Florina kept it with her all the time. They came to my house to get it.'

❧

'Drug dealers? Well, it would explain why Florina was shot in the back of the head. And one of the drug dealers mentioned Jacko?'

'Yeah, does the name mean anything to you, Conor?'

'The head of one of the largest crime families in Dublin is called Jacko. When things got a bit tough for him here, he ran off to Spain, but he still controls most of the drug trade in Ireland.'

'So that's proof, then? The boyfriends were drug dealers.'

'It's possible, but, Aoife, you have to be very careful if you investigate anything that involves Jacko. His guys don't fool around. I don't want you ending up with a bullet in the back of your head too.'

FORTY-FIVE

FLORINA'S DEATH WAS consuming Aoife's thoughts to such an extent that when she saw 'Conference' marked in her diary, she had no idea what it referred to. She shrugged and went back to cleaning up after breakfast. Ten minutes later she shouted, 'Damn!', slammed the door of the dishwasher so hard the glasses rattled, grabbed her bag and ran to her car.

Forty minutes later, she was seated at the back of the conference room, barely listening to earnest corporate types, mostly men, trying to convince an audience of about five hundred people that their organisation was the best in the world; nobody could match their expertise or their success record. Aoife couldn't concentrate enough to find out what they were talking about. She scanned her programme. It would be Edgard's turn to speak in eighteen minutes.

Aoife watched Edgard closely as he gave his presentation. He was confident, friendly and professional. If she had any idea what he was selling, she might be persuaded herself. He finished his presentation to a decent smattering of applause, stood at the back of the auditorium for the first few minutes of his colleague's presentation, then slipped outside. Aoife followed.

'Edgard,' she called as he headed for the hotel lift.

He turned. He ran his eyes the length of her body, then he looked into her face and smiled. 'Yes. How can I help you?'

His English was perfect. It clearly wasn't his first language, but there were so many accents mixed together, Aoife couldn't even guess at his nationality.

'My name is Aoife Walsh. I've been trying to get in touch with you for some time.'

'I'm sorry. My secretary is usually very good at passing on messages.'

'It's not a business matter. I emailed you a few weeks ago. I'd like to discuss your stay at the Colonnina Hotel in Italy.'

The smile disappeared and tiny beads of moisture appeared on Edgard's forehead.

'My job requires me to travel extensively throughout the US and Europe. I couldn't possibly remember any specific hotel. Excuse me.'

As he pushed past her, Aoife raised her voice. 'Do you often check into hotels under an assumed name?'

Two guests waiting for the lift turned to stare. Edgard gave them an apologetic grin. 'That's not funny, dear. People will think you're serious.' He grabbed Aoife's arm so tightly she winced, and led her to a table in a quiet corner of the hotel lobby.

'What the hell are you trying to do to me?' he snarled.

'I'm trying to find out why you used a false name and address when you checked into the Colonnina Hotel.'

'Are you the police?'

'No, I'm a journalist.'

'A journalist! Oh my God! What do you want?'

'Information.'

'Why? What do you care what hotel I stay in?'

'You checked into the Colonnina for a week, but you left the following morning. Why?'

'That's none of your business.'

'I believe it is my business. I'm investigating the murder of Matt Gallagher.'

'That name means nothing to me.'

'You and Matt were guests in the same hotel. You checked out hours after he was murdered.'

'Coincidence. I told you I didn't know that man.'

'You didn't tell me why you checked out early and why you used a false name.'

'I'm not going to tell you anything. You have no right to question me.'

'I don't have a legal right to question you, that's true. But the police have that right. If I tell them you checked into a hotel using a false name and a man was murdered that same day, I think they'd find that interesting.'

'Your police have no right to question me. I'm not Irish.'

'Of course they can question you. They can arrest you too, and in this country you can be held for up to seven days without being charged.'

'That can't be right.'

'But it is. Check it out. It's up to seven days for serious offences. I'd call murder a serious offence, wouldn't you?'

'I didn't murder anyone.'

'No? Then tell me why you checked into the Colonnina under a false name.'

'I didn't. I used my own name.'

'You're saying somebody else changed the records?'

'Yes.'

'Why would they do that?'

'How should I know?' He stood. 'I answered your question, now I'm going to my room.'

'Okay.' Aoife took out her phone. 'I have contacts in the police, so I should be able to get them here within ten minutes. You might want to wait for them outside. I imagine you'd rather your colleagues didn't see you dragged away in handcuffs.'

The beads of perspiration returned. 'Why are you doing this? I just answered your question.'

'No, you didn't.'

Edgard looked towards the lift, then the hotel entrance, as if calculating his odds of escape. 'Fine, call the police.' He headed for the lift.

'Okay. Don't worry about your family. I'll phone your wife and let her know what's going on and I'll ask your colleagues to pass on a message to your manager.'

Edgard muttered something under his breath. He returned to the seat he had abandoned seconds earlier.

'I had absolutely nothing to do with that man's murder. I've never met him in my life.'

'Yet you checked out of the Colonnina the morning after his death and the hotel records show you gave a false name and address.'

'I admit I didn't want anybody from that hotel to be able to trace me and, yes, I arranged for my contact details to be changed, but that was for a personal reason. It had nothing to do with murder.'

'If you want me to believe that, I need more information.'

'So you can print it in your newspaper? Forget it.'

'If all I was after was a story, why would I bother talking to you? I could have already written a piece about your suspicious behaviour that weekend. I might even have mentioned your name, where you lived, your wife's name, even the name of your employers. I didn't do any of that because I want to know the truth.'

'And if I were to tell you that, you'd have two stories.'

'I'm not interested in any other story.' When Edgard looked unconvinced, Aoife added, 'Your options right now are pretty limited. Either you explain everything to me or you explain it to the police, your wife and your employers.'

Again, Edgard muttered under his breath. 'Alright.' He looked around to make sure they couldn't be overheard. 'I used my own name when I checked in. Later I picked up a girl in the bar. We went back to my room, spent about an hour together and then she demanded money.'

'She was a prostitute?'

Edgard raised an eyebrow. 'Do you know of any other reason why women demand money for sex?'

'Go on.'

'I was appalled. I don't use hookers. You could pick up anything from them, and how would I explain that to my wife?'

'Did you pay her?'

'Not until she threatened to claim I'd raped her. I had fifty quid in my wallet. She seemed perfectly happy with that and she left.'

'That's it.'

'Yes. I didn't want my wife finding out I had been with a prostitute, so I bribed the night porter to remove the photo of my passport from the hotel files and to change my name on the hotel computers.'

'That seems a bit of an overreaction.'

'I believe in being cautious.'

'I believe you're lying. How could your wife find out? Unless the prostitute threatened to tell her.' From the expression on his face, Aoife knew she had guessed correctly. 'The woman said she would tell your wife you had been with a prostitute? But how would she get her hands on the hotel records?'

'When I thought about it afterwards, I realised that girl knew her way around the hotel. She asked for my room number and then she led the way. What if the hotel knows what she's up to? She might give them a percentage of everything she earns.'

'You think they'd risk their business for a percentage of the odd fifty quid? And why would you be afraid to speak to the police? If that girl was a prostitute, she's probably already got a police record. There's no way the police would take her side.'

'I couldn't be sure of that.'

'I don't believe you. Something else is going on here.'

'That's all there is to it.'

'No. To go to all that trouble, you must have been terrified the police would believe the girl. So either you really did rape her, and even then the chances of the police believing her are slight or… oh my God!'

Edgard paled at her horrified expression. 'It wasn't my fault,' he wailed. 'I didn't know.'

'She was a child, wasn't she?'

FORTY-SIX

EDGARD LOOKED LIKE he wanted to throw up. 'It wasn't my fault.' His voice shook. 'How could I have known? I met her in a bar. She looked like she was in her mid-twenties.'

'What age was she?'

Edgard looked away.

'If she was allowed into a bar, she must at least have been in her teens.'

When Edgard still wouldn't meet her gaze, Aoife said, 'Please tell me the girl was older than twelve.'

'Fourteen,' Edgard muttered.

'She told you that? She must have looked pretty young if you believed her.'

When Edgard finally met her gaze, his face was ashen. 'I swear, she looked like she was in her twenties. I don't have sex with teenagers. Not even ones who are legal. I don't need the hassle.'

'So why did you believe the girl was fourteen?'

'I couldn't sleep that night. I kept worrying how I would explain to my wife if I'd caught some disease. Around four in the morning someone slipped a piece of paper under my door.' He paused, looking like he wanted to throw up.

There was a carafe of water and some glasses in the centre of the table. Aoife pushed them towards Edgard. He poured himself a glass and drank for so long Aoife wondered if he was playing for time.

'Go on.'

Edgard took another quick gulp. 'It was a passport photo. There was a circle drawn around her date of birth and a note that said "leave five hundred euros under the door of Room 402 by ten a.m. or we're calling the police".'

'You paid?'

'Certainly, I paid. After I'd stopped vomiting. I bribed the night porter to destroy all trace of my real identity and then I went to the cash machine. I packed, put the money under the door of that room and left the hotel.'

'You were that scared?'

'Of course. The note said "we". I watched that room for over an hour. Eventually a man used a card to open the door. He took the envelope and disappeared. I recognised him. He was one of the hotel waiters. The hotel was part of the scam.'

Aoife nodded. 'I don't think that's likely, but some of the staff could be involved. They could make quite a lot of money blackmailing people who had sex with underage girls.'

'And they wouldn't have stopped at five hundred. They would have taken my contact details from the hotel computer and bled me dry for every cent I had. When I ran out of money, they'd probably have turned me in to the police.'

Aoife went over the story in her head. It made sense. 'Okay. I believe you didn't know the girl was a child. I won't tell anybody.'

For a second, Edgard looked like he might collapse with relief, then he regained his composure. 'Thank you.'

'Did you see Matt Gallagher at all that weekend?'

'No. I saw his wife on the beach, but she was alone. Later I heard her tell the receptionist that her husband had already disappeared by then.' Now Aoife was no longer a threat, he seemed anxious to chat. 'I think his wife had something to do with that man's death.'

'Why do you think that?'

'It's just a feeling. I watched her lying on that sunbed and she seemed very relaxed. Then all of a sudden, she was rushing back to the hotel. Who goes from relaxed to panic in seconds? And when she was talking to the hotel staff, it seemed a little over the top. Do you know what I mean? Like those old black-and-white movies where everybody overacts. All those extravagant gestures. The girl was doing that. Her hands were flying every which way. It all seemed a little theatrical to me.'

FORTY-SEVEN

'Okay, so you think Nicole is the murderer now?' Conor picked up Amy's bike helmet and put it in the hall cupboard.

'I don't know. She doesn't strike me as a killer, but I can't be certain. If I had been there when she'd found out Matt was dead, I'd have known from her reaction. And I keep remembering how upset she was when she found out she wouldn't inherit anything.'

'You said she was upset Matt was keeping secrets.'

'That's what she said at the time, but maybe she was panicked that she'd committed murder for nothing. Another possibility is that Matt got mixed up in the blackmail scam. He had an affair with Katie. Maybe he picked up a girl in the bar, the same way Edgard did?'

'He was on his honeymoon, Aoife.'

'I know it seems unlikely, but it would explain why Matt left the beach that day. He needed to get to the bank so he could pay off the blackmailers.'

'I don't think that's very likely. Matt and Nicole would have been together twenty-four hours a day. Unless you're saying he got up in the middle of the night and went looking for someone to hook—'

'Moaney, can I talk to Blainey?'

Conor checked his watch. 'He has practice tonight, Amy. He might not be home yet.'

'Can you try? Please, Moaney. Please!'

Conor FaceTimed Blaine. He tried to have a conversation, but Amy kept pulling at his arm. 'My turn! My turn!'

'Amy! Stop that! Wait until Conor's finished.'

'It's okay. We can talk later.' Conor handed her the phone.

'Blainey, look what Supergirl can do. Look!' Amy shouted, running from the room.

'She's never going to learn if you give into her like that, Conor.'

'Yeah, you're right. It's going to take us a while to adjust to the stepfather/stepdaughter roles. Talking of which…'

'What?'

Conor looked away.

'Is something wrong?'

When he met her gaze, Conor looked slightly embarrassed.

'I know the wedding's only a month away, but I was thinking of taking Blaine on holidays for a week so we could have some time together while it's still just the two of us.'

'You're going to take him out of school?'

'The school was broken into on Friday. All the taps were left on for the entire weekend. There was lots of other damage. The school's had to close down for almost two weeks. I thought it would be a good opportunity for us to get away.'

'Where were you thinking of going?'

'Blaine's often mentioned he'd like to see Italy. Sardinia should be nice at this time of year. I thought we'd try it out.'

'Sounds lovely.'

'Do you mind?'

'Of course not. Why would I mind, Conor? Your relationship with Blaine is important to me too.'

Amy ran into the room.

'Where's my phone, Amy?'

'I don't know.'

Conor sighed. 'Okay, let's go look for it.'

Amy skipped out of the room, hand clasped in Conor's. Aoife smiled. Conor would be a great stepfather. He was a brilliant father to Blaine, and that wasn't easy given they had never lived in the same country. It was good they would have this time together. Although it was odd that Conor had seemed embarrassed mentioning his plans. Was he worried she expected him to spend less time with Blaine after the wedding? She never wanted to come between Conor and his son. She would have to make sure Conor understood that.

FORTY-EIGHT

THE FOLLOWING MORNING Aoife returned to Florina's apartment block. She spoke to Florina's neighbours on each side. They were both furious about the previous tenants.

'This used to be a nice, quiet place to live. Most of us are retirees. It's no place for a load of young girls even if their boyfriends weren't drug dealers.' The elderly woman who walked with a cane was fuming. 'Nobody cares. I rang my local T.D. All I got was a form letter telling me he would look into my concerns immediately. That was eighteen months ago and I haven't heard from him since. The police are useless. It's enough to make you want to take the law into your own hands.'

A younger woman, Aoibhinn, who lived in the apartment opposite Florina said she had tried to speak to one of the girls when they'd first arrived but her boyfriend had grabbed her arm and pulled her away.

Aoife flicked through her phone until she found Greg's Instagram account. She chose a picture of Greg in the airport. He stared straight ahead, unsmiling, as if somebody was taking his passport photo.

'Have you ever seen this man?' she asked.

Aoibhinn took the phone and enlarged the photo. 'I'm not sure. Somebody of about the same age was talking to one of the boyfriends a few months ago. It might have been him. I barely glanced at him.'

'Was he speaking English?'

'All I heard was a hum, but they sounded Irish to me.' She smiled. 'Is that ridiculous? When I'm in a queue, I amuse myself by listening to people who are just out of earshot. I think I can tell from the tone if the speakers are Irish or not.'

'And you thought this man was speaking English?'

'Yes.'

'How often are you right?'

'About fifty percent of the time.'

'Were these people having a friendly conversation or were they arguing?'

'Well, as I said, I couldn't really hear them. The boyfriend was talking when I walked nearby. He wasn't shouting, but the other young man was rigid. I remember thinking if he moved a limb it might snap, he was so uptight. My guess is the boyfriend was threatening him.'

FORTY-NINE

Aoife decided she'd done enough for one day. She'd go home early and collect Amy from school. That would be a nice treat. Her phone rang. It was an editor of a small newspaper who sometimes sent work Aoife's way. Aoife had chosen him as the most likely of her contacts to be interested in the prostitution in Ireland articles she planned to write.

'Hi, Aoife. I've been thinking about our last conversation. Legalising prostitution is a hot topic these days. A series of articles on the subject is a great idea.'

Aoife was so excited she drove to Tatiana's immediately. Tatiana's car wasn't in the car park, so Aoife waited for her to turn up.

It was almost an hour later when Tatiana parked nearby and, laden down with bags of groceries, headed for her apartment block.

'Want some help?' Aoife asked as she got out of the car.

'Go to hell!'

'I've got a business proposition for you, Tatiana.'

'Don't tell me. You need a lap dancer for your hen night, right?' Tatiana cackled as she walked away.

'I have a plan to make us both money.'

Tatiana stopped. 'What plan?'

'I'm doing an article on prostit—'

'Over my dead body. No.' She thrust her face within inches of Aoife's. 'It will be your dead body if you mention one word about me.'

'I've spoken to some people who work in Ruhama. They're a charity that help victims of trafficking and prost—'

'More bloody useless do-gooders.'

'I think you should talk to them, Tatiana. They've helped a lot of women like you.'

'Not interested.'

'Okay, it's up to you. They liked my idea of writing a series of articles about legalising prostitution.'

'Typical.'

'How do you mean?'

'You're another bloody do-gooder, getting involved in things you know absolutely nothing about. How could legalising pimps be good for women?'

'Exactly. That's why I need your help, Tatiana. You don't have to use your real name. Your story can help me explain to people who think they are doing a great thing that this law will only harm those who find themselves trapped in prostitution.'

Tatiana paused.

'I'll share my fee with you. You have my number. Think about it and phone me if you're interested. We can have a chat about the best way to approach the subject. The longer we can keep the series running, the more we'll be paid.'

⁂

On her way home, Aoife phoned Orla and told her about her conversation with Florina's neighbours.

'What do you think? If the drug traffickers were threatening Greg, and one of the boyfriends was aggressive with his girlfriend, maybe she was yet another girl Greg was having an affair with?'

'Why would you think that? How would Greg ever get to know her?'

'He might have called to the house to see the apartment. If the girls were planning to leave, the landlord might have insisted they show it to prospective tenants.'

Orla laughed. 'And in the time it took to walk around a smallish apartment, he'd picked up the girl? That doesn't seem likely.'

'I know, but Florina told me she heard Greg on the phone to a Romanian girl. She was crying and he was screaming at her.'

'He was probably yelling at one of his cleaners.'

'That's what I thought, but Florina heard the girl say "home". What if he had an affair with one of the drug dealer's girlfriends? The boyfriend finds out and he assaults her. She phones Greg in tears and says she wants to go home. Greg might have been shouting because he was furious she was attacked. He goes to the apartment to get her and he's greeted by the drug dealer who threatens him. It all fits.'

'It doesn't, Aoife. You've twisted the facts to fit your theory. Florina said he was really angry when he told Katie about the phone call. Would he tell Katie about his girl on the side? We don't even know that Greg was ever near that apartment or even met any of the drug dealers.'

'We know he rented the apartment they used to live in. Is that just a coincidence?'

'I'm sure people rented the apartment before those girls moved in. Does that mean that they must have ties to organised crime?'

FIFTY

ORLA'S LACK OF enthusiasm had no effect on Aoife. She was onto something. She was sure of it. She could kick herself for not interviewing Greg earlier. When she'd found out he had been in Dublin the weekend Matt was murdered, he'd dropped to the bottom of her priority list. How stupid was that?

A quick call to Vicky and she learned that Greg was staying in his brother's house in Terenure. Aoife pulled up outside the door at 2 p.m. She rang the bell several times before Greg answered. He looked like he had just gotten out of bed. He was naked from the waist up and barefoot, and tufts of his short blonde hair were sticking straight up like soldiers standing to attention.

'Yes?'

'I'm sorry, did I wake you?'

'No.'

'I'm Aoife Walsh. We met at the airport.' She thought it better not to mention witnessing his marriage breakup.

'I remember.'

'Can I speak to you for a moment, please?'

'Go ahead.'

'May I come in?'

Greg hesitated, then opened the door and led the way to

the first room off the corridor. It was a complete mess. The table was covered in the remains of the previous night's meal. Aoife glanced at the empty bottle of wine, half-eaten cartons of Chinese food and unwashed glasses. Greg ignored it. He sat on an armchair and pointed at the sofa. Aoife picked up a navy-and-white striped jacket with ornate silver buttons and moved it to one side. Underneath was a white bra.

Greg grabbed the clothes from her hand. 'My brother had a girl over last night.' He flung the clothes into a corner. 'What do you want?'

'Katie said—'

Greg scowled. 'Don't mention that bitch's name to me.'

'How did you find out about Matt and Katie?'

Surprise flitted across his face. 'A friend told me.'

'How did your friend find out?'

'It's common gossip, apparently.'

'Nobody in the apartment block knew about it.'

'They were seen around town.'

'Where exactly?'

'Does it matter? That bitch was cheating on me. That's all I need to know.'

'You were cheating on her too.'

'What's that got to do with anything?'

'You don't think that might have been the reason Katie turned to Matt?'

'I don't know and I don't care.'

'Katie thinks you were having an affair with Florina.'

'She's wrong. Florina was little more than a child.'

'Did you like her?'

'I don't have personal relationships with the staff. She did a good job. That's all I cared about.'

'Katie believes you had affairs with two of the other cleaners you hired.'

'Yes, well, that was different. They never actually worked for us. My relationship with them was completely personal.'

'Did you have an affair with anybody else?'

'What right do you have to ask me who I'm sleeping with?'

'I don't have any right, but if you answer my questions, I can cross you off my list of suspects and I'll never come near you again.'

'You can hang around here as much as you like. I have nothing to say to you.'

Soft footsteps moved across the floor overhead.

'Your brother's girl is still here?'

'Probably.'

'My guess is she's listening to every word we say. You'd rather keep her out of this, wouldn't you?'

Greg snorted in derision. 'I don't care what she listens to.' But Aoife heard the hesitation in his voice.

'Did you ever visit Florina's apartment?'

'A few times.'

'Why?'

'There were several little things that needed to be done. I'm pretty good with my hands.' As if suddenly realising what he had said, Greg burst into laughter. 'In more ways than one.'

'Did you ever visit the apartment before Florina moved in?'

'No. Why would I?'

'To check out the place before you put down a deposit.'

Greg looked momentarily confused. 'I don't have time to look at every single house we rent. We have an estate agent who takes care of that. If he says the apartment is suitable, I take his word for it.'

'Did you ever meet the previous tenants?'

'No, of course not.'

This line of questioning wasn't getting her anywhere. Aoife changed tack.

'How did you feel when you found out Matt and Katie were having an affair?'

'What kind of a stupid question is that? How do you think I felt?'

'I'm assuming you were very angry. You probably felt like you wanted to get revenge.'

A smirk crossed Greg's face. 'Oh, you really think I'm an idiot, don't you? Is this where I'm supposed to say, "Oh yes, I was so angry I wanted to blow Matt's head off and by the way, did I mention that I found out about the affair long before he was murdered?"'

'Florina mentioned you wanted her to do other work.'

Greg seemed thrown by the change of subject. He blinked, picked up a wine glass stained with pink lipstick and downed the remaining mouthful in one gulp.

'Other work?'

'Presumably there were other clients you wanted Florina to take on.'

Greg gave her a wary look. 'So what if I did? How many cleaners do you know who have only one client?'

'Did you know Florina planned to go out on her own?'

'Katie mentioned it.'

'How did you feel about that?'

Greg shrugged. 'It meant I'd have to take another trip to Italy, but that's hardly the end of the world.'

'So you didn't mind?'

'I'd have preferred she stayed, but it was no big deal.'

'Who do you think killed Florina?'

'No idea.'

'Do you care?'

'As much as I care when any stranger is murdered. It's sad that a young girl was killed, but it doesn't affect me personally.'

'The police think she was executed.'

Greg frowned. 'By whom?'

'Organised crime, they think.'

'That's unlikely. Florina was a teenager and she'd only been in Ireland a few weeks.'

'You knew her in Italy. What kind of people did she hang out with there?'

'What makes you think I knew her? She occasionally helped out with breakfast in the hotel I stayed in.'

'What hotel was that?'

'The Colonnina.'

'Matt stayed in that hotel the weekend he was murdered.'

'No doubt the bitch told him about it. They were probably planning a weekend away together. We have an account there.'

'When did you first see Florina in the hotel?'

'I don't remember. Probably about a year ago.'

'So it took a while to convince her to go to Ireland?'

'Yes.'

'Why?'

'She said it was a long way from home.'

'How many times did you and Florina discuss it before she agreed to relocate?'

'Four or five, maybe.'

'So presumably Florina didn't just work on the five days you stayed in the hotel. She was probably friendly with several of the hotel staff.'

'I wouldn't know.'

'Don't you think it's curious that Florina and Matt both stayed at the Colonnina and they were both shot in the head, execution-style?'

'Why would I? They were murdered a year apart and in different countries. I'm sure lots of Irish people have stayed in the Colonnina. They all have to die sometime.'

'Do they all have to be shot in the head?'

'Probably not. I'd love to spend the rest of the day discussing unusual coincidences, but I have things to do. Is there something else you want to ask me?'

As Aoife was leaving, she glanced up the stairs. The wall was lined with family photos. The closest was of a couple with a young baby. The man looked like an older version of Greg. As Aoife walked back to her car, she saw two young boys riding their bikes on the footpath.

'Hi.' Aoife smiled. She nodded towards the house she had just left. 'Do you know who lives in that house?'

'Dylan and Ian. They've gone to Trabolgan. My cousin had his birthday party there. We played soldiers and they gave us huge laser guns. My team won.'

'When are they coming back?'

'Dylan said he'd be in school on Monday.'

'Did they go away with their mum?'

The boy nodded. 'And their dad and their little sister. She wants to see Peppa Pig but Dylan said that's for babies.'

So the woman upstairs was obviously Greg's girlfriend. Aoife wondered if she was another of the Romanian maids.

FIFTY-ONE

CONOR WAS SHOPPING for his trip to Italy when Aoife phoned him. 'Do you want me to change my flight home? I could take the train to Bari. I might be able to find someone in the Colonnina who knew Florina. The journey's only about four hours each way.'

'No. Spend what time you have with Blaine. The Italian investigators can check it out. They already have contacts with the hotel staff.'

ꕥ

Aoife was on her way to Nicole's when Tatiana phoned.

'Alright, I'll do it, but you'd better not mention my name.'

'Great. Can you meet me next week?

'Okay. How about Bewley's in Grafton Street?'

'See you then.'

ꕥ

'I know you don't want to be involved, Nicole, but all I'm asking is that the private investigators speak to the hotel staff.'

'This girl, Florina, she was in Italy when Matt was murdered?'

'I think so. It can't be a coincidence that all three of you are connected to the hotel.'

'Do you think she and Matt knew each other?'

'She worked the breakfast shift. Do you remember any of the breakfast waiters?'

Nicole shook her head. 'One night I drank too much. I had a hangover the next morning, so Matt went to breakfast without me. He could have met the girl then.'

'Did Matt seem on edge that day?'

'No. Although once or twice during the week he seemed a bit distracted.'

'Did you ask him about it?'

'He said it was a work problem and he'd sort it out when we got home. I assumed a client hadn't paid him. That's the biggest problem with working freelance. Sometimes I feel like a debt collector.'

'But otherwise he seemed fine?'

'Yeah. We had a really good time.'

'I think it would help if the Italian investigators spoke to the hotel staff. At least we'd know if he and Florina had ever spoken to each other. And while they're at it, I found out recently that some of the staff are running a blackmail ring from the hotel. Could they check that out too? It might have something to do with Matt's death.'

FIFTY-TWO

TATIANA WAS ALREADY sitting at a table, a cappuccino in front of her, when Aoife arrived.

'Hi.' She looked wary and a little embarrassed.

'Hi.' Aoife thought it best to adopt a professional approach. She removed a notebook from her bag. 'I thought we might begin with you telling me how you ended up on the streets.'

It was a long, sad story of neglect and child abuse. Although she tried, Aoife was unable to maintain a dispassionate manner.

'Oh, Tatiana,' she said at one point, reaching out to touch the girl's arm.

Tatiana jerked her hand away. 'I've been thinking about what you said about dragging out the series as long as possible.'

'Do you have any ideas?'

'Lots of women are forced onto the streets. Why don't we get them to tell their stories too?'

'That would be great. Do you know anybody who might be interested?'

'Not yet, but I had an idea. I phoned Rhuama. They do lots of classes and free counselling and stuff. I've been dropping in there, and I got to know some of the other women. I could tell them about you. They'd get paid for their interviews too, right?'

'No, Tatiana. Apart from the fact that I don't have the money, I could end up with people pretending they were prostitutes just to get the cash. It's a small paper. They don't have the resources to do background checks.'

'You have to give them something.'

'Okay, how about we meet in a pub and I'll buy them a few drinks? I might be able to pass that off as expenses.'

'It's better than nothing. I'll get extra for introducing them, right?'

'No. I'm already splitting my fee with you. I can't afford to give you more. But the longer the series runs, the longer you'll be paid.'

Aoife's phoned pinged. She smiled at the selfie Conor had sent her. He was sitting at a beach bar sipping something very red. The sky above was so blue it merged seamlessly with the ocean. Aoife texted back a string of emojis. She could do with a day lounging on a beach, especially now the weather was getting quite warm. But that wouldn't get her work done. Now she had two stories going at the same time, Aoife was almost glad Conor was in Italy. Her article was due in two weeks' time. She had typed up pages of notes, but she still hadn't written a single word. This was her big break. She couldn't afford to mess it up. Amy was with Jason this weekend. That gave her two full days to work on it. By Monday she needed to have produced a rough draft, something she could work on over the next two weeks. Saturday afternoon, Nicole phoned.

'The investigators got back to me. They're still looking into the blackmail thing, but you were right about Florina. She was working in the hotel when Matt and I were on our honeymoon. The staff didn't know her very well. She only worked there occasionally.'

'Does anybody know if she spoke to Matt?'

'No, but Matt told one of the waiters that he was from Ireland. The waiter knew Florina was thinking of coming here. He said he meant to mention it to Florina, but they were very busy that day and he never had the chance.'

'Did he mention it to any of the hotel staff?'

'He says he might have, but he really can't remember.'

'But it's possible Florina might have heard about Matt from someone in the hotel. Did the investigators talk to all the staff?'

'They say hotel staff come and go. It was over a year ago. A lot of them have moved on.'

'Well, thanks for asking, Nicole. I'm not sure how it helps us, but the fact that they were both in the hotel at the same time makes it likely their murders were linked.'

'If Florina and Matt spoke, surely it could only have been for a few minutes? What could she say that would get Matt killed? And how come she wasn't killed for another year?'

'I don't know, Nicole. Maybe it took them that long to figure out Florina was the one who blabbed.'

'Blabbed about what?'

'I have absolutely no idea.'

There's one other thing, Aoife. One of the waiters said he thought he might have seen Matt in the hotel the day he disappeared.'

'You mean after you both went to the beach?'

'Yes. He never mentioned it because he only saw the man from behind.'

'What made him think it was Matt?'

'He was wearing an Irish rugby t-shirt. The waiter is fanatical about rugby and he'd seen Matt wearing it before.'

'Was Matt the only Irish man in the hotel that week?'

'No but Matt wore that t-shirt to the beach the morning he disappeared. Do you think it's a coincidence that a man who looked like Matt from behind was wearing an identical t-shirt the exact same day Matt disappeared?'

FIFTY-THREE

THAT NIGHT AOIFE told Conor all she had discovered while he was away.

'You've been busy. Have you even had time to miss me?'

'Of course I missed you, sweetheart. The more work I do when you're away, the more time we'll have together when you get back. Do you want me to collect you from the airport?'

'No, thanks. I left my car there. I'll be flying into London on Sunday. I'll stay overnight there so I can drop Blaine home. I'll be in your house Monday afternoon. I can't wait to see you, my love.'

On Saturday night, Aoife met Tatiana in O'Gorman's pub in the city centre. Aoife had suggested the pub because it had only opened the previous week and was one of the few city centre pubs unlikely to be packed on a Saturday night. She had been right. The pub was large and spacious. There were tables in the centre and booths in the corner for those who wanted a little more privacy. Aoife chose one of the booths. Tatiana was accompanied by Selena, Carmel and Deirdre, three women she'd met through Rhuama. The three young women perched on the edge of their seats, as if ready to flee should the conversation take an unpleasant turn. After a few drinks, they began to relax. Tatiana brought the subject around to their time on the streets. After listening to their stories, Aoife needed a drink herself. She got up to order another round. As she was passing one of the booths, she heard a familiar laugh. It was Katie. She and her companion were locked in an embrace. As they pulled apart, Aoife got a good look. The man with her was Greg.

'What happened?' Tatiana asked as Aoife put the four glasses on the table. 'You stood in the middle of the floor for so long we began to wonder if you'd taken root.'

'I saw a couple I knew. I thought they split up, but it looks like they're back together again.'

'That's nice,' Selena said.

'I suppose.'

'You don't seem too sure.'

'I thought she was better off without him.' Aoife shrugged. 'It's none of my business. I guess Katie knows what she's getting herself into.'

Two hours later they prepared to leave. As they waited for Tatiana and Deirdre to return from the ladies', Aoife said, 'Thank you so much for helping me. I know it can't be an easy thing to discuss.'

'Our names won't be mentioned, right?' Selena asked.

'No. There will be no names mentioned at all. You can read the article before I send it to the newspaper if you want.'

Selena and Carmel exchanged glances. 'Yes, we'd like that,' Carmel said. 'Tat was right, we can't let fear stop us. Nothing will ever change unless people speak up.'

'You mentioned that you volunteer with Rhuama. Would you like to work there eventually, Carmel?'

'No, I don't think so. I'm not like Tat. I couldn't be a counsellor. I'd find it too depressing. Coping with my own issues is enough for me.'

'Tatiana wants to be a counsellor?'

'I think so. We're all trying to talk her into it. She'd be brilliant. She's so caring, especially with the younger girls.'

Selena rooted in her bag for her phone. 'Well, she knows what it's like, doesn't she? It's hard on the streets at any age, but lots of teenagers don't survive it. Tat was lucky.'

'Not lucky,' Carmel corrected her. 'Tat's tough.'

'Of course she is.' Selena glanced up from the screen. 'If she wasn't, she'd be dead now.'

'Tatiana plans to go back to full-time education?'

'No. She thinks she's too dumb for that, but she's agreed to talk to a support worker about a career progression plan. It will take a while, but Tat will get there in the end.'

'I hope it works out for her.'

'It has to. Tat was made for that kind of work.'

'Did I hear someone mentioning my name?' Tatiana said as she reached behind Selena to get her bag.

'Your friends were telling me you'd make a great counsellor.'

Tatiana's cheeks reddened. 'Okay, if you two are saying nice things about me, you've obviously had way too much to drink. Let's go. I don't want to miss my bus.'

As they were walking out of the pub, Aoife glanced into

the booth again. Katie and Greg were still there. The three girls followed her gaze. 'I know…,' Tatiana began.

'I know him too,' Selena chimed in.

'Ex-client?' Carmel asked.

Selena shook her head. 'Not one of mine, but I've seen him somewhere. Where do you know him from, Tat?'

'He's turned up at a few of my stag do's—oh hell, that's my bus.' Tatiana raced across the street, shouting over her shoulder. 'I'll phone you later.'

Aoife shuddered. Greg was a sleaze. What was Katie thinking of, taking him back? Although, Aoife reminded herself, it wasn't as if she had the right to judge anybody. She'd not only married Jason, she'd had a child with him. At least Katie had the sense not to make Greg the father of her kids.

As Aoife watched, Katie and Greg rose. He helped her on with her jacket. It was navy and white with ornate silver buttons. Wasn't that the jacket she'd seen in Greg's brother's house? What the hell? Did Greg gift every woman in his life the same jacket, or had he been with Katie the day Aoife had called? But if Katie and Greg had been back together by then, why had he told Aoife she was a bitch he never wanted to set eyes on again?

On Sunday morning, Nicole phoned.

'The Italian investigators got back to me. They said at first none of the staff would talk to them, but when they offered money for information, a few said they had suspected something was going on for a while.'

'Who were they suspicious of?'

'Mostly the bar manager. They say he has far more money

than you'd expect from someone in that role, and a few of the waiters seemed to be living way above their income too.'

'Were they able to find out any details?'

'The investigators asked if they thought prostitutes hung out in the bar. Everyone mentioned one young woman they often see around. She's very friendly with the bar manager.'

'Do they know her name?'

'One of the investigators pretended to be a client. Then he offered her cash to speak. She said her pimp brings her to Bari every few weeks. At some stage during the weekend, she's told to pick up a specific man. When that happens, she has to use the camera on her phone to record everything from the moment she enters the room until she leaves.'

'How did she meet Matt?'

'She didn't. She says she never heard of him until his picture appeared on TV. Her pimp didn't bring her to Bari for months afterwards.'

'Can the detectives be sure she isn't lying?'

'They say she was very convincing. They believe she never met Matt.'

'Does her pimp have other girls working for him?'

'Yes, but not in Bari.'

'So her pimp is running a blackmail scam?'

'No. He gets a phone call telling him what men she should pick up.'

'It's the bar manager who picks the marks, then?'

'No. The girl doesn't know who the calls are from, but they're definitely not from the bar manager.'

'How can she be sure?'

'Because whenever he gets a call, her pimp says, "The Irish have another job for you."'

FIFTY-FOUR

JASON DROPPED AMY home. She ran in, hugged Aoife, spent ten minutes telling her about her weekend and then said, 'I want to tell Blainey about my new friend.'

'Blaine's probably in the airport now.'

'Please, Mummy. Please!'

'I'll try, but he might not be able to answer.'

Amy hopped from one foot to the other while Aoife rang Blaine.

'Hi, Blaine, are you on your way to the airport?'

'Not yet. Dad's plane doesn't land for another three hours.'

'Land where?'

'Heathrow.'

'You're on your way to Heathrow?'

'Not yet. Mum's at the supermarket. She'll drive me there when she gets back. I'm going to spend the night in the hotel with Dad.'

'You're in London?'

'I live in London, remember? Aoife, are you alright?'

'I'm fi—I thought you were in Italy with Conor.'

'I wish. I begged Dad to let me come, but he wouldn't take

me out of school. Dad can be very unreasonable sometimes. It's not like I'd miss anything. The term is almost over.'

'I suppose. Amy would like to talk to you.' Aoife handed the phone to her daughter and went up to her bedroom. Conor had lied to her. Why had he said he was taking Blaine to Italy? When she could no longer hear Amy's prattling, Aoife went downstairs and found her phone abandoned on the bottom step. She switched off the caller ID, googled the Italian hotel Conor had told her he was staying in, and asked to be put through to Conor's room.

'Mr Moloney checked out twenty minutes ago.'

Aoife was about to hang up when a thought struck her. She asked to be put through to Orla. The receptionist said, 'One moment, please.' Aoife's heart pounded. Lots of Irish people went to Italy. The receptionist could be putting her through to somebody with the same name.

The phone rang, once, twice, three times. On the fourth ring, a slightly breathless young woman said, 'Hi.'

Aoife's heart missed a beat. Her best friend, the girl she had known since she was four years old, was in Italy. In the same hotel as Conor.

'Hi, this is Orla. Anyone there?'

Aoife tried, but she couldn't make a sound. It felt like her throat was closing up. She sat there, phone in her hand, mouth opening and closing as she tried to swallow the lump in her throat. After a few seconds, Orla disconnected the call.

For a few minutes, Aoife tried to think of a scenario that wouldn't destroy all her plans for the future. Orla had mentioned she would go on holidays. It was possible she and Conor happened to go away at the same time. It was even possible they had chosen the same hotel. Maybe Orla had mentioned the hotel to Conor and he'd remembered it when he'd decided to go to Italy. Aoife gave a hollow laugh. How could she be so pathetic? It was quite obvious what was going on. Conor had told her he was taking Blaine to Italy. He'd lied so he could spend a week in Italy with Orla. You didn't need to be a genius to work that out.

Aoife didn't cry. She didn't scream. She sat on the bed, staring straight ahead. She just couldn't get her head around it. All the years Conor had spent patiently breaking down her defences, and for what? So he could cheat on her with her best friend?

It took Aoife a few seconds to realise Amy was climbing on her. 'Mummy! I'm hungry.'

Aoife picked her up and carried her downstairs. She hugged her so tightly Amy squirmed and demanded to be put down.

Amy was eating dinner while Aoife shoved her food around the plate when Conor rang. Aoife rejected the call.

'Let's watch a movie, Amy.'

When Amy ran into the sitting room to switch on the TV, Aoife listened to her message.

Blaine told me he spoke to you. Aoife, I know it doesn't look good, but I can explain everything. Just talk to me, okay?

Aoife deleted the message. She was about to turn off the phone when she changed her mind. Her fingers flew across the keyboard, stabbing out her anger: *I never want to hear from either you or Orla again. Do not call me. Do not try to speak to me. EVER!!* She switched off her phone and joined Amy in the sitting room. She spent the entire movie concentrating on trying not to cry. Halfway through the movie, Amy curled up in her lap and fell asleep in her arms. Aoife carried her upstairs. There was no need to pretend now. She could go to her room and let it all out.

Aoife had assumed she would bawl the moment she closed her bedroom door, but now that she had the freedom to express her grief, the tears wouldn't come. She couldn't sleep, she couldn't cry. All she could do was stare straight ahead, going over and over the events of the day. How could Conor lie to her? How could her best friend betray her? How was she going to get through the next few hours, let alone the weeks and years ahead? It was 2 a.m. when the crying started. At first it was tiny whimpers, almost like a cat mewing. The mewing gave way to heart-wrenching sobs. The sobbing grew so loud, Aoife had to stuff her head in the pillow in case she woke Amy.

The following morning, Aoife felt completely drained. After dropping Amy at school, she considered going back to bed. No. She'd never sleep. A half hour later, Aoife decided if she was going to spend the day pacing the house, she might as well work off her energy outdoors. At first, she was able to keep her mind blank by walking so fast her legs hurt, but after a while she tired and she could no longer control her thoughts. How could Conor betray her? Was Orla the first? Had he been cheating on her all these years? Her phone buzzed. Tatiana. Aoife put the phone back in her pocket. She was in the middle of an imaginary conversation with Conor and Orla where she called them every expletive she had ever heard when Tatiana phoned a second time. Aoife disconnected the call. Her train of thought broken, she decided all this fuming was a waste of energy. Conor was scum and Orla was just as bad. Neither deserved one second of her time. Her phone buzzed again.

'Hi, Tatiana, I'll call you back.'

'There's no need to call me. The girls are asking when we'll meet again.'

'Work out a few dates that suit you all and text me.'

'Okay, where do you want to meet?'

'Same place.'

Tatiana paused. 'I'd rather go somewhere else. I don't want to risk running into that guy again.'

'Greg?'

'Yeah. He and I had a run-in a few months ago. It was at one of the stag do's. If the bouncer hadn't interfered, I could have been seriously hurt. I think it's best to stay well out of his way.'

'Greg tried to rape you?'

'No, nothing like that. He took a swing at me.'

'Why?'

'I got talking to a girl he was with and I tried to help her. I always bring a change of clothes with me to these things, and I gave them to her. Somehow he found out about it and he went off his head. It's a long story. I'll tell you about it the next time we meet.'

FIFTY-FIVE

Aoife continued her walk, but her mind kept drifting back to her conversation with Tatiana. Greg had been furious that Tatiana had given his girlfriend second-hand clothes? That was bizarre. She remembered the navy-and-white jacket she'd seen in his brother's house. Maybe it wasn't Katie's. Maybe Greg gave the same jacket to everyone. Was he so controlling that he wouldn't allow any of the women he was involved with to wear clothes he didn't choose for them? But to get so angry that he tried to attack Tatiana? That was unhinged. Aoife turned towards home. She needed to talk to Katie again. Now was not the time to give up on her career. She had a daughter to support. She needed to put Conor behind her. She was done with him. That part of her life was over, and wallowing in her grief wouldn't change anything.

⁂

Aoife strode home full of determination. When she reached her gate, she came to an abrupt stop. How dare he! Conor was standing at the front door, hand pressed on the doorbell. His face flooded with relief when he saw her. 'Thank God, I thought you were ignoring me. Aoife, let me explain.'

He looked terrible. His face was pale and drawn and his jacket looked like he'd slept in it. A few days ago, Aoife would have been full of concern. Now she felt rage bubble up from the pit of her stomach. It wasn't bad enough that he'd ruined her life. He couldn't do the one thing she asked of him. She was not playing his game. She didn't give a damn how he rationalised his behaviour. The least she deserved was that he leave her in peace to come to terms with her grief. Bastard! Of course it was all about him. A lying snake like that would never think of her feelings. Aoife raced to her car, started the engine and reversed at speed. Conor ran after her shouting, 'Wait!' In her rear mirror, she watched him run back to his car.

Conor stayed behind her as she joined the motorway. He wasn't much better than a stalker. He knew she didn't want to speak to him, but there he was following her to Dublin. She took the first exit for Naas. When she reached the roundabout, Aoife waited until a large truck was almost on top of her, then she darted in front of it. The driver honked furiously. Aoife didn't care. The truck had been holding up a stream of traffic, and it would be several minutes before Conor was able to follow her. Aoife circled the roundabout and rejoined the motorway to Dublin. She checked her mirror several times, but there was no sign of Conor. She felt a momentary thrill at having outwitted him, but it was replaced with a pang of loss. She bit her lip to stop the tears. Conor wasn't worth crying over. He was the past. She had to concentrate on the future. Later she'd find a place she and Amy could stay for a few days until he gave up trying to talk to her. She didn't want Amy witnessing any arguments. It would be hard enough having to tell her that Conor would no longer be in their lives. How could a five-year-old be expected to understand that the kind man she'd loved for as long as she could remember was actually a two-timing bastard? Damn Conor! How dare he pretend to love her and Amy and then let them down? She would never speak to him again. Not one word. Not ever.

ঌ

Aoife tried Vicky's door. When there was no reply, she phoned her.

'Vicky, I'm at your place. Where are you?'

'At work. I'll be home tomorrow if you want to pop around then.'

'Okay. Vicky, I've been meaning to ask you for ages. When did you first hear that Matt was having an affair?'

'I'm not sure. Not long before you asked me about it. Why?'

'Just wondering. By the way, what's going on with Katie and Greg?'

'Still fighting as far as I know. Gotta go, Aoife. Talk to you tomorrow.'

ঌ

Aoife took the stairs to the third floor. If Greg had moved back home, Vicky would know about it. She had to talk to Katie now while there was still a chance to get her on her own. If Greg was completely out of control, then it was possible he was Matt's murderer. As he had been in Ireland that weekend, he must have hired a hitman. He might even have hired a hitman to kill Florina. But that meant he must always have known about Matt and Katie's affair. So why wait a year to have the big fight? Was there another reason they'd fought? Could it have been because

Katie had found out that Greg was a murderer? But then why had Katie claimed the breakup was Aoife's fault? As she climbed the stairs, Aoife considered Katie's dilemma. She could hardly have said, 'We broke up because my husband killed my lover.' The weird thing was, how had Greg talked her around? They had been all over each other in that pub. It was going to be hard to get Katie to understand that her life was in danger. Turning Greg in to the police was her only option. As Aoife knocked on the door of Katie's apartment, a hand touched her shoulder.

'Aoife, please talk to me. Just for five minutes and then if you want me to, I'll go away and never bother you again.'

Damn it! She should have known the bastard would guess where she was going. Aoife shook off his hand as Katie opened the door. Barely acknowledging her, Aoife slipped inside Katie's apartment. She tried to slam the door, but Conor caught it.

'What's going on here?' Katie asked.

'I'm sorry. I won't be long. Aoife, I promise you have nothing to be upset about. I didn't—'

'Nothing to be upset about! How dare you! I trusted you. Long after anybody with any common sense would have run a mile, I still believed in you. Pig!'

'Long after? Run a mile? What are you talking about?'

'Okay.' Katie stood between them, hands on her hips. 'You guys need to take this outside.'

'Yes, of course. We'll leave now. Aoife?'

'I'm not going anywhere. Don't interrupt me while I'm working. I'm here to speak to Katie.'

'We have nothing to say to each other, Aoife. Both of you, get…' Her voice trailed off as she looked at a spot behind Conor. He turned to see what had startled her. A small skinny man in his late fifties met their gaze. Katie paled. Conor went very still. For a moment all three stood frozen, then the man pulled down the hood of his bottle green hoodie, stretched his face into something resembling a smile and sauntered towards them.

'Having a domestic, are we, Detective?'

Conor attempted a laugh. 'Afraid so, Jacko. You know what it's like.' He jerked his thumb at Aoife. 'This one is my ex. I've been trying to get rid of her for months, but she keeps turning up like the proverbial bad penny. We'll get out of your way. Come on, you,' he said, reaching for Aoife's arm.

'A bitch, is she? Well, let me help you with that, Detective.' Jacko drew a gun from his pocket and aimed it at Aoife's head.

'No,' Conor yelled, jumping in front of her.

'Yeah, that's what I thought.' Jacko raised the gun and brought the barrel down on Conor's skull.

Aoife screamed as Conor slumped to the ground and lay there motionless.

FIFTY-SIX

Jacko wiped the gun on his jeans and put it in the pocket of his hoodie. He searched Conor's pockets, took out his phone and removed the battery. Grabbing Conor by the shoulders, he dragged him across the threshold and kicked the door shut with his foot.

'Where's the key for this?' he asked Katie. She pointed at a hook behind the door. Jacko locked it. Putting the key in the back pocket of his jeans, he stepped over Conor, yanked Aoife's bag from her shoulder, removed her mobile and shoved it in his pocket.

'Now, Katie, my beauty.' He took a seat on the couch. 'Where is that scumbag of a husband of yours?'

'I don't know. We split up.'

Jacko laughed. 'Sure you did.' He picked up the phone Katie had left on the breakfast bar and tossed it to her. 'Phone him now. I didn't come all the way from Spain to be told that scumbag has more important things to do.'

Katie held the phone to her ear.

'Speaker.'

Obediently she hit the speaker button. Greg answered on the second ring.

'I was just about to phone you. Chris was telling me about a new restaurant he and Lily went to recently. It might be worth checking out.'

'Jacko's here.' Katie's voice wasn't much more than a whisper.

After a moment's silence, Greg said, 'Are you okay?'

'Yes.'

'On my way.'

ൾ

While Jacko was listening to Katie's call, Aoife examined Conor's wound, then headed for the bathroom. She returned with disinfectant and cotton wool. Jacko looked up as she headed for the kitchen sink but made no attempt to stop her. Aoife got a basin of lukewarm water, added the disinfectant and dabbed at Conor's head wound. She had no idea how to treat him, apart from a vague notion that all wounds had to be kept clean. After a few seconds, Conor groaned and Aoife's heart lifted. At least he was conscious. When Conor tried to sit up, Jacko got up from the couch and stood looking down at him.

'Well, Detective. Not a good day for either of us, is it?'

'Let Aoife go,' Conor croaked. 'She's never done you any harm.'

'Too late for that. You've both seen me, and let me tell you I went to a ridiculous amount of trouble to make sure everyone thought I was still in Spain. If I let either of you go, the police would be here in seconds and the mysterious deaths this morning of some of my associates would suddenly become a whole lot less mysterious.'

'Aoife won't tell anybody she saw you.'

'I know.' Jacko nodded grimly. 'Neither will you.'

Katie gasped.

'Don't you worry, my lovely.' Jacko put his arm around her. 'The detective and his woman deserve special treatment. But while we're on the subject of what people deserve, I'm concerned you didn't keep a better eye on that loser husband of yours. I don't like it when people try to cheat me.'

'Greg wouldn't—'

'Oh, but he did. I found out yesterday that he's been running a blackmail scam behind my back. I'm guessing you found out before I did. That makes me very—'

They heard the scraping of a key in the lock, then Greg crashed through the door with such force that the door banged behind him. He ran straight at Jacko and pushed him to one side. Looking Katie up and down, he said, 'Are you alright?'

Katie nodded.

'Well, now.' Jacko had stumbled against the glass doors that led to the balcony. He straightened up. 'Quite the hero, aren't we?' He pointed the gun at Greg's head. 'As I was just saying to your lovely wife, I get very angry when somebody cheats me.'

Greg swallowed. He wiped his hands on his chinos, leaving damp patches on the beige material. 'We didn't cheat you.'

'No? So why is it I hear you've been running a blackmail scam out of the Colonnina?'

'Katie had nothing to do with that. She didn't even know what was going on.'

'She should never have taken up with a loser like you.'

'I didn't mean any harm, Jacko.' He pushed his fringe out of his eyes. 'I'll pay you back. Every cent.'

'Yes, you will.' Jacko took a piece of paper from his pocket and put it down on the kitchen countertop. 'My account number. Transfer everything in your account.'

'Yes, yes.' Greg hurried out to the balcony, where Katie had been working on her laptop.

'Bring it inside.'

Greg carried the laptop inside and put it on the table. From the opposite end of the room, Aoife watched Jacko pull the balcony door shut and rest his back against it.

Greg clicked on an online banking logo and looked at the screen helplessly.

'I can't remember…'

Jacko raised the gun and pointed it at Greg's head.

'I'll do it.' Leaning over Greg, Katie entered the codes with one hand. She grasped his shoulder with the other. Her grip was so tight, Aoife could see her knuckles turning white. Greg rested his hand on top of hers. They exchanged a glance as Katie returned to Jacko's side.

'Now we wait,' Jacko said.

'For the money to transfer?' Aoife could hear the note of panic in her voice. 'That takes twenty-four hours.'

Jacko grinned. 'All my associates use UK banks. They're faster. It can take up to twenty-four hours, but transfers usually go through in two. For all our sakes, let's hope it takes two hours today. Nice and all as it is to get home occasionally, I need to get back to Spain. Every bloody guard in this country has been trying to get their hands on me for years now.'

'I wonder why that might be,' Conor mumbled.

'Don't get smart with me, Detective. You'd do well to remember that I'm the one with the gun. Now, Katie, my beauty, we can't have detectives running around the place. Not even ones with a dented skull. Find me something to tie him up with.'

Katie went into the bedroom.

'Leave the door open.'

Katie kicked the door open with her foot. She pulled out a small red suitcase. She tried four different pockets before finding what she needed. She returned to Jacko with a set of zip ties. Jacko grinned.

'Handy things to have around the house. Is this what that useless piece of crap'—he gestured towards Greg—'needs to get excited? Interesting. I might try that myself later when the business part of our transaction is complete.'

Katie's hand began to tremble.

'Don't you dare touch her.' Greg ran towards them, fists clenched.

'Not to worry, my dear.' Jacko patted Katie's arm. 'I never mix business with pleasure. And there's a possibility you and I might continue to be business partners. We'll have to see how things work out. But for now, the detective's woman will help me celebrate.'

'Jacko.' Conor shifted so his back was against the door. His voice was ice cold as he said, 'Lay one finger on her and you sign your own death warrant.'

'Always the threats, Detective. Just for that, I'm going to make you watch.' He took the zip ties from Katie and yanked Conor's feet towards him. Conor put his hands out to balance himself. His head was inches from the floor when Aoife caught it and laid it gently on the ground.

'Good hands.' Jacko grinned at her. 'You and I are going to have a really great time later.'

'I'm not making idle threats, Jacko. You touch her, you die. If it's the very last thing I do, I'll make damn sure of that.'

Jacko kicked him in the groin, then dragged him about a

foot away from the door. 'Threaten me again, Detective, and the girl pays.'

A soft moan escaped Conor's clenched lips. Jacko yanked Conor's hands behind his back and used the zip tie to secure them.

'Get me more of these, Katie.'

When Katie returned with another set of zip ties, she said, 'That's all we have.'

Jacko pulled Aoife's hands behind her.

'I bet your mother would be proud of you, Jacko.' Conor spoke through clenched teeth, his face contorted in pain. 'It's not enough to tie her up, you have to twist her hands behind her back? Do you get a kick out of hurting women?'

'Do I have to shoot you to shut you up, Detective?'

Conor continued as if Jacko hadn't spoken. 'Or are you scared of any woman who doesn't faint in terror every time you open your mouth?'

'Shut up,' Jacko said, but he released Aoife's hands and tied them in front of her. Katie returned with a woollen scarf. 'I couldn't find anything better.'

'For the love of God, Katie. A scarf? Get me duct tape.'

'I don't have any. Would sellotape work?'

'God save me from women!' Jacko did a quick scan of the apartment. 'Well, her hands are secure,' he said, tying the woollen scarf around Aoife's legs. 'That's the main thing.' He took the other set of zip ties and, yanking Greg's arms so roughly that he gasped, tied them behind his back.

'There's no need for that, Jacko. Greg wouldn't try to escape.'

Jacko grabbed Greg by the collar and shoved him against the wall. Greg eased himself onto the ground, his panicked eyes never leaving Katie's.

'It wouldn't do him much good if he did. Where would he go? My guys would find him in no time.'

'So why tie him up?'

'The snake double-crossed me once, Katie. I'm not taking the chance he does it again.'

'He made a mistake. You've known him longer than I have. You know what he's like. He doesn't think sometimes. I wanted to buy a house and he thought I'd be okay with him cheating you. But the minute I found out, I told him if he ever did anything like that again, I'd phone you immediately. He can't hide anything from me for very long and I'll watch him like a hawk from now on. You can trust me.'

'Can I? You two have been nothing but trouble lately. You're supposed to be a recruitment agency, for God's sake. The least you could do is recruit people who don't cause me any trouble.'

'I admit we've had a bit of bad luck, but that happens sometimes. We sorted it.'

'What! I was the one who sorted it. Even before that scumbag cheated me, I was beginning to think you two were more trouble than you're worth.'

'We'll do better in future, Jacko. I promise. There'll be no more screw-ups. You have my word.'

Jacko gave her a hard look, then he sighed. 'I don't blame you, Katie. It's that idiot you married. He's leading you astray.'

'I haven't changed, Jacko. I'm still the girl who helped you recruit all those college kids. How much money did they launder for you?'

'Those were the good old days, Katie. Ever since you two married, it's been one problem after another. He pointed at Greg. 'Thanks to that piece of crap you married, I'm going to have to get some guys over here to take care of the detective and his woman.'

'Do you have to kill them? Couldn't you just leave them tied up until you're out of the country?'

'No. I couldn't. I have no desire to be on the run for the rest of my life. When I've got my money, I'll send some of my guys over here to take care of them. And don't think about helping them. My guys are going to have orders to kill two people. If those two aren't here, you'll be taking their place.'

'You can trust us, Jacko. Greg made a stupid mistake, but we can fix this. Greg's transferred everything in our bank account. We have nothing now. Greg did all the work and you got all the money. That's good, right?'

Jacko gave a non-committal grunt.

'I wanted to tell you when I found out about the Colonnina, but I was afraid you'd hurt Greg.'

'Damn right I'll hurt him! I'll wring his bloody neck.'

'Jacko, there's a steady stream of men through that hotel. Greg knows all the staff. He could run that blackmail scam for years without anybody being any the wiser.'

'Katie's right. You won't find a better spot.'

Aoife wished Greg could keep the pleading out of his voice. You didn't show weakness to men like Jacko. It could only make the situation worse. Katie obviously agreed. She motioned to Greg to be quiet, but he ignored her.

'The hotel's near the beach, the town and the airport. It gets both business people and tourists. Believe me, you could make a fortune.'

'Working with a treacherous scumbag like you?'

'Forget about me, Jacko. Katie can run it for you. You always said she was bright.'

'The world is full of bright people. It's loyalty that's hard to find.'

'You can trust Katie.'

'Oh shut up, you prat.'

'But—'

Katie interrupted him. 'Jacko, I know you're thinking you don't need either of us. You're right. You could run the scam without Greg, but why would you want to? Why take the time and trouble to build new relationships? And what makes you think you could trust somebody new?'

'I—'

'Yes, I know you don't trust Greg, but you don't need to. I'll watch him night and day. Even if he was dumb enough to try to cheat you again, he'd never get the chance. And the best thing is both of us will work for free. You'll have a fortune rolling in and you don't have to pay out anything at all.'

As they were speaking, Aoife watched Conor. He was twisting his feet, trying to weaken the zip tie. She shifted on her behind to get closer to him. 'Move in the opposite direction,' Conor whispered. 'Get as close to the door as you can. When I distract him, tighten the zip tie with your teeth.'

'Tighten it?'

Conor nodded. 'It's the only way it will work. You can get free easier now your hands are tied in front. Put your arms over your head. Stick your elbows out so they are wider than your hips and bring your arms down in one quick movement. Do it a few times and the tie will break.'

'How are you going to distract him?'

'I don't know yet, but the minute it happens, free your

hands and run. Greg came through that door so fast, he must have left the keys in the lock. Turn the lock on your way out. That will give you time to get out of the building before Jacko goes after you. Call the police when you're safe.'

'I can't just leave—'

'You have to, Aoife. It's the only chance either of us have of surviving this.'

'But if I leave, he'll kill you.'

'No. I'll use the distraction to get free. I'm a lot bigger than Jacko. I can look after myself. But not if you're here. He'll hold a gun on you and I won't be able to touch him. Once you're free, he doesn't stand a chance.'

'Are you sure?'

'One hundred percent. Promise me you'll run straight out the door. Don't look back.'

'Okay.'

They were silent for a moment, then Conor said, 'Nothing's going to happen, but just in case, I want you to know that I love you.'

'That doesn't matter now.'

'It matters to me, Aoife. I didn't cheat on you. Orla and I went to Italy to make the final arrangements for the wedding. There's not much chance Jason would show up in Italy uninvited, and as you never wanted a formal affair, we thought a wedding on the beach would be more your style. It was meant to be a surprise.'

'Oh, Conor!' Tears gathered in Aoife's eyes and she shifted closer so their bodies touched.

'I wanted you to know in case anything happens. But it won't. I'll distract Jacko and you'll run for the door, right?'

Aoife nodded.

'Go now. Get as close to the door as you can without attracting attention. I'll roll to the wall opposite.'

As they moved apart, Jacko looked up. From across the room he called, 'What are you two doing?'

'How could we do anything tied up like turkeys?' Aoife hoped her trembling voice would be put down to the terror of her situation.

'Hmm. I'm watching you, so don't try anything stupid.' Jacko refreshed the computer again, but from the disappointed look on his face, it was clear the money still hadn't transferred.

While Jacko was refreshing the screen, Aoife saw Greg gesture at the front door and mouth 'run'. So Conor wasn't the only one determined to save his partner. Katie shook her head. Aoife saw Greg mouth the words 'go' and 'now', but Katie turned her head away.

'Jacko, can I make you a cup of tea?'

'Why not, my beauty? Nothing like tea to pass the time. Make one for yourself while you're at it.'

Katie picked up a hoodie and slipped it on. She filled the kettle. 'No sign of the money yet?'

The kitchen area was midway between Jacko and Aoife. When Jacko turned to check the screen, Aoife saw Katie's hand move to the knife block. With one swift movement, she pushed the smallest knife up her sleeve. Then she turned on the tap, letting the water drip into the basin.

'Two sugars, just the way you like it.' Katie handed Jacko the mug.

Jacko took a seat at the table. He threw his eyes up to

heaven as Katie sat on the ground beside Greg and held her mug to his lips.

'What's that dripping?' Katie asked. 'Oh hell, I left the tap running.'

Jacko glanced over. The basin in the kitchen sink was beginning to overflow. He got up and turned it off.

'If you want biscuits, there are some on the top shelf on the left,' Katie said.

Aoife focussed on Katie. As Jacko rooted around in the cupboard, from across the room Aoife saw Katie slip the kitchen knife from her sleeve.

'There aren't any biscuits here, Katie.'

'Greg keeps moving them. Try the lower press.'

'Ah!' As Jacko gave a satisfied grunt and slit the packet of chocolate biscuits open with his teeth, Katie cut the ties that bound Greg's hands.

FIFTY-SEVEN

'WANT ONE?' JACKO offered the biscuits to Katie.

'No, thanks. Did I hear the computer ping?'

When Jacko turned his back to check the laptop, Greg rose, the knife Katie had used to free him clasped in one hand. He tiptoed towards Jacko, knife raised in the air. Aoife wanted to scream, 'No! He'll see your reflection in the computer screen.' She bit her lip. Screaming would only alert Jacko. Besides, her job was to free herself and Conor. If Greg and Jacko wanted to kill each other, that could provide the distraction she needed.

Aoife figured she had guessed correctly because as Greg was raising the knife into the air, Jacko roared, 'What the—!' Jumping to his feet, he grabbed Greg's arm. Greg twisted to one side, forcing Jacko's hand backwards. When Jacko released his wrist, Greg slammed his body into Jacko's, knocking him to the ground.

'Run, Katie,' he shouted.

Katie didn't move. Greg flung himself on Jacko, knife raised above his head.

ꗃ

Aoife was already on her feet. She glanced at Conor. He was struggling to his knees. He bent forward, raising his hands behind his back, trying to perform the same action he had explained to Aoife. As his hands were tied behind him, it was a far more complicated manoeuvre. He needed to get his hands as close to his neck as possible, and even then, there wasn't space to get much momentum into the downward swing. Aoife spread her elbows and raised her hands over her head. She brought them down in one sharp movement. Nothing happened.

'Keep at it,' Conor whispered between grunts as he attempted to free his own hands.

Aoife raised her hands again. Nothing. By the fourth attempt she wanted to scream in frustration. She took a deep breath, shut her eyes and pictured Amy. They both had to get home to Amy. *Concentrate.*

'Every time you do it, the bond weakens. Two or three more times and you'll be free,' Conor muttered.

༄

As Aoife and Conor struggled to free themselves, Jacko and Greg were rolling on the ground. Greg still had control of the knife, but he was now on his back, Jacko looming above him. Jacko raised a foot to kick the knife from Greg's hand.

༄

Katie watched Jacko and Greg's struggle. When one of Jacko's kicks caused Greg to cry out in pain, Katie's eyes ran frantically around the room. She picked up a lamp, raised it in the air and brought it down on Jacko's head. Greg rolled free. As he got to his feet, he shouted at her, 'No, Katie, run!'

Aoife and Conor exchanged worried glances. Leaving space

between himself and Jacko was the worst move Greg could have made. Now he was no longer in imminent danger of being stabbed, Jacko had the time to remove the gun from his pocket and aim it at Greg.

'Run, Katie. Please!' Greg pleaded. 'Please run.'

❧

On her seventh attempt, Aoife's ties broke. She glanced at Conor.

'Nearly there,' he whispered. 'Don't worry about me. Free your legs and get out of here.'

❧

When Greg pleaded with her to run, Katie hesitated. Whatever she saw in Greg's eyes made up her mind. She raced for the door. As her hand touched the handle, a shot rang out. Katie fell to the ground, inches from Aoife's feet.

Jacko fired at her again. Greg screamed and, abandoning all caution, flung himself on top of Jacko, jabbing the knife at anything he could reach.

'I got it,' Conor shouted to Aoife as the gun went off again. He waved his free hands at her and bent down to untie his legs.

Legs free, Aoife was getting to her feet as Greg and Jacko struggled for the gun. The gun fired a third time. Greg swiped at Jacko, leaving a thin cut the length of his arm. Jacko jumped backwards and stumbled. The gun flew out of his hand.

❧

Aoife was heading for the door when the gun that had flown out of Jacko's hand skidded across the floor. Without thinking, she ran over and picked it up. Jacko reached out and grabbed her wrist as Greg made another lunge with the knife. Still maintaining a vice-like grip on Aoife's wrist, Jacko used his legs to defend himself. While his eyes were on Greg, Aoife grasped the gun with her left hand. The movement caught Jacko's attention. He kicked Greg in the groin. As Greg doubled up in pain, Jacko turned on Aoife. It would only be a matter of seconds before he took the gun from her, and then what? If she was lucky, Greg would have recovered enough to provide a distraction. If not, she would die. And what about Conor? If she could turn around, she was sure she'd see him racing to her defence. Jacko wouldn't think twice about shooting him. She only had one option.

Aoife held her breath as she raised the gun. Even when she had use of her right arm, Aoife's aim had always been dreadful. With her left, there was no knowing what she might do. 'Please! Please!' she muttered as she used all her strength to fling the gun towards the kitchen area. She let out a breath when she heard the loud splash. Bingo! The gun had landed in the basin of water.

With a howl of rage, Jacko punched Aoife in the face and sent her reeling. As she landed, Aoife's head banged against the sofa. She barely felt it. The punch had landed under her nose. Her vision blurred and it felt like her entire face was on fire. When she touched her nose, drops of blood landed on her hand. She shook her head to clear her vision. If her nose was broken, it would mend. That was the least of her worries. She struggled to her feet. Her heart was beating so fast the room spun. Why hadn't Conor tried to save her? Why hadn't he made a single sound when she was struggling for her life? She already knew the answer. She just couldn't face it. She walked slowly towards him. Conor was slumped on his back unmoving.

FIFTY-EIGHT

'Conor,' Aoife whispered.

Conor groaned.

As gently as possible, she turned him over. Aoife didn't know much about gunshot wounds, but even she could tell he'd been shot. His once-white T-shirt was now red. One of the stray bullets must have hit him. Where the hell was the blood coming from?

ꕥ

As Aoife searched the kitchen for a clean towel, located the source of Conor's bleed and attempted to stem the flow, she was vaguely aware of the fighting in the background. Greg had managed to trip Jacko and was now leaning over him, knife clasped in both hands. Jacko raised his feet. The kick sent Greg flying towards the doors leading to the balcony. He got to his feet as Jacko lunged at him. His only escape route was the balcony.

ꕥ

Now that Jacko and Greg were on the balcony, this was Aoife's chance to escape. But what then? She could go to a neighbour's apartment, call the police and tell them a detective had been injured. But wouldn't the neighbours have called the police by now? True, there was a silencer on Jacko's gun, but the neighbours on both sides and the people in the apartment below must have heard all the crashing around. Unless everyone was at work. Nicole said the building was mostly empty during working hours. If Jacko overpowered Greg and noticed Aoife had escaped, he'd be in such a rage, he'd kill Conor. She couldn't leave Conor on his own, completely helpless. He could be dead before she even found a neighbour who was at home in the middle of the day. Maybe their best chance was if she helped Greg.

Greg and Jacko struggled for control of the knife. If Katie had chosen a larger knife, the struggle would have been over long ago, but as it was, Greg couldn't do any damage without getting up close. Jacko was at least thirty years older, but he was strong and wiry and this clearly wasn't his first fight. Even Aoife could tell that Greg had never used a knife before and she was pretty sure he hadn't been in a fight since childhood. As Aoife watched, Jacko charged at Greg, head lowered like a bull charging at a matador. Greg flew backwards. As he fell, he dropped the knife. They both scrambled for it and in the struggle the knife slipped off the balcony and got stuck in the gutter outside the railing. Now he no longer had to worry about the knife, Jacko moved in for the kill. Fists flying, he delivered three sharp punches, driving Greg backwards against the railings.

As she watched them struggle, Aoife considered her options. Could she lock Jacko outside? There was no key in the door and she had no idea where to find one. There was no time to search. A knife! She needed a knife. Aoife ran to the knife block. Grabbing the largest knife she could find, she ran out to the balcony just as Jacko, with a strength that was surprising for such a small man, raised the younger man's legs and flung him over the railing.

Aoife covered her mouth with both hands to suppress a scream. Jacko would come for them now. If Greg couldn't fight him off with a knife, what chance had she? But Jacko didn't turn. He was leaning over the railings and Aoife realised she hadn't heard Greg fall. She hadn't heard residents running out to see what had happened. She moved closer. Greg had grabbed the railing as he was falling. He was now hanging by one hand from the third-floor balcony.

'Well, well. You're a stubborn one, aren't you?' Jacko sneered as he slammed his foot against Greg's hand. Greg screamed but he didn't let go. Jacko raised his foot again, then stopped. Dropping to the ground, he ran his hand along the gutter, searching for Greg's knife.

Aoife sneaked up behind him. Both hands gripping her knife, she raised it in the air.

FIFTY-NINE

AS AOIFE RAISED the knife, Jacko realised his arm wouldn't reach and he scuttled an inch to his right. He jumped up in surprise as Aoife's knife nicked his arm. Aoife had put so much momentum into the swing that she went flying into the balcony railings. The knife fell from her hand. Jacko stared at her for a moment, mouth open, then his face creased into a grin.

'The detective's woman has some fight in her. I like that.' Grabbing her by the neck, he muttered in her ear. 'We'll have our fun later, my girl.'

Aoife's mouth twisted in disgust, but before she could reply, Jacko drove his fist into her stomach. As Aoife fell backwards, she tripped over the leg of one of the balcony chairs and landed on her back midway between the balcony and the apartment. Before she had time to gather herself, a foot slammed into her ribs. Aoife pulled her knees into her chest and covered her head with her arms. She felt four kicks before Jacko snorted in disgust and stomped out. When she heard his boots on the tiled balcony, Aoife uncurled. Everything hurt. Maybe she should run for help. Her attempt to disarm Jacko had been an utter disaster. But Greg couldn't hang on to that railing for much longer. When he hit the ground, the neighbours would call an ambulance and the police would be notified. Was it worth the risk of leaving an undefended Conor behind for the sake of alerting the police a few minutes earlier? Another scream from the balcony and Aoife hobbled outside. Jacko had picked up her knife. He was now leaning over the edge, knife clasped in one hand, swinging wildly at Greg. At first Aoife assumed he was trying to cut Greg's arm so he'd release his grip on the railing—then she realised Jacko had a different plan. If Greg fell from the third floor, there was a good chance he'd survive. Jacko wanted him dead.

As Aoife watched, Jacko leaned further over the balcony. Greg swayed to one side in an effort to avoid the knife. His face was screwed up in pain as he tried to maintain his grip on the railing. Jacko was aiming for Greg's armpit, eyes or neck. His short arms made the reach difficult, so he stood on his tiptoes. Right leg raised off the ground and his stomach balanced on the railing, Jacko stretched his arm towards Greg's eye. It was now or never.

SIXTY

AOIFE KNEW THIS would be her last chance. If she failed a second time, she would die. She took a deep breath and ran towards them. She grabbed Jacko's left leg with both hands and, using every ounce of strength she could muster, raised it in the air. Jacko screamed as he went over the railings. She heard a dull thud, then silence.

As Jacko fell, Greg's grip on the railing loosened, and with a piercing screech, he plunged to the ground. Windows opened and residents came racing into the car park. There were shouts of 'I called an ambulance!' and 'Are they dead?' and 'My God! It's Greg! Is Katie okay?' Some of the residents looked up at the balcony. Aoife yelled, 'Call 999. Tell them there are two injured people here.'

Everyone in the car park looked up at her.

'What's going on?' a man she had never met shouted.

'And call the police,' Aoife replied. She hobbled inside and, taking another knife from the block, cut Conor's zip ties. When the police arrived, she was cradling his head in her lap.

SIXTY-ONE

THE HOSPITAL STAFF wanted to examine Aoife, but she refused to leave Conor's side. A nurse wiped the blood from her face. Her nose wasn't broken, but it would be swollen and bruised for a few weeks. Aoife thought of her wedding and vowed she would walk down the aisle looking like the victim of a car crash if only Conor was well enough to be there.

Fifteen minutes after they arrived in the hospital, Grainne rushed into the ICU, face stiff with fear. Conor's father and siblings arrived within the hour. By that evening, Blaine, his mother and his stepfather had joined them.

Aoife didn't leave Conor's room for the entire first day. On day two she took the stairs to the shop on the ground floor. It was the most exercise she'd had in twenty-four hours. At first her legs felt stiff and achy, but they were back to normal by the time she reached the shop.

The shop was busy and Aoife had to queue for several minutes to get a coffee and a bottle of water. Afterwards she walked up and down outside the hospital entrance as she spoke to Amy, who had spent the previous evening in Maura's house. Amy was delighted with the change to her routine and excitedly listed all the things she had done that day. Aoife had to chew on her thumbnail for the entire conversation to avoid bursting into tears. How could life go on as normal outside the hospital? How could people worry about work and paying bills when Conor was lying in a bed in ICU? Only yesterday she'd been part of that world. It was difficult to believe she'd ever been that carefree.

When Aoife returned to Conor's room, she found Grainne and Sarah sitting on Conor's empty bed. Both were red-eyed and teary. Rory and Conor's dad were trying to comfort them.

'What's wrong?'

'Conor's in surgery.' Rory's voice shook. 'The doctor said something about his breathing. They're operating on him now.'

Aoife felt the bile rise in her throat. She took a deep breath. 'He'll be okay. Conor's young. He's fit and he's strong. He'll be just fine.'

Surgery seemed to take forever. 'What are they doing?' Grainne paced the floor. 'Even heart surgery wouldn't take this long.'

'I'll see if I can find a doctor,' Conor's father said.

Aoife didn't speak. She sat totally still, concentrating on a vision of Conor sitting up in the bed, chatting and laughing. The others in the room barely registered with her. She would keep Conor alive by the sheer force of her will if necessary. Realistically Aoife understood this was impossible, but she refused to listen to her rational side.

When Conor returned from the operating theatre, Aoife felt like she had dragged him back to life all by herself. Her will had kept him safe and now everything was going to be fine. There was nothing to worry about, she assured his frantic family. Setbacks were an inevitable part of recovery.

'I think that only applies to addiction,' Rory muttered, but Aoife ignored him.

She badgered every doctor she saw for information. Afterwards she googled the information she'd received so she could understand what was going on. She kept the Mayo Clinic website open on her phone, consulted it constantly and assured everyone that Conor was progressing even better than could be expected under the circumstances.

It was the following evening when Conor's doctor asked to speak to them. They waited in the corridor as the young doctor checked Conor's chart and scribbled a note. Grainne gripped her husband's arm. Rory moved closer to Sarah. Blaine's mother stood behind him, her arms wrapped around his neck. Aoife stood alone, leaning against the wall for support.

'His vitals are good,' the doctor said. 'We should be able to move him out of ICU in the next day or so.'

For a second nobody reacted, then Grainne said, 'Oh, thank God. Thank God!'

Conor's father shook hands with the doctor. Sarah and Rory hugged. Blaine pumped his fist in the air and looked slightly embarrassed when his mother kissed him. Aoife watched, mouth open. Conor was going to be okay. Her legs felt too weak to support her weight and she lowered herself to the ground. 'He's going to be okay,' she muttered to herself. She felt something bubbling up from within. Her hands shook, her mouth opened, seemingly of its own volition, and she bawled. Three days of pretending everything was alright had taken its toll. She covered her mouth with both hands in an attempt to stifle the sobs, but it had the opposite effect—the sobs just grew louder. Conor's family crowded around her. Grainne muttered, 'There, there, everything's going to be okay. She's been through so much,' she told the doctor by way of apology.

'Why don't you take her to the waiting room?' the doctor suggested.

Aoife was vaguely aware of people putting their arms around her, shushing her, telling her it was all over now. Sarah handed her a cup of tea that was so sugary Aoife gagged. Everyone urged her to go home and get some sleep, but Aoife wasn't ready to leave Conor, so they insisted she sit in the armchair. They pulled up a chair for her to rest her feet. Aoife's last thought before she fell asleep was that if Conor had wanted to integrate her into his family, he couldn't have chosen a more effective method. After their seventy-two-hour vigil at Conor's bedside, she felt she'd known them all forever.

The next thing Aoife knew, it was morning. The second she realised where she was, Aoife jumped up, but Conor was sleeping peacefully. He was still pale, but his breathing wasn't laboured. Rory looked up from his phone.

'Hi. Feeling better?'

Aoife nodded. 'Did you stay here all night?'

'No. Dad did the night shift. I've been here since eight.'

Aoife felt Conor's forehead. No fever.

'Your friend Orla came by again. The nurses told her to call back in a few days. Conor should be in the general ward by then.'

'I'll phone her.'

'How long is it since you've had anything to eat, Aoife? Go down to the canteen. The food's dreadful, but it's better than nothing.'

ॐ

Aoife phoned Amy again. Then she called Orla. At first Orla was shocked Aoife thought she would have an affair with Conor, but within minutes she saw the funny side. 'Oh, Aoife! I can just picture your face as I walked out of Conor's house. Why on earth didn't you phone me?'

'I did. You said you were busy.'

'Well, yes. I can see that might appear a little suspicious, but Conor really wanted to surprise you and we figured the less people who knew the wedding would be in Italy, the less chance there was that Jason would find out.'

'I know, and I do love the idea of being married on a beach. Though, to be honest, I'd happily agree to having the ceremony in Buckingham Palace if it would get us out of this hospital.'

'Don't worry. I've taken care of everything. We had to move hotels, but the wedding's been put back for two months. That will give Conor time to recover.'

'I hope so.'

'Oh, I spoke to your editor.'

'The article! Oh my God, I'd completely forgotten about it. What date is it? Have I missed the deadline?'

'I took care of that too. I know somebody who knows somebody at the *Times*. They agreed to close the series with your article, so you have another four weeks to turn it in.

'Oh, Orla, that's brilliant. Thank you.'

'It will give you a chance to break the news to Nicole. You wouldn't want her finding out what happened from strangers. She deserves to hear it from you.'

It was 11 a.m. when Aoife finally made it to the canteen. The place was almost deserted. She chose rubbery scrambled egg and wet toast for her breakfast. Strangely enough, they tasted quite good and she went back for seconds. She was scrolling through her phone when a man took the seat opposite.

'Hi, Aoife. I'm Fionn. I work with Conor.'

'Of course I remember you, Fionn. How are you?'

'We were all thrilled to hear Conor's going to make it. That scumbag Jacko will be locked up for a long time. You can trust us to make sure of that.'

'He's here?'

'Yes, but don't worry about that. There's a guard with him day and night. Besides, he broke his leg, ankle and elbow. He won't be going anywhere for a long while.'

'Conor told me weeks ago that Jacko was a drug dealer. Why did he hate Conor?'

'We've been investigating him for years now. Two years ago, we thought we finally had the proof to put him away for a long stretch, but our chief witness disappeared and Jacko ran off to Spain. When he was gone, a few of his underlings tried to take over. Jacko came home to sort them out. He killed four of them before turning up at Greg and Katie's apartment.'

'What happened to Katie and Greg? Did they survive?'

'Oh yeah. Greg broke both his legs. The bullet went right through Katie's shoulder, but she lost a lot of blood. They're both here. We're looking into the money laundering allegations. We should have enough to arrest them in the next few weeks. We passed on the information about the Italian blackmailing scam to the Mutual Assistance Unit. They'll liaise with the Italian authorities.'

'Will they go to prison?'

'For money laundering? It depends on the judge, but probably not. Technically they could each get up to ten years in prison, but the courts tend to be sympathetic to young people like them.'

'Why?'

'It happens a lot these days. Criminal gangs target college students. They say all you have to do is let us lodge money into your account and leave it there for a while. When we move it out, you'll get a percentage. When you're young and stupid you think it's easy money, but once the gangsters have their claws into you, they don't let go easily.'

Aoife said she could handle the afternoon shift on her own, so Rory left. Conor's eyes fluttered open when the nurse checked his wound, but he was asleep within minutes. Aoife found her mind wandering to her conversation with Fionn. She found it hard to see Greg and Katie as victims. When Jacko had told them he planned to kill herself and Conor, Katie had barely objected. Greg had said nothing at all. Aoife reached for her phone.

'Orla, do you believe Florina had an affair with Greg?'

'I don't know. We could communicate, but because of the language barrier, our conversations didn't have much depth. Still, Florina had enough English to say she was in love and girls that age usually want everyone to know that.'

'When we were in their apartment with Jacko, Greg didn't act at all like I would have expected. He was prepared to sacrifice his own life to save Katie, and she did everything she could to protect him too. And did I tell you that Katie stayed overnight in Greg's house a few days earlier?'

'Maybe they fought and made up.'

'I don't think so. I remember Vicky saying they were rock

solid. That's how they seemed to me. And Greg didn't appear to be the type who would tie her up either.'

'What?'

'Katie had zip ties in the house. Jacko assumed they were for bondage. I don't think Greg would ever hurt Katie.'

'Maybe she enjoyed hurting him?'

Aoife pictured Katie sitting on the ground beside a bound Greg, holding the coffee mug to his mouth.

'No. They're not like that with each other. They're very caring. And that's another thing. Why would they pretend to hate each other? And if Greg wasn't sleeping with those maids, why did he have them live in the apartment for the first two weeks? Did Florina ever mention her time there?'

'It never came up.'

'I remember meeting the girl before Florina. Gabriela? Something like that. She stayed with Katie for the first fortnight. Greg wasn't even in the country at the time.'

'How did she seem?'

'Happy, relaxed. She was eating ice cream and texting her friends.'

'That doesn't sound very suspicious to me.'

'No. Me neither. But why was she there in the first place? Katie said it was because she was so young they wanted to reassure her parents that she would be okay so far from home.'

'It's possible, I suppose.'

'Maybe. But I don't think so. Something weird was going on there, Orla.'

SIXTY-TWO

When Grainne arrived to do the evening shift, Aoife phoned the reception desk. Fifteen minutes later she stood in the corridor outside Greg's hospital room, trying to get the courage to enter. When Jacko had said he intended to shoot her and Conor, Katie had at least asked if that was necessary. Greg hadn't said a word. Greg had had his own problems at the time, obviously, but what Aoife couldn't forgive was that their imminent death hadn't even registered with him. Greg cared about himself and Katie. He barely acknowledged the existence of other people. Was there anything she could say that would get through to somebody like that?

Greg lay in the narrow hospital bed. His face was covered in bruises. The floppy fringe had been combed back, giving him an old-fashioned appearance, like a blonde Humphrey Bogart. One leg was in plaster, the other was raised over his head on a type of pulley. His hands were swathed in bandages, but they were about double the size of normal hands. Aoife remembered Jacko slamming his boot down on Greg's fingers and wondered if they were broken. Greg opened his eyes as she approached.

'I'm not in the mood for visitors.'

'I can see that. You must be in a lot of pain.'

Greg glared at her but didn't reply.

'A friend of mine says she knows you. You tried to attack her a few months ago.'

'What? That's crazy. I'm not in the mood for games, Aoife. Get out!'

'In a minute. You puzzle me, Greg. Katie told me you sleep with teenage maids and at times she even seemed scared of you. That was certainly Florina's impression.'

'I don't care how puzzled you are. Go away.'

'But when Jacko turned up at your apartment, you risked your life to save her.'

Greg closed his eyes.

Aoife inched closer. Greg didn't react. Watching Greg carefully to make sure his eyes remained shut, Aoife grabbed the mobile that sat on top of his locker and stuck it in her pocket. She pulled up a chair and sat beside his bed.

'You know, I spoke to Florina's neighbours. They told me about the girls who lived in that apartment before Florina. They also told me about the men who lived with them.'

Aoife waited, but there was no response from Greg.

'They saw you talking to one of those men, Greg. They thought the man was threatening you.'

'Are you still here?'

'Aren't you curious about my friend? The one you tried to assault? She met you at a stag do. You brought a girl with you. My friend gave her some second-hand clothes and you lost it.'

'I have no idea what you're talking about.'

'You know, I've been so distracted lately, I haven't been paying enough attention. When my friend told me that story, it never occurred to me to wonder what kind of man would bring a girl to a stag do.'

'Go away, please.'

'Or what kind of girl would want to attend one. Because it seems to me the only girls who would be at a stag do are girls who work there. Like my friend.'

Greg's eyes opened. 'Your friend's a prostitute?'

'She's a lap dancer. But I can see why you might assume she was a prostitute. I'm sure there were several prostitutes there. That's why you brought the girl, isn't it, Greg? You're her pimp.'

SIXTY-THREE

GREG'S EYES OPENED wide. For a split second, Aoife saw the fear, but he closed them immediately.

'The men who used to live in Florina's apartment, they weren't boyfriends, were they?'

Silence.

'They were the girls' pimps. Aoibhinn, one of their neighbours, said she tried to speak to one of the girls, but the man pulled her away. They weren't allowed speak to anybody, were they?'

Greg gave a loud, fake snore.

'And those men sat outside the apartment day and night because they were minders. Their job was to keep the girls under control and make sure the customers paid. Isn't that right?'

Greg opened his eyes again. 'I was never in that apartment before Florina moved in. I don't know who the other tenants were and I don't know what they did. Now, I would like to rest. I'm in a lot of pain and I don't have the energy to listen to your rambling.'

'Florina told me you'd promised her "other work" that would pay well. I thought she meant other work as a maid.

When I mentioned the "other work" to you, I remember you looked worried. I should have guessed then. Florina agreed to be a prostitute, didn't she?'

'Please go. You're talking nonsense.'

'So, what did you promise her? She'd have two clients each day and in between she'd be free to go to English classes and meet up with her friends. In time she'd have enough English to get a good job, maybe even go to college. Is that it?'

Greg closed his eyes again.

'I've read about girls like that. They think they're going to be in control, but then they're locked in a house where they're watched twenty-four hours a day. They're forced to service men all day and most of the night, for which they receive no payment. They're not even allowed to own clothes in case they try to escape.'

Greg turned his head away.

'That's why you tried to attack my friend, isn't it? She felt sorry for the girl, so she gave her clothes. You found out. You knew the girl was trying to escape and you flew into a rage. If she escaped, she might go to the police and you'd all end up in prison. Even if you caught her before she spoke to anybody, Jacko would be furious and he'd blame you. And we both know how Jacko reacts when he's furious.'

Silence.

'Jacko mentioned that your recruitment wasn't going well and I remember Florina saying you were screaming at some crying Romanian girl on the phone. Was she the girl who had tried to escape? Is that why Katie looked scared when you told her about the call? You were becoming a liability, weren't you?'

Still no reply.

'Greg, if you don't talk to me, I'm going straight to the police and telling them everything I know.'

It took a few seconds before Greg opened his eyes. Aoife could see immediately that he had decided to call her bluff. His expression was a mixture of anger, determination and fear.

'Tell the police anything you like. Just get out of my room.'

SIXTY-FOUR

Aoife phoned Fionn. He agreed to meet her in the hospital. He also made a call to the policeman sitting at Jacko's bedside. When Aoife entered Jacko's room, the young policeman nodded, rose, and left them alone.

Jacko's right leg and left arm were plastered, but it didn't seem to bother him. His bruised face lit up when Aoife entered.

'Ah, the detective's woman. They tell me your old man's going to make it.'

'No thanks to you.'

'Hey, I never meant to shoot him. The gun went off in the struggle. I've spoken to my lawyer. No court on earth could call it attempted murder, and as for the untimely death of my associates, it was just coincidence I happened to be in Ireland at the time.'

'You don't seriously think you're going to get away with this, do you?'

Jacko shrugged. 'If we had a fair justice system, I'd have a pretty good chance. Unfortunately, the likes of me go straight to the special criminal court. We're not even allowed to put our case in front of a jury. The European Court of Human

Rights should get involved, but they don't give a damn about the little guy.'

'Millionaire gang leaders who used to threaten every jury they faced, so they walked away free each time they were arrested? That's your definition of the little guy?'

'Some people may have issued threats, but a jury trial is a basic right in a free society. Doesn't it bother you that our justice system denies me my human rights?'

'I can live with it.'

Jacko laughed. 'I'm sure you can. I like you. In different circumstances, I think we could have been friends.'

'I don't.'

Jacko's lined face creased into a grin. Either he was too macho to show any pain, he was over-medicated or, more likely, the prospect of being locked up in Ireland's overcrowded prisons made him determined to enjoy the relative privacy of his spartan hospital room.

'I've just been to see Greg.'

Jacko's face darkened. 'I should have known that idiot would be the ruin of me. If I'd any sense, I'd have gotten rid of him years ago. My old man always said never mix business and pleasure. If only I'd listened to him.' He scratched at the skin above his cast. 'I wasn't dumb enough to get involved with Katie, but I let my feelings for her affect my judgement. A pretty girl can destroy a man. My old man used to say that too.'

'Greg told me about your prostitution ring.'

'No idea what you're talking about.'

'The police are with him as we speak.'

'Even Greg's not that stupid.'

'He was very slow to admit anything, that's true. But when

I told him I could prove he murdered Florina, he spoke so fast I had difficulty writing it all down.'

Jacko didn't reply, but his eyes narrowed.

'Florina didn't want to be a prostitute. She discovered she could make a reasonable living as a cleaner and that was enough for her. You couldn't let her go, though, could you? If she went to the police, that would be the end of a very profitable business. Your goons would end up in jail. Your empire would be disbanded. The police might even have managed to get you extradited.'

'I was in Spain when that girl died. How could I possibly know what happened to her?'

'Why did you have her killed in Orla's house? Were you worried Florina's neighbours were too nosy? They might see your goons making their escape? They saw them in Florina's apartment once already, you know. Her neighbours thought Florina was out, but she wasn't, was she? You sent your goons to threaten her. That's when she said she would go to the police, isn't it?

'I think it's time for my nap. Guard!'

When the young policeman stuck his head around the door, Jacko said, 'The detective's woman is leaving now.'

SIXTY-FIVE

As she took the stairs to Katie's room, Aoife checked Greg's phone. It was password protected, but that didn't prevent her from turning down the volume. For her plan to work, she had to make sure Greg and Katie couldn't communicate. Katie was her last chance. It was time to get inventive.

Katie was propped up in the bed with pillows. Her shoulder was bandaged and her left arm was in a sling. A drip was attached to the hand she was using to flick through a glossy magazine. Surprise, anger and wariness crossed her face when she saw Aoife at the door. Then her mouth stretched into a huge smile.

'Hi, Aoife. I was so happy to hear your fiancé is going to be okay. That was a close one, wasn't it?'

'It was.'

Katie seemed a little taken aback by her lack of enthusiasm. 'Don't think I blame you for anything, Aoife. Of course you told the police we'd been money laundering for Jacko. It would all have come out anyway, and it was our own stupid fault for getting involved with him. Kids are dumb, right?'

Aoife closed the door and stood with her back against it.

'I've just spoken to Greg.'

'The poor love is in so much pain. Who would have thought I'd be the one with the lesser injuries?'

'You know, Katie, the Greg I saw in that apartment was very different from the Greg you told me about.'

'In what way?'

'He risked his life to save you.'

Katie smiled. 'He did, didn't he? I have an amazing husband.'

'Who sleeps with teenage girls but walks out on you when he learns you're having an affair with Matt?'

Katie's eyes flicked to her magazine. She turned the page before saying, 'Greg's not perfect. Neither am I. But we love each other. That's all that matters.'

'When you two split up and Greg was staying at his brother's house, I went to see him. He had a girl there. She'd left her jacket on the sofa. I saw you wearing the exact same jacket a few days later.'

'So what? I'm sure half the women in Ireland wear the same clothes as me. It's not like I can afford to buy designer wear.'

'This jacket didn't look like it came from Penneys. I've certainly never seen anybody wear it before. So, my question is, why pretend you and Greg split up when you obviously did nothing of the sort?'

'And my question, Aoife, is what is your obsession with our relationship? Why do you care when or why we break up?'

Aoife smiled. 'You're right. It is becoming an obsession. I've thought about your relationship most of the day. I even went through both your Instagram profiles. I keep remembering that you were the person who told me about Matt's affair.'

'I already explained that. I thought if I told you, it wouldn't occur to you that I was the person he was having an affair with.'

'Yes, I remember. But it always struck me as strange that everyone seemed to know Matt was having an affair, yet nobody ever saw him with you or any woman other than Nicole.'

'Matt and I had a one-night stand. What were the chances anybody was in the corridor at the exact moment he left my apartment? Especially when I checked the corridor was empty before I let him leave.'

'Greg seemed to think it was more than a one-night stand.'

'He's wrong.'

'Leaving that aside for the moment, it was a sensible precaution to make sure nobody was in the corridor before Matt left your apartment. And you're right. How could anybody know Matt was having an affair? And yet everybody did, which leads me to believe that somebody wanted everyone to know.'

'What does that mean?'

'I checked with Vicky and the rumours of Matt's affair started around the time I began my investigation. They were designed to distract me. And when I discovered Matt was your employee, you claimed to have been his lover. And if that wasn't enough of a distraction, you then told me Greg was sleeping with the maids.'

'I'm not sure what you're getting at.'

'And then everyone was convinced Matt was a domestic abuser, yet nobody ever heard him even raise his voice to Nicole.'

'I wouldn't know anything about that. Nicole never mentioned that Matt was violent.'

'Probably because he wasn't. Just like he wasn't having an affair with anybody either.'

Katie nodded. 'I agree. A one-night stand is not an affair.'

'But I never asked Nicole about any of that because both you and Vicky convinced me that it was true and that Nicole would be destroyed if she discovered Matt had betrayed her. Being friends with a gossip can be very handy sometimes, can't it?'

'I'm not sure what you're getting at. Vicky is a gossip, but she has a good heart, so it's something her friends accept. I doubt any of us would call it "handy".'

Aoife ignored the interruption. 'And then somebody drove Matt's father off the road.'

'I didn't even know that happened.'

'No? A young man was driving the car. Yet another distraction that sent me off on the wrong track. So what were you trying to distract me from, Katie? The fact that Matt worked for you?'

SIXTY-SIX

KATIE GLANCED AT her phone.

'I'm afraid you've lost me, Aoife.'

'I don't think I have. Nicole said Matt mentioned a problem he had at work. Something he would sort out when he got home. He'd found out about Greg's prostitution ring, hadn't he?'

Katie's eyes opened wide. 'Aoife, are you feeling alright? I know you've been under a massive strain. It seems to be affecting your mind. You honestly think Greg runs a prostitution ring?'

'Greg said he'd been trying to recruit Florina for months and she'd told the hotel staff she was thinking of moving to Ireland. We finally got confirmation from one of the waiters that Florina and Matt spoke. She told him all about Greg's proposition.'

'What proposition?'

'Greg already admitted to me that he's a pimp.'

Katie sat up, groaned, touched her shoulder and eased herself back against the pillows. 'Are you crazy? That's ridiculous.'

'Jacko didn't deny it.'

Katie paled. 'You can't be serious. After all that monster did to us, how could you trust a word he says?'

'I don't. But when I told him that you and Greg murdered

Florina, he didn't think twice about handing you over to the police. According to Jacko, Greg asked him for the name of someone he could hire to kill Florina. Jacko refused to help him.'

'You can't possibly believe that, Aoife.' Katie picked up her phone. It took her a moment to get it into the right position, but she quickly clicked out a message. Aoife felt Greg's phone vibrate.

'If you're texting Greg, you're wasting your time. The police should be taking his statement around now.'

'I don't believe you.'

'Okay, I can wait.' Aoife pulled out a seat and sat down. Katie waited a few minutes, then made a phone call. The phone in Aoife's pocket vibrated again.

'I told you. He's not going to answer.'

Katie tried the phone again. 'Answer!' she muttered.

Aoife told herself to take it slowly. Katie was beginning to lose it. This was good. All she had to do now was keep her nerve. It was only a matter of time before Katie cracked.

'Oh God!' Katie threw the phone on the bed. 'Greg's not a pimp. If he said he is, it's because he's terrified of Jacko. Jacko is the one who was pimping those girls.'

'Really? Then why did Greg take them to the stag do's?'

'He didn't take them. Jacko's guys did that. Greg went along occasionally to make sure everything ran smoothly. Jacko blamed us if there was any trouble.'

'Like the girls trying to escape?'

'Those girls agreed to work for Jacko. If they changed their minds later, that was between them and Jacko. It had nothing to do with us.'

'Even though you were the ones who forced them into prostitution?'

'We never did anything of the sort. Greg and I spoke to the girls online, but we never forced them into anything.'

'You just told them prostitution was the way to improve their lives?'

'It wasn't like that. Those girls were miserable. They lived in poverty, with no way to make a better life for themselves. Greg and I discussed their options with them, that's all. We didn't meet with anyone under the legal age of consent in Ireland. Nothing we did was illegal. It was the girls' choice to come here.'

'Of course it was. And they knew exactly what they were signing up for, didn't they? That's why you invited them into your home. You showed them the life they could aspire to. And when they were happy and relaxed and had told their family and friends about their lovely new employers, you handed them over to Jacko's goons. I'm guessing the pimps made them send the odd text home, or maybe they sent texts for them. By the time the girls disappeared without a trace, nobody would suspect the lovely young couple who took them into their own home, would they?'

'Those girls chose to meet Jacko's guys. It's a free world. If they want to be prostitutes, who has the right to stop them?'

'You never wanted those girls spending time with anybody who could understand them. I should have noticed how upset you got when you realised Orla spoke Romanian.'

'This is all nonsense, Aoife.'

'You only allowed Florina to work for Orla because you were worried I was getting suspicious. What kind of a cleaning agency won't let any of their staff work for their friends? It was a risk, but you weren't that worried. Florina knew about Jacko's business, of course, but as she'd never met any of his people and she had very little English, you figured it was safe enough. But

Jacko didn't agree, did he? He thought you were endangering his business. He even had to shut down one of his houses. And then Florina threatened to go to the police. You both knew Jacko would murder you if he found out. That's why Greg killed Florina, isn't it?'

Katie's eyes were glued to her phone as she texted furiously. 'I've told you. Greg and I offered those girls options. Nothing more.'

'You were already in Jacko's bad books. His associates were furious the house was shut down. One was overheard calling you a bitch and saying you were going to get yourself killed. Greg knew you were in danger, so he killed Florina to save you. That's what Jacko told the police.'

Katie hit send on the text and immediately tried to make a phone call. Again, Aoife felt Greg's phone vibrate.

'For God's sake!' Katie flung the phone down on the bed again. 'Greg didn't murder anybody. It was Jacko. The police in Romania have no interest in protecting prostitutes. Girls disappear all the time and nobody cares. When Florina discovered it was different in Ireland, she threatened to go to the police if she wasn't allowed to work for Orla. All Greg did was report back to Jacko. He assumed Jacko's guys would have a word and Florina would realise she had to stick by their agreement. It never occurred to him that Jacko would have the girl killed. And even when she was murdered, we couldn't be sure Jacko was involved.'

'I see. And that explains why you didn't go to the police. You had no idea a murder was going to take place, and afterwards you weren't covering up for Jacko because you had no proof he was involved?'

'Exactly.' Katie gave her a wary look as if doubting her problems could be solved so easily. 'And remember, Greg was arrested the day Florina was murdered, and I spent most of the day in the police station. We couldn't possibly have had anything to do with Florina's death.' She reached for the water jug and filled a glass. 'I'm getting tired now, Aoife. I'd like to sleep.'

'I'll go soon. I'm curious about Greg's arrest. Isn't it odd that somebody in the complex would call the police? They all know you. You're all good friends. Why call the police because you had a domestic?'

Katie shrugged. 'Maybe they were afraid Greg would hurt me?'

'The way I heard it, you were the one throwing things. Vicky never said anything about Greg trying to hurt you. And why were you fighting in the first place? Greg knew you weren't having an affair with Matt, and you knew he wasn't sleeping with the maids, so what was the problem?'

'You're wrong about the affairs, but it's true that's not the reason we were fighting. I'd just found out Greg was trying to steal from Jacko. I was terrified he'd get us both killed.'

'Ah yes, the blackmail scam. How long were you running that before Jacko found out?'

'I wasn't running anything. I wasn't aware there was any blackmail operation going on until I discovered all the money Greg had hidden away in a secret account.'

'That's interesting. Because as I remember it, Greg didn't even know how to access that account.'

'Of course he knew. Pretending to forget was a delaying tactic.'

'Not a very clever one. Jacko was holding a gun to his head at the time.'

'It was a very stressful situation. Greg wasn't thinking clearly.'

'You were stressed too, but you had no problem entering the

password. You did it with one hand, like it was something you were so accustomed to doing, it didn't even require thought.'

'Greg used the same password for all his accounts. I'm used to accessing the business account.'

'Oh yes, the business Matt worked for. You went to so much trouble to distract me from the fact that Matt was your employee. I was suspicious at first. That's why I checked your Instagram accounts. You were both invited to your friend's stag and hen do. It took me a while to notice that Greg was in almost every photo taken that weekend, but you were only in the pics taken on Friday.'

Katie shrugged. 'I'm not big into photos.'

'So I asked Conor to check with immigration. That's why I came to your apartment to talk to you. I wanted to ask why you flew into Bari on Saturday morning. The day Matt disappeared.'

SIXTY-SEVEN

KATIE SWALLOWED. 'I felt like a holiday.'

'I can understand that. I'm sure lots of people decide to go abroad in the middle of their friend's hen do.'

'They're Greg's friends. I barely know them.'

'And as there's no record you were in the Colonnina that weekend, I presume your friend, the bar manager, arranged a room for you.'

'I didn't stay in the Colonnina.'

'Really? So why were you seen leaving one of their hotel rooms? Were you visiting somebody?'

'I stayed on the other side of town entirely because there were no vacancies at the Colonnina.'

'Where did you stay?'

'In a friend's house.'

'Well, I'm sure the police can check that out. Although they might not think it's necessary since Greg has already confessed to killing Matt.'

'What? I don't believe he ever said that.'

'The police have proof.'

'They couldn't have. It never happened.'

'Well, their proof wouldn't stand up in a court of law, but it doesn't have to because Greg is signing a confession as we speak.'

Katie reached for her phone again. As she called a number, Aoife was unsurprised to feel Greg's phone vibrate.

'You see, the police can prove Matt phoned you the day before he disappeared, and they can prove on the day he disappeared, you phoned him.'

Katie put the phone down on the bed and smiled. 'Now I know you're lying. Nicole told me that Matt's phone was never recovered.'

'That's true. And, as their apartment was broken into and both their computers stolen, the police couldn't get any information from Matt's computer either.' As she spoke, it occurred to Aoife that Katie probably had a key to Nicole's apartment, but she decided to let that go for the moment.

'So why did you make all that stuff up, Aoife?'

'You didn't let me finish. A few weeks ago, Conor told me about this new technology that allows you to trace phone records as long as you have the correct number. You don't need a SIM card anymore.'

'I never heard of that.'

'Neither had I. It's very new, apparently. Anyway, Conor had the police tech guys check out Matt's number. That's how we know about the calls between you and him.'

'I didn't get any calls.'

'Greg explained that. He said he borrowed your phone that weekend, so the call that appears to be from you was actually from him.'

'No! Greg would never say that. It's not true.'

'Greg says he spoke to Matt on Friday. Matt mentioned his conversation with Florina. Greg panicked. He was terrified Matt would contact the police, so he said he was in Italy and would meet him in Bari on the Saturday.'

'Greg never left the country. Everybody at the stag do can swear to that.'

'I know. Greg says he hired a prostitute to take a room in the hotel and then he phoned Matt and suggested they meet in that room. When Matt arrived, the prostitute said Greg would be back in a minute. She spiked Matt's drink and called Jacko's men. They disposed of the body.'

'No! No! No!' Katie winced as she sat up in the bed and pulled at the needle in her hand.

'Are you going somewhere? The police won't let you speak to Greg and there's a detective outside this door. He wants to interview you when I'm finished. Fionn!' Aoife called, hoping she'd given Fionn enough time to reach the hospital. She was in luck. Fionn stuck his head around the door.

'Yes?'

'It's okay. You remember Katie? I believe you spoke a few days ago. I was just telling her you're waiting to interview her again. We're not ready yet, though.'

'Okay, give me a shout when you need me.'

Katie sank back against the pillows. 'What are you trying to do to us, Aoife? You know Greg's lying. He thinks he's protecting me.'

Aoife nodded. 'I know. I just don't care.'

'What?'

'When Jacko said he was going to murder Conor and me, Greg couldn't have cared less. I want him locked up. I don't give a damn whether or not he killed Matt. He was responsible for Florina's death and he tried to run Matt's father off the road. That's enough for me.'

'Greg didn't want Florina murdered. That had nothing to do with him.'

'One of you called the police before you staged that fight. You both knew Florina would be murdered and neither of you lifted a finger to stop it.'

'We didn't know anything.'

'Tell that to a jury.'

Katie put her head in her hands. They sat in silence for several minutes, then Katie said, 'Greg had nothing to do with the blackmailing scam. He didn't even know it was going on.'

'I don't believe you.'

'Jacko blamed Greg because it never occurred to him that I'd turn on him. Do you remember when Jacko first held the gun to Greg's head? Greg said "'we' didn't cheat you". He was willing to die to protect me. Would he have said "we" if I had no involvement?'

Aoife pretended to give this some thought. 'It seems unlikely.'

'You see, Greg had nothing to do with it. That's why Greg couldn't even access our bank account. He never knew the password.'

'He wasn't surprised when Jacko mentioned the blackmail scam.'

'I'd told him I was making some money on the side, but I didn't give him any details. The less he knew, the safer it was for him.' She paused as if trying to decide how much it would be safe to admit. 'Jacko has an operation running out of Bari. It's always handy to be near a port in his line of business.'

'I'm sure.'

'Jacko's been running a blackmail scam in most European capitals for years. One day I was talking to one of the goons and he told me he sometimes works protection for the girls. I was desperate for money to put a down payment on a house and I suggested we borrow one of the prettier girls occasionally and run the scheme from the Colonnina.'

'So, you sent a child out to seduce middle-aged men.'

'She was already doing that. I couldn't save her. Hell, I couldn't save myself. But I helped the girl by letting her earn some money on the side. She jumped at the chance.'

'How did the barman get involved?'

'There's a limit to how often I can go to Bari. I needed somebody on the ground. That was my mistake. Too many people got involved and somebody told Jacko.' She picked up her phone and sent another text. Aoife felt Greg's phone vibrate. 'Okay, I'm ready now. You can tell the detective I'll make a complete confession.'

'I'm not sure what good you think that will do. The police will still charge Greg with Matt's murder.'

'But I told you, he didn't even know there was a blackmail operation going on.'

'We only have your word for that.'

'Aoife, don't do this. Greg is innocent. He never tried to kill Matt's father. You were right. It was a distraction. He made sure the man wasn't seriously injured.'

'He killed Matt.'

'No. Jacko's goons did that. Matt phoned me. His Italian was quite good, so he'd got a lot of information from Florina. She was too embarrassed to admit she'd agreed to be a prostitute, but she'd given enough away that Matt knew none of our girls were cleaners. I was worried, so I told Jacko. He sent some of his goons to sort it out. I didn't know he planned to kill Matt. That's why I went to so much trouble to help Nicole. I felt it was my fault Matt was murdered.'

'Greg's story is pretty similar, except you had nothing to do with it.'

'But that's not true. Greg was in Ireland the entire time. Loads of people saw him. The whole prostitute in the room is nonsense. If Matt had seen a prostitute, he would have left. I was in the room waiting for him. I spiked his drink, and then I called Jacko. But I swear I had no idea Jacko was going to kill Matt.'

'Really? I thought it was weird you had zip ties in your suitcase. I knew you and Greg weren't into bondage. You bought them when you flew out to meet Matt. When he was unconscious, you tied him up and waited for Jacko's goons to come and get him.'

'That's not true, Aoife. They brought their own zip ties. I removed any trace we'd ever been in the room. They'd left some zip ties behind, so I stuck them in my suitcase and forgot about them.'

'And Matt sat beside you patiently and didn't even put up a struggle when Jacko's men came to kill him?'

'He was unconscious.'

'And you were prepared to take the chance that he'd wake up and not leave the room?'

'Oh for God's sake, does it matter who tied him up? The important thing is I didn't kill him.'

'I'm sure you didn't. You just phoned his killers, opened the door for them, led them to a man who was bound and gagged and then walked out of the hotel. Nothing that happened to Matt was your fault at all.'

'God! You're some bitch. I didn't kill anyone and Greg didn't even know Matt was dead until it appeared in the papers. He didn't know I'd even been to Bari that weekend until I told him you believed I was having an affair with Matt.'

'Why the big breakup scene?'

'Nicole told me you were calling to her apartment that afternoon. I figured you'd call to me afterwards, so I told Greg to be ready. I thought blaming you for our breakup would make you think there was more going on than you realised. The more distractions we could provide, the better. None of it was Greg's idea. He's completely innocent.'

'Of murdering Matt, maybe. But I'd hardly call him innocent. Fionn!'

Fionn stuck his head around the door again.

'Katie just told me she was involved in Matt Gallagher's death. She'd like to tell you all about it.'

As Aoife headed for the door, she heard Katie mutter, 'Bitch.' She turned in time to see Katie give Fionn a broad smile. 'Detective, Aoife is a little confused. Jacko murdered Matt. I was aware of it, and yes, I know I should have reported it, but you understand that I was terrified of Jacko, don't you? Greg had nothing at all to do with it.'

SIXTY-EIGHT

AOIFE TOOK THE stairs to the ICU. Grainne would be waiting for her to take over so she could go home. As she walked, Aoife went over Katie's confession in her head. She'd taken a big chance lying to her. If Katie had called her bluff, there would have been no way Aoife could prove her guilt. Who knew what would happen now, but one thing was certain—Katie and Greg wouldn't be able to walk away from this. They'd be charged with accessory to murder at the very least.

How was she going to break the news to Nicole? The past few days had given her a better understanding of what Nicole must have gone through this last year. And now Aoife would have to tell her that her best friend was responsible for Matt's death. What would that do to her? So much needless pain, and for what? Money? The life Nicole and Matt had planned, destroyed. Florina dead at seventeen. How could any amount of money be worth that? But if she hadn't chosen Matt as the subject of her article, Katie and Greg would have gone on with their lives with barely a thought for the people they had ruined. Jacko was the criminal in their minds. They were just as much victims as Matt and Florina. Aoife thought of all the young girls whose lives they had helped to destroy. Not to mention Florina, who had no chance of a life at all. As she opened the door to Conor's room, Aoife had a sudden image of Florina dressed in white, laid out in her coffin, family and friends surrounding her weeping parents. She blinked back the tears. It took her a moment to work out what was in front of her. Conor's bed was empty. A young nurse was changing the sheets.

Aoife covered her mouth with her hands.

'What? Where?'

'It's okay. The doctor decided Conor was well enough to move to the general ward today. He's in—'

ꟹ

The first thing Aoife was aware of was voices. She felt so exhausted she had to force her eyes open. Two nurses and a worried Grainne looked down at her.

She sat up. 'What happened?'

A nurse gently pushed her head between her knees. 'You fainted. Stay like this for a moment and then we'll get you a nice cup of tea.'

ꟹ

Aoife sipped at tea that was only slightly less sugary than the stuff Sarah had forced on her.

'The poor girl hasn't slept in her own bed in days. She's barely eaten,' Grainne whispered to the nurse.

The nurse checked Aoife's pulse. 'You're okay now, but you need to go home, Aoife. Conor is fine. We're taking great care of him.'

Aoife stood. 'I'll just stay here for a few more hours, then I'll leave.'

Grainne helped her to her feet. 'Conor would want you to get some rest. I'm driving you home right now. No arguments.'

SIXTY-NINE

Aoife woke in her own bed, the sun shining through her window. The smell of baking drifted up from the kitchen, and she could hear Amy's animated chatter. Aoife pulled on a dressing gown and went downstairs. Grainne was taking a cake out of the oven and Amy was jumping up and down beside her.

'Can I eat it now?'

'Hi, sweetie.'

'Mummy!' Cake forgotten, Amy ran to Aoife and jumped into her arms.

'I missed you so much, sweetie.'

'Grawny took me to the playground and she bought me a big ice cream and I helped her make a cake. Do you want some?'

'That would be nice. Did you thank Grainne for the ice cream?'

'Thanks, Grawny. Mummy, you were in bed forever. I thought you were never going to wake up. Just like Sleeping Beauty.'

Aoife laughed. 'I was very tired, but I'm fine now.'

'Grawny said Moaney will be home soon and then we'll have the wedding. It's going to be on a beach in a country where it can't rain and I can wear my swimsuit under my dress and then I can swim afterwards.'

'Of course you can, sweetie. It's going to be a wonderful day.'

Amy frowned. 'Can I be a flower girl on the beach?'

Aoife hugged her. 'We'll work it out, sweetie.'

'I'm going to practise now.' She ran out of the room and a few minutes later could be heard singing 'Here Comes the Bride' as showers of potpourri floated around the corridor.

'Thanks for taking care of her, Grainne. Conor's still okay?'

'Yes, thank God. He spoke a few words today.'

'Really! Oh my God, I wish I'd been there. I'd better get back. I need ten minutes to shower and get dressed, then I'll drop Amy off at her grandmother's. Oh hell!'

'What?'

'I've no idea where my car is. It must still be parked outside Nicole's apartment.'

'It was, but some guy, Fionn I think he said his name was, dropped it around here last night.'

'That's so nice. I must remember to phone him. Do you want a lift back to the hospital?'

'No, thanks. I'll do the night shift. There's no need to ring Maura. If it's okay with you, I'd like to take Amy back to my place. I still have some of Sarah's old toys to keep her entertained. I'd like to spend a little time with my very first granddaughter.'

Aoife's eyes filled with tears.

'Oh, no. Don't start that again. Go on!' She waved Aoife away. 'Shower!' Grainne cut the cake into small slices and put one on a side plate. 'Amy, the cake's ready.'

Amy bounded into the kitchen. She took a slice of cake

and insisted that Aoife have some too. 'Isn't it lovely, Mummy? I made that.'

Aoife nibbled it and proclaimed it the nicest cake anybody had ever made. So nice that she would bring it upstairs so she'd have something sweet to eat while she got dressed. As she was climbing the stairs, Aoife heard Grainne say, 'Your mum says you can come back to my house. I think the trampoline Conor used to play on is still in the garage. How about we ask your grandad to put it up again? Would you like that?'

From her bedroom, Aoife could hear Amy's excited squeals. She blinked away tears. Who would have thought Grainne would ever refer to Amy as her granddaughter? Of course Grainne could never replace Maura in Amy's eyes and Aoife doubted Grainne would ever consider Amy her "real" grandchild, but they seemed to be getting along well. That was enough for now.

Aoife stepped into the shower. As the hot water rained down on her still-bruised body, she felt days of tension drain away. Things had been tough there for a while, but that was all behind them. She thought of Conor, now in a general ward. She couldn't wait to speak to him again. Aoife felt her heart soar. It took her a second to recognise the feeling as happiness. She smiled at the realisation that she was humming her mother's favourite song - 'Happy Days Are Here Again'. It was going to be a good day. A good week. A good life.

Hi,

Thank you for choosing Dying To Tell. If you enjoyed it, I would really appreciate it if you had a moment to write a review. One or two words would be perfect. Reviews mean the world to authors. It's how other readers find us.

Dying To Tell is the fifth book in the Aoife Walsh Thriller Series. All five books are standalone thrillers and can be read in any order. The other books in the series are Girl Targeted, Only Lies Remain, The Silent Speak and Where Loyalties Lie. You can check out all my books on my website here: https://valcollinsbooks.com/books/

If you would like to get in touch you can contact me here:

https://valcollinsbooks.com/contact/

or on Instagram:

https://www.instagram.com/valcollinsbooks/

I'm also on Facebook:

https://www.facebook.com/ValCollinsBooks

and, although I'm not very active on other platforms, I have some presence on almost every social media platform.

I really love hearing from readers, so please do get in touch.

Val

As always I would like to thank my friends:-

Tina, the first person outside my family to read all my books. Tina is my typical thriller reader and can always be counted on to spot ways to make my books more appealing to voracious thriller readers like herself. As friends go, she's one of the best.

John who is always so generous with his extensive knowledge of the Irish gardai and who once again came to my rescue when I had no idea how the Irish police would handle a situation.

Yvonne who very generously took time away from her busy family to offer advice on a variety of subjects.

Most of all I am, and will always be, forever grateful to my family – those who are still with me and those who are gone.

CPSIA information can be obtained
at www.ICGtesting.com
Printed in the USA
JSHW081947100223
37570JS00002B/82

9 781838 353452